The Trouble with Dad

Kidnap Caper #3

Peg Herring

The Trouble with Dad is a work of fiction. The names, characters, and incidents are entirely the work of the author's imagination. Any resemblance to actual persons, living or dead, or events, is entirely coincidental.

Editor: Trish Zanczak

Copy Editor: R. Hodges

ISBN: 9781393560210

Printed in the USA

Chapter One

Just after midnight, two figures clothed in black tiptoed into a room where a woman sat up in bed, apparently reading a novel called *The Laird's Lusty Wife*. The room smelled of peanut butter cups, and several wrappers had been wadded up and left on the night stand.

As the figures entered, they passed two men leaning against the wall. One was checking his phone, though he'd muted the sound. The other one, who was chewing on a toothpick, toyed with the idea of tripping the nearer figure as she went by, but professional courtesy—or perhaps common sense—prevailed, and the figures passed without interference.

The occupant of the bed wore a flannel nightgown, and she'd stacked pillows behind her back and pulled the covers up around her waist. Completely absorbed in the novel, she didn't seem to notice the interlopers at first. When the slighter of the two made a throat-clearing sound, the reader looked up, and her eyes went wide.

"Aaaaaahhhhh!" The book fell from her hand and thumped to the floor as she pulled herself to a crouch at the center of the bed. "Who are you?"

"Who we are doesn't matter." Altered by a mechanical device, the voice sounded like a kid's toy robot.

The woman raised clasped hands to the ceiling. "Lord, help me! Help me now in my time of need. I'm counting on you, Lord!"

"We aren't going to hurt you."

"That's a lie." She pointed an accusing finger at the larger of the interlopers. "He's going to rape me and then slit my throat." Knitting her hands again, the woman hollered, "Help me down here, Lord. I need an angel to rescue me from some big-time trial and tribulation." There was something off in the delivery, but it didn't lack volume or emphasis.

The intruders looked at each other. The larger one shook his head, and the smaller one rolled her eyes. "Hey. Hey!" The volume decreased, but their target's calls for Divine Intervention went on. "Stop that," the intruder ordered. "You need to listen."

"I ain't listening to you," the woman hollered. "You're straight from the Devil. I can see it in your squinty little eyes."

"My squinty…" The figure shook that off. "We're here to talk to you about something important."

Clutching the neck of her garment, the woman asked, "What?"

"Your city commission meets on Monday, Mayor Gessing. We know about the bribe you were offered to support one bidder for the new project. They asked you to convince your co-members to ignore their reputation for sloppy work and cost overruns."

The woman gasped. "I would never take a bribe. I am an honest person."

"You haven't accepted it yet, as far as we can tell, so we want you to remain honest. Reject the money Lawson offered and vote your conscience at the meeting. Will you do that?"

The woman released the grip on her nightgown and dropped into her original position, making a soft plop when her back hit the pillows. "Sure thing," she said, her tone suddenly bored. "Y'all talked me right into it."

"There, Robin." Cam pulled his ski mask off and rubbed his spiky hair. "She agreed. We're done."

"Nice entrance this time. Completely silent," Hua said from where he and Tom had watched the rehearsal. "But, Luca, you gave in very easily."

"It's like the twelfth time we practiced this," Luca complained. "One time I cried, another time I screamed for the cops. I got mad, and once I even pulled a ball bat out from under the pillows. I'm plumb worn out with playing the hysterical target."

Tom, who was helping Robin untangle her earring from her ski mask, offered their newest member positive reinforcement. "You've been great, Luca. You were convincing every single time."

"Loud, for sure," Cam commented. "This last one hurt my ears."

Robin countered Cam's brutally honest comment with more praise. "You played the role very well."

Luca leaned down to pick up her book. "If there's one thing girls like me learn how to do, it's act convincing."

The others made no comment. Luca didn't often refer to her former occupation as a hooker, and no one else did either. Back then she'd done what she had to. Now she was part of the Kidnap Gang, as they called themselves. Though Robin had been reluctant to accept the term, a gang was what they were.

In addition to Luca, the gang consisted of Robin, once a middle-class law clerk; Tom, a wounded Iraq War vet; Hua, a former slave from Thailand; and Cam, a Georgia farm boy with Pervasive Development Disorder. Not part of the gang but living in their house were Mai and Jai, Vietnamese sisters they'd rescued from human traffickers during a caper. Part of the gang but not living in the house was Robin's brother Chris, whose main job was finding people the legal system couldn't or wouldn't deal with, criminals who needed a wake-up call.

The vigilante group had begun by accident when Cam encountered a crooked politician and kidnapped him, largely by mistake. He'd called Robin for help, and together they'd made the man face his dishonesty and promise to reform. Liking the idea that they might force other criminals to reconsider their behavior, they went on to a second "caper," and from there the gang grew. After researching a potential "target," they swept in, isolated the offender, and made him or her admit to their crimes. The confessions were recorded to keep the offenders honest going forward, and "fines" were levied to make the experience financially painful and therefore more memorable. The amount charged was split 50-50; half to charity and half toward the gang's living and operating expenses.

Cam addressed the room in general. "We're ready, right?"

"We'd better be," Robin answered. "We leave in the morning."

Her words were met with a rebellious silence that hinted the others weren't fully behind the current plan. Finally Luca spoke. "Can you all get out of my room and give me some quiet time now? I've been trying to finish this book for the last three days."

Chapter Two

As Cam tossed Robin's suitcase and his gym bag into the trunk of the car, less gently than she'd have liked, they answered the barrage of questions aimed at them as patiently as possible. "Did you pack your ski mask?" Hua asked.

"Got it."

"And your outfit? You won't find big and tall men's black sweats at most stores."

"Got it," Cam repeated. "I've got everything, Hua, honest."

"Did you check the batteries in the voice-changer, Clarabelle?" Tom used Robin's clown name, a practice they'd developed during capers to prevent identification. "You don't want equipment trouble in the middle of everything."

"I checked this morning." Robin's tone hinted he was irritating her. "And I packed extras too."

Unconsciously, Tom massaged the spot where his flesh-and-blood stump met his prosthetic hand. "I still think two people isn't enough. What if something goes wrong?"

"Nothing's going to go wrong," Robin said calmly. "We go in, do our thing, and leave."

"I could hide my tats," Luca offered for the tenth time. "If I wear long sleeves and take out my nose and eyebrow rings, nobody will even notice me."

"It's a small town." Robin kept her tone neutral, though she'd said it all before. "Strangers are a novelty unless it's tourist season, which it isn't." She phrased her final argument tactfully. "Cam and I fit the local demographic."

Luca's brow rose "Y'all are what they're used to, so the home folks won't guess you're up to no good."

"We're not kidnapping anybody this time," Cam reminded her. "We're just going to let the mayor know we're watching her."

"But you don't have to do it by yourselves," Hua argued. "The rest of us could go along, in case there's trouble. Jai and Mai have kept the house going on their own before."

Robin ran a hand through her hair. "Guys, Brandell, Indiana, is kind of like Mayberry, R. F. D. Everyone in town would notice a black woman who favors booty skirts or an Asian man in pastel leggings who smells of ginger. Since we plan to commit unlawful entry and threaten a city official, we need to be as inconspicuous as possible."

Hua crossed his arms. "I can tone down the flames, Robin. You know that."

"I do." She looked to Tom, silently pleading for help. Though he was no happier than the others with her decision to proceed without backup, she knew he'd set aside his doubts and judge her arguments fairly.

"They've done their homework," he said reluctantly.

"They sure practiced it often enough," Luca agreed. "Over and over and over."

New to the group, Luca was coming to understand how important practice was to Cam. Because of his disorder, he needed repeated rehearsals to become confident about a caper. Over and over he would ask, "What if this happens?" He'd listen carefully as the others discussed what they might do in different situations. The apparent negative had become a positive, since the group was forced to consider every possible scenario. That was good for all of them, but for Cam, it was like a vaccine. Once he knew his part thoroughly and had walked through it several different ways, he suffered no anxiety during the real event. Even when things went wrong, he coped, having considered ahead of time what the right thing to do would be.

Robin was the complete opposite. No matter how often they practiced, she worried before, during, and after each caper. She tortured herself with questions that had no firm answers. Might they scare a target so much that his health suffered? Were the fines she levied too easy on criminals who had no mercy toward their fellow citizens? Had she risked the safety of one of the gang members unnecessarily? And on and on. By the end of a caper she was a bundle of nerves, exhausted and enervated.

"You're going to be fine." Tom put a reassuring hand on her arm. Because he didn't often do that, Robin felt her face warm. She suspected Tom Wyman was everything she'd ever wanted in a man, but, fearing a relationship between them would undermine the gang's purpose, she hadn't let herself respond to her emotions. He seemed to understand that the work they'd chosen to do had to come first, at least for now.

Robin and Cam drove off, kicking up a light cloud of dust, as their five housemates and their dog, Bennett, watched with various degrees of concern. As Cam guided the car smoothly from the narrow, two-lane road onto a state highway and then toward I-70 East, the GPS screen indicated it would take seven hours to drive from Kansas City, Kansas, to Brandell, Indiana. "Should be there by six," Cam predicted. After a moment he added, "But you said they haven't got much for fast food there, right?"

Turning her face toward the side window, Robin smiled. While she fretted about all the things that might go wrong, Cam was concerned because there'd be no Taco Bell. Still, he'd matured a lot since they met. Raised by parents whose version of love was protecting their "damaged" son from outside influences, Cam had been left adrift when they died. With the support of the gang, he'd become much more confident in the past year. Fiercely loyal to his friends and especially to his partner Hua, Cam had found talents in himself that helped the gang and furthered their cause. His growing confidence didn't alter the fact that his main concerns in life were vehicles, video games, and "vittles," preferably the order-at-the-counter kind.

"It's been a while since I was in Brandell, but I doubt there's a big choice in restaurants." Reminded of food, Robin opened the sack Hua had provided and got each of them a cream puff. Biting into its gooey chocolate center she said, "We'll stop in Terre Haute for dinner. You can choose the franchise."

Cam swallowed half of his cream puff in one bite. "You said your uncle had a cabin in that town?"

"My dad's uncle," she corrected. "My brother couldn't find it in the records, but that's because neither of us remembers Uncle Tim's last name."

"But the town has a crooked mayor."

"She isn't a crook, at least not yet."

"I thought Chris said we need to make her behave."

She refreshed Cam's memory, since he usually played video games while the rest of them discussed the reasons for a caper. "Chris wasn't looking for a criminal. When he saw an article online about a proposed development in Brandell, he read it because we spent time there as kids."

"And he figured out the mayor is going to do something crooked." Cam hadn't missed all of it, just parts.

"Maybe. There are two major bidders on the project, one local guy who's apparently known for honesty, and one state-wide company with some less than honest dealings in their past. Chris got curious and hacked the large firm's internal emails. He found the top guys emailing back and forth about offering the mayor a bribe to push acceptance of their bid. Chris passed the information on to me, and I brought it up to the group for a vote. Since this mayor doesn't seem to be a bad person, Tom suggested a gentle warning rather than a full-on kidnap, and we all agreed."

"So you and I visit the mayor's house, tell her we know what's going on, and make her turn it down." Cam licked a last smear of filling off his thumb and then wiped his hands on the napkin Robin had provided.

"Since the mayor has been honest until now, we thought it was only fair to warn her we know about the bribe she's been offered. We warn tonight, and tomorrow we head for home. Easy-peasy."

"Why don't we stay at your uncle's cabin? Then no one would even know we're in town."

Robin shivered. "Even if I could remember how to find it, the place wasn't much fifteen years ago, and I doubt it's gotten better.

No electricity, no running water, lots of dirt. The lake was pretty, but no thanks on the cabin."

"Did you and your brother fish there with your father? My dad and I used to do that a lot."

"He wasn't a fisherman." Mark Parsons had been everything a parent shouldn't be, and nothing he'd ever done benefitted anyone but himself. Robin had been terrified of the dank, dark cabin, but she, her mother, and Chris had several times been forced to stay there after one of Mark's cons went wrong and got him into trouble.

Things would be going well in a new place. Robin would have a few friends, and she'd know the neighborhood and the school pretty well. Then out of the blue Mark would come home and announce, "Pack your bags, kiddies. We need to drop off the face of the earth for a while."

Mom's face would go tight with anxiety, but she never argued. Loading the car in the dead of night with whatever fit, they'd leave a place that had been home for a year or two at best. They'd live in the crowded cabin for weeks, sometimes months, until Mark found them a new place where no one knew his cheating ways. Then the scams would begin again, often with Robin and Chris forced to act as accomplices.

Their con-man father was cheerful when "on a roll," but it wasn't wise to trust his smiles. If a scheme was successful, Mark often left them on their own for a while, living high on the money he'd scammed from some sucker. Those were better times for Robin and Chris, though there was no money and their mother cried a lot, wondering what they'd do if "Daddy" didn't come home soon.

"Not get knocked around," Chris would answer, and Mom would cry harder.

"Don't talk like that," she'd say. "He's your father."

"Sperm donor," Chris would mutter, but their mother never saw the truth about Mark.

Brandell, Indiana, had few pleasant memories for Robin, though she recalled the smell of lilacs in the spring and the nice woman who worked at the library and seemed thrilled to have two avid readers visit. Cam would not understand that. He'd had two loving parents and a settled life on a small farm in Georgia. She could never explain what being the child of a volatile, narcissistic, flim-flam man had been like, so why try?

After Terre Haute the car smelled of fries and chicken nuggets, but Cam was happy. They arrived at the Brandell village limit at six-thirty and began looking for a motel. The first one they saw, the Lucky Angler, was nowhere near a lake, though there were lots of them in the area. It sat in the center of town, near a gas station, a family market, a dollar store, two bars, a Head Start preschool, and two resale shops. The other buildings were shuttered, with signs announcing businesses that hadn't made it: a pie shop, an ice cream parlor, a fishing tackle store, and a movie theater.

Expecting more than a six-unit, shabby motel with a leaping fish atop its sign, Cam passed the Lucky Angler and drove all the way through town. When they reached the second city limit sign, he pulled in at the abandoned Mike's Bait and Tackle and asked, "That's it?"

"Yup. The Lucky Angler it is," Robin said. "We're sure to get a room this time of year, but I'll bet it's musty and at least one of the lamps doesn't work."

When they entered the lobby, a bell over the door called a woman from behind a curtained space to wait on them. With her came the smell of something spicy, perhaps lasagna. She seemed neither pleased nor displeased to have guests but accepted the cash payment Robin offered without asking for any sort of identification. "One night, you said?"

"Possibly two. My husband and I are nature photographers, and we need some specific shots for an article on deer season. We'd like to get in and out before the hunters take over the woods."

The motel owner almost smiled. "I don't leave my yard when they're here, running around in overpriced camo and blasting away with guns they haven't sighted in since they bought 'em." She licked her teeth before adding, "Bunch of grownups acting like they're John Rambo."

"Can we get two double beds, please?" Robin tilted her head at Cam. "He's a restless sleeper."

The woman eyed Cam's oversized frame. "I ain't got one big enough his feet won't hang off the end."

"No problem," Cam told her. "I'll sleep crosswise, corner to corner. I do okay like that."

Chapter Three

Just after midnight, two figures clothed in black tiptoed into a room where a woman lay, reading a book called *The Sultan's Lusty Slave*. The room smelled of popcorn due to a large bowl near the woman's knees. A few bits had escaped and lay on the floor beside the bed. The occupant wore an oversized T-shirt and rested her head on one hand as she held the book with the other. Completely absorbed in the novel, she didn't notice the intruders for a few seconds. Silently, the larger one circled the room, outside the spill of lamplight, and stopped at the far side of the bed. When he was in place, the smaller figure made a throat-clearing sound.

When she looked up and saw Robin, the woman gasped. The book fell closed, and the almost empty bowl of popcorn spilled across the blankets. As Robin opened her mouth to speak, the woman's hand slid under the pillow. It came out holding a pistol, but that was one of the scenarios they'd practiced. Reaching over her, Cam twisted the gun from her hand and set it on the dresser behind him.

"Ow!" Rubbing her wrist, the mayor of Brandell demanded, "Who are you?"

"Who we are doesn't matter," Robin said in her robot voice. "We're not here to hurt you."

"Then what's this all about?"

"Lawson Construction offered you a bribe. We're here to tell you it isn't a good idea to accept it."

"But I haven't told—" She stopped, realizing she'd said too much already.

"Ms. Gessing, we know exactly what's on the table."

The response sounded like something the mayor had been rehearsing. "Lawson's offering a good deal for the citizens of Brandell. Better than the local guy can do."

Cam took a document from his pocket and handed it to Gessing as Robin went on in her robotic voice. "If you take their money, we'll send copies of that to every news outlet in the area. At best you'll be embarrassed. At worst you'll go to jail."

Gessing bristled. "I haven't done anything wrong."

"Not yet," Robin allowed. "Refuse the money, look at the bids honestly, and help your city choose a contractor who'll do a good job for everyone."

Gessing's face clouded. "What gives you the right to invade my home and make demands?"

"Absolutely nothing," Robin replied honestly. "We represent a group that promotes the general welfare wherever we can. It's up to you to protect your own reputation." With that she and Cam backed out of the room, leaving Brandell's mayor with a lot to think about.

Chapter Four

The city commission met at 9:00 a.m. Monday morning, and by 10:00 the word was out. Brandell would award the bid for the new housing development to a contractor who'd entered the second lowest bid but promised to use local workers and materials to complete the project. Satisfied, Robin called to report they'd soon be on their way home.

"You scare this bad woman very much," Jai crowed. "She did what you said, yes?"

"We encouraged her to put integrity over greed." Robin felt guilty on two counts. They'd scared the mayor (though she hadn't seemed all that frightened), and Jai clearly enjoyed their use of threats to incentivize good behavior. They had to work on developing the girl's compassion.

"You are okay?" Jai asked. Robin heard the clink of silverware and guessed she was doing dishes as they talked. "Tom is very worry."

"Things went well, but I'll be glad to get home. Any news?"

"Em called. I told her you were at work. Is that okay to say over the phone?"

Retired FBI agent Emily Kane had left the gang recently, declaring herself too old and disabled to be of help. Though Robin missed her grumpy friend, she was pleased that Em was now living happily with the man she'd been in love with for years.

"Em will know what you meant," she told Jai. "How are she and Bennett doing?"

"She says it is good, living in California." There was a pause. "She want Mai and me to come out there for a visit. Maybe to stay. She says I won't be cold there like here."

Along with complaints about not being allowed to help with capers, Jai often voiced strong opinions about moving somewhere warmer than what she usually called, "Kansas, Kansas." Tom joked that she had more clothes than the rest of them put together and wore all of them at once.

Robin tried to sound surprised. "Em wants you to move out there?"

"Yes. Em's Bennett has a…guest house near the swimming pool. She says we could live there and go to school." Her tone changed abruptly. "But I say, 'What can school do for Mai?'"

Before Robin could explain that specialized teachers help those with Down syndrome become more independent, Jai said, "I told Em we must stay and help you fight bad people."

Robin made what she hoped was an agreeable sound. The adults in the household spent a good deal of time discussing what to do with the sisters. Since their rescue, Jai was determined to become a member of the Kidnap Gang. She had never lived as a normal teenager, however, and Robin believed she'd benefit from attending high school with others her age. Formal education would develop her natural intelligence and hopefully instill the accepted social norms of American society. At the very least she might learn not to suggest beheading their enemies or "cutting off little parts they will not miss much."

Em's invitation was the first step in what might be a solution, but there was no sense pushing the idea long distance. "How is the other Bennett doing?"

"He is a good dog. He goes with Mai when she walks in the woods, so I don't worry she will get lost or eaten by a bear."

"Jai, we don't have any bears."

A louder clink signaled more silverware and strong disagreement. "If you don't see a bear, doesn't mean there's no bears. They are very sneaky."

"I see. Well, it's best that Bennett goes along then."

"Like I said, he is a good dog."

"Everyone else is okay?"

"Hua is with his computer, like always. Tom is working in the barn. Luca is doing something called Hop-Hop Funk, and she lets Mai do it too. They are very funny."

"Hip-Hop," Robin corrected.

"Yes, that. They moved all the dining room furniture into a corner. This is okay, right? Tom said, because we never eat in there."

"That's fine."

"Luca says I should do it too. She show me booty pop. I am very good at this, she says."

"I'm sure you are."

"I told her I am too busy with housework to play hop-hop—uh, hip-hop with them."

Robin smiled at Jai's definite tone. She wanted so much to contribute to the group's welfare. "We count on you to keep the place running, and you always get it done."

"I rearranged the place for sheets and things, the, uh…"

"Linen closet?"

"Yes, that. It is very efficient now."

"I can't wait to see it, Jai. We should be home by dark, but I'll check in when we stop for lunch."

Chapter Five

Robin and Cam put their bags in the car. As Robin tidied up the room, Cam stood outside. The day was mild, and the breeze smelled faintly of smoke from some nearby homeowner's burning leaves. Cam watched pickups and cars pass, mentally tagging the make and model of each. After a while he went back inside, where Robin was checking one more time to make sure they had everything. "There's a guy standing across the parking lot. I think he was checking you out."

Robin froze. "This is the first you're mentioning it?"

"You're pretty," Cam said in a matter-of-fact tone. "I don't think I need to tell you every time some guy watches you walk away." After a pause he said, "This one's old, though. He could be your—"

Robin had moved to the window and angled herself so she could look out without being seen. "Dad."

"What?"

"We have to go now." Grabbing her jacket, she fumbled to get her arms into the sleeves. "Is everything in the car?"

"Yeah, but don't you want to say hi?"

"Cam." She felt like someone had placed a strong rubber band around her head, immobilizing her jaw. "Mark Parsons is a bad person. He's…he's like poison."

"Is that any way to talk about your father?"

The man they'd been discussing appeared in the open doorway. Cam had never seen Robin react so violently. She froze, one hand fisted at her chest, the other spread at her side as if ready to push herself away. Her breath came in ragged gasps, and she seemed unable to function.

Not understanding the danger but sensing Robin was temporarily unable to deal with it, Cam stepped forward and took a protective stance between the man and Robin.

"Imagine my surprise, finding my long-lost daughter here in my old stomping grounds."

"We're leaving." Robin found her voice, but it was oddly high. "Whatever you're here for, we want nothing to do with it—or you."

"A little vacation with your…husband? Boyfriend?"

"My husband," she replied, but it came too quickly. The man's eyes flicked to Cam and back to Robin, assessing. She dropped her arms to her sides in an attempt to look relaxed, but they hung unnaturally, like they didn't belong to her. She tried to brazen it through, though Cam heard a tremble in her voice. "We did some local photography for a magazine article, and now we're finished. We need to get back home."

The interloper stepped into the room and raised a small pistol he'd had concealed in his jacket pocket. "I don't think that's going to happen, Robbie. The three of us are going to get into your car and go for a ride."

"People are expecting us."

"I doubt that." His smile seemed friendly, but Robin's obvious distress told Cam they were in trouble.

Though as upset as Cam had ever seen her, Robin tried again. "It's true. Our boss told us to stop by and show him the photos we got."

"Then he'll be disappointed. You're going to help me make a really big score, and then I'll leave you and Mr. Universe here alone forevermore." He put up a hand in a sarcastic mime of a pledge. "Scout's honor. Now both of you, hand over your phones and sit down on the bed."

When they'd given them up, the man, who Cam assumed was named Parsons like Robin, did something with her phone, possibly a text message. When he'd finished, he demanded any other electronic devices they had with them. That led them to the car, where Robin and Cam dug out their tablets, which he stuffed, along with the phones, into an overloaded, smelly trash can at the corner of the building. Noticing the GPS device, he told Robin to toss that into the trash as well. Once that was done, he ordered them into their car. Cam looked to Robin, who gave him a tight nod, indicating he should follow orders.

He considered a sneak attack. Parsons was half his size, and Cam might be able to wrestle the gun away if he came at him from the side. But Robin knew their captor and no doubt had a better idea of what his capabilities were. Besides that, Parsons seemed competent with the pistol, holding it level and close to his body. He pointed it directly at Robin, tacitly indicating she'd be his first target if they didn't do as he said. Cam couldn't imagine the guy would really shoot his own daughter, but Robin's tense posture signaled caution. Cam did as he was told.

Starting the engine, Cam backed out of the parking spot. Closed in the car, he noticed Parsons' body odor was strong, like an old farmer who had lived down the road when he was a kid. Mr. Turner hadn't believed frequent bathing was necessary, and Cam's dad had joked that might be the reason there was no Mrs. Turner.

"Turn left onto Main Street and drive until you see an auto repair shop. Turn right there, onto Butler." Once they'd traveled a few miles down the roughly paved road, Parsons directed Cam down a series of smaller and bumpier roads. Finally he ordered him to pull into a grassy drive that led to a cabin that had to be the one Robin described earlier. Though the lake beyond it was picturesque, the structure itself brought to mind an old song his mother used to sing about a tumble-down shack. Behind it was an even more tumble-down outhouse.

"Home, sweet home," Parsons said. "Pull around the back, where the car won't be visible from the road." Cam obeyed. "Hand me the keys. Now, precede Robin and me to the back door. It isn't locked. Sit down at the kitchen table and put your hands flat on the top. If you do exactly as I say, I won't have to put a hole in my daughter's hide."

Again Cam obeyed, fearful for Robin's safety. It was dark inside, owing to the fact that there were only two windows, both small, both filthy. Cam's nose twitched at the musty, mousy smell, overlaid with hints of decaying food.

Parsons fetched a length of clothesline rope, cut it into lengths with a butcher knife, and ordered Robin to tie Cam to the chair where he sat. "Hands tied to the uprights, feet to the legs. Put a few loops around his chest and the chair back for good measure."

Murmuring an apology, Robin did as she was told. As she worked she asked, "Why are you in Brandell, Mark?"

"The usual reason," he said airily, but his tone sobered a bit as he added, "I ran a con in Florida that should have let me retire somewhere nice." He frowned. "It failed, through no fault of mine, and as it turned out, the mark has some nasty associations. He sent a couple of thugs to hunt me down. Since this place was a good hideout in the past, I figured it would work for me now."

Robin rolled her eyes. "When will you learn?"

Parsons shrugged as if to say, "Who knows?" After a moment, he gestured at their surroundings. "My cousin never sold the property after Uncle Tim died. Not sure what she's holding onto it for, since she always despised sunshine and fresh air. Anyway, I figured I could come here, stay off the grid for a while, and regroup." He finished with a horrible Bogart impression and a mangled quotation: "Of all the boring burgs in the world, you had to walk into mine."

"Bad luck for me," Robin's tone was bitter. "Coming anywhere near you when you're in trouble."

"My luck always turns good when I need it most." He gestured with his free hand. "As happened today. Now let me tell you what I have in mind."

Cam tried to listen, but he was learning that being tied up was a lot more uncomfortable than he'd ever imagined. His hands started going numb almost immediately, and it was awful not being able to move his feet. He felt like a Thanksgiving turkey, all trussed up with an unhappy future. He hoped Robin was already making a plan for how they were going to get out of this, because it looked like their escape would be all up to her.

Chapter Six

"Robin's three hours late for her check-in," Hua spoke loudly to be heard over the scrape of a wire brush Tom was using to remove old paint from a trim board.

Tom set the brush aside and turned to Hua. "She didn't call when they stopped for lunch?"

"No. She spoke to Jai this morning, said the caper went well and they'd be leaving Brandell soon. Since then our calls go directly to voicemail. The apps that locate their devices indicate they're still at the motel."

"Did you check the website?"

When a phone call wasn't possible or advisable, gang members could send messages at a website called KIDNAP.org. "Under construction" to most users, each of them was listed as an administrator and could therefore see any messages left for the group. "I checked," Hua said. "Nothing there."

Tom's gray eyes were troubled. "I assume you tried to call Cam too."

"Several times."

"Damn," Tom said softly. "We shouldn't have let them travel without backup."

"Who should go?" Hua's question revealed that he knew what their next move would be.

"I vote we take all the talent: you, me, and Luca. What do you think?"

Hua looked around to assure himself they were alone. "I think you shouldn't say that where Jai can hear you. She believes she is part of the talent."

Tom smiled grimly. "True, but sixteen is a little young for crime-fighting. I'll tell her we need them to guard the house." After a moment he added, "Maybe Bennett should come along. A dog is a good excuse for a lot of things, and his nose might be helpful."

Hua ran a hand through his dark hair. "What do you think is wrong?"

"The mayor might have come after them, in which case they could be under arrest. If they realized something had gone wrong, they might have had to leave without their belongings."

"They might leave their tablets behind, but they are seldom without their phones," Hua commented. "And if they were arrested, they'd have contacted us."

"True. The other possibility is that something came up we didn't predict. If that's the case, they'll deal with it as best they can, but they'll probably need help to get away without being identified."

Hua turned toward the house. "I'll tell Luca to be ready in half an hour."

They assembled at the van, Hua laden with electronics. Bennett danced excitedly, pleased to be included. Luca looked almost prim with only three pairs of earrings, an auburn wig, false eyelashes, and a long-sleeved top that covered most of her tattoos. The smell of

Beyoncé Rise in her immediate area was stronger than Tom would have liked, considering the long ride ahead.

Mai and Jai came outside to see them off, shivering in the nippy fall air. Peeping out from a tightly-tied hood, Jai pouted at being left behind, but Tom stressed again the need for her to remain vigilant. Their oversized, slightly run-down mansion on a dead-end road north of Kansas City, Kansas, was supposedly an artists' colony. That explained the odd mix of residents, but locals sometimes showed up to see the place for themselves. Late at night, it was carloads of curious teens. During the day, it was civic-minded citizens with pamphlets and business cards. Both were largely ignored.

"Tell anyone who stops by that we're having a week of solitude to spur artistic expression," Tom told Jai.

"If they do not leave," she said, "I will beat them with Hua's frying pan."

Tom shook a finger at her. "No beating anyone. Use the skills we've taught you. Diplomacy works better than violence."

"Yes. I will use my diplomacy," Jai promised. Though she preferred brute force as a first response, anything Tom said was gospel to her.

Chapter Seven

It resembled a scene in a *B* movie, one hero tied to a chair, the other helpless before the grinning villain's snub-nosed .38. Munching on a candy bar, Mark asked, "How's your mother, Robbie?"

"Great," she lied. "She's remarried and very happy." He didn't need to know the woman he'd abused and mistreated for fifteen years had died in an auto accident.

Robin and Tom had practiced techniques for handling an armed opponent. One way was stepping forward unexpectedly, twisting the gun from his hand, and kneeing his groin. Or she might distract him with a ploy, pick up a makeshift weapon like the ancient drip coffeepot near her elbow, and use it to knock the gun away. Doing either of those things might allow her to escape, but Cam would be left behind, helpless. The occasional scrape of his chair legs against the floor told her he was working to free himself, but she saw no sign that he was having any success. For the moment, she could do nothing.

Unaware of Robin's rebellious thoughts, Mark asked, "What's my boy Chris up to?"

"He has a very successful internet business." Again, Mark didn't need to know Chris had lost both legs in Afghanistan and was only now learning to walk with prosthetics.

"Good," Mark said. "Although he treated me badly, I never wished him any harm, Scout's honor." Leaning his rear against the dry sink, Mark said, "I couldn't believe it when I spotted you."

Robin bit her lip, wishing she'd seen him first so she could have turned and walked away.

"I stumbled onto an opportunity that requires an attractive young woman as bait. I was trying to think of some sweet young thing I might send for, and out of nowhere, poof! There you were."

Before she could think of a nasty enough comment, he went on. "You'd never expect anything good to come of hiding out in this crappy burg, but fifty miles from here is a guy who made a fortune in electronics. Now he's old and alone. He sits in a wheelchair all day, looking out his window and waiting to die. And do you know what? He's got no one to leave all his lovely money to. Not a living soul."

"You learned this how?"

Mark raised a shoulder in a coy pose. "As you know, I'm a people person. This girl I met in the local watering hole is a home care nurse. Recently the guy, his name is Harrison Robeson, had a bout with pneumonia, and she got him as a client. He's a sweetheart, Lola says, but he's got this live-in caregiver who's a pain in the ass. After a month he convinced Robeson he didn't need a visiting nurse, and she was out of there."

"Sounds like the caregiver could be a stone in your path."

"Your path, Robbie." Mark pointed at her. "But I'm sure you can handle him."

"Me?"

“You. Lola the Nurse was peeved about being ousted from the job, and she talked a lot about Robeson. I think maybe she’d started hoping she’d be named in the will, and all of a sudden her dreams were shattered. Anyway, being a polite sort of fellow, I listened.”

“You were trying to get her into bed,” Robin corrected.

A sly grin admitted that. Mark opened a cooler that sat near him, felt around inside, and came out with a soda, which he set on the table in order to pop the top with one hand. He took a long drink, and Robin realized how dry her own throat was. Not that she would ask her father for anything, even a sip of Sprite.

“As I said,” Mark went on, “Robeson is loaded.”

“So you want a chunk of his money. How does that involve me?

“He and his wife had one daughter, Dolores. She was a real handful, and at seventeen she ran away from home. They were living in California then. Despite doing everything they could, the parents never located their little girl. In 1982, the police found Dolores dead in a rat-trap apartment building in L.A.”

“End of story.”

“Not necessarily.” Mark's eyes burned with excitement. “Who's to say Dolores didn't have a child during the lost years? The child could have grown up and had a baby of her own. Who's to say that baby isn't you?”

Robin gave him a disgusted look. “DNA, for one thing.”

“I've got a way around that, as long as Robeson isn't too savvy about the testing process.” Mark pointed a finger at Robin. “A regular DNA kit can be done at home. There's a more secure version with witnesses and chain of custody, but we're going to hope he doesn't go that direction. Getting the results we want will take a little sleight of hand, but it's manageable."

"You want me to pretend to be this man's long-lost granddaughter—no, wait. I'd be his great-granddaughter." A shiver of dread traveled down Robin's back. "Then what? Are you going to suggest I smother him with a pillow or something?"

Mark looked hurt. "You know me better than that."

"I haven't laid eyes on you for fifteen years, Dad. You were a low-life back then; I can't predict how much lower you've fallen." She nodded at the pistol. "For example, you never carried a weapon before."

He frowned at the gun as if seeing it for the first time. "I told you. I'm being hunted by some bad people." He met her gaze. "If they catch up with me, they're going to kill me."

Robin grimaced sarcastically. "I'm devastated to hear it."

Mark's eyes, so much like her own, darkened. "I didn't choose to abandon my family. Remember that."

"Like any con man, you needed us to act as shills, to make you look legitimate." Robin's tone was harsh. "Mark Parsons wouldn't cheat his friends or steal from his employer. He's got that sweet wife, an earnest son, and a cute little girl. He can't be a crook."

Though Cam frowned at the bitterness in her tone, Mark merely took another drink and belched lightly. "Think what you want, say what you like," he responded. "You're going to help me score with Harrison Robeson. When it's done, I plan to leave the country. Neither you nor the hired guns from Florida will ever see me again."

"Why would I help you?"

Using the gun, Mark pointed at his prisoner. “Because your husband's life depends on it, my dear. Either we get a healthy chunk of Robeson's money, or Cam here starves to death.”

Chapter Eight

As Tom drove through the afternoon and into the night, Luca sat in the passenger seat. Hua and the dog rode in the back of the cargo van, seated on cushions that would later serve as beds. A Black woman, an Asian man, and a one-handed white guy made an odd trio, so they did what they could to avoid notice. Tom pumped the gas. They got dinner at a drive-thru, and they took turns exiting and entering the van at rest areas along the way. At each stop, one of them walked Bennett, who sniffed at everything from dead squirrels to discarded food wrappers with equal interest, perfectly content to be on a trip with his humans.

"Only Cam's tablet is registering a location now," Hua reported. "It thinks it's still in Brandell, but you know how unreliable the locators are. It will say you're in Los Angeles when you're actually in San Diego."

"It's a place to start," Tom said grimly.

Though they tried to remain positive, anxiety grew as the hours passed with no word from Cam or Robin. Had they been arrested? Had an accident? Misjudged the mayor's reaction to their visit? With no way to know until they reached their destination, they focused on practical matters rather than torturing themselves with what-ifs. Tom and Luca scanned the ditches for signs of recent accidents. Hua studied his tablet for news of some calamity along I-70. Nothing they saw explained their friends' silence.

They'd formed a rough plan. Luca would take a room at the motel where Cam and Robin had stayed and learn what she could about when and how they'd left. "I'll say I'm waiting for a friend to give me a ride to Detroit," she told the men. "That way I can say she got delayed if we need to stay longer than one night."

"Good idea, Lily." Tom used her clown name now that they were technically on a caper. He was Homey, and Hua was Bubbles. Along with Robin as Clarabelle, Cam was Bozo, and Robin's brother Chris was Ronald. Luca had chosen Lily for her clown name, a tribute to Lily Tomlin. When Cam pointed out that Tomlin wasn't really a clown, she'd shrugged and said, "She's funny. Clowns are funny."

Though new to the team, Luca was a fast learner who'd turned out to have a talent for...lying wasn't a term Tom liked. Dissembling, maybe. In addition to that, Luca had a shrewd sense of people and often amused the others by analyzing guests on TV talk shows. "He ain't got half as much money as he pretends," she'd say, or "When the doctor put in her cheek implants, some of her brain power ran out the slits."

Tom and Hua intended to pose as hikers and camp at a small city park. "The website says there is a shower facility," Hua reported. "I hope it is in good repair."

"And I hope the temps don't drop too low at night," Tom said. "I can do without a shower for a day or two, but I hate sleeping in the cold."

"Why don't you buy an extra car battery and one of those little heaters?" Luca asked. "I used to know a guy who lived in his car, and that's how he got through the cold nights."

It was a matter of a five-minute stop to do as she said, and Tom felt a little more optimistic with a heat source for night-time. Though he'd never shared it with the others, he suffered Post Traumatic Cold Intolerance in his damaged arm. Once he got chilled, it took a long time for his core temperature to normalize, and the stump ached like crazy.

They reached Brandell just before eleven p.m. Tom dropped Luca off at the blind side of the motel, and she went in to register. He and Hua quietly searched the motel lot, following the locator for the single device that was still sending out a signal, Cam's tablet. They found it in the trash can, along with Robin's tablet, the car's GPS device, and both phones. The inoperative devices rested in a few inches of water at the bottom of the can. Cam's tablet had escaped drenching, but it offered no hints to where they were. Its last use was a game he liked, which showed that Cam had been relaxed up to the moment when whatever had happened to them interrupted their plans.

"Do we have any other way to track the car?" Tom asked.

"No," Hua replied as they got back into the van. "We decided it was safer to not be traceable by the police or any enemies who might be looking for us." He punched the dashboard with a fist. "It's my fault. I never considered that we might need to be able to find our own vehicles."

"It isn't your fault," Tom told him. "They had phones. They had other devices. They should have been able to get us a message."

"But they couldn't," Hua said sadly. "And now—where are they?"

Leaving the motel, Hua and Tom went on to the city park. It appeared deserted, which they'd expected in late October. An honor system drop box asked them to deposit ten dollars for an overnight stay, which Hua did, filling out the card with one of the many false identities he created for such situations. The place was nicely wooded, a knoll with perhaps twenty campsites scattered around its base. Atop the knoll was a bath house with lights set into the ground around it, providing security without making the sites themselves too bright for sleeping.

Hua got out his tablet and began consulting various apps that might tell him where Robin and Cam were. "I've done everything I can think of," he mumbled, more to himself than to Tom. "In the future we should wear some sort of tracking device on our bodies, perhaps a watch or a piece of jewelry that sends a signal."

"Yeah." After a second Tom asked, "How long do you think we'll be doing this?"

Hua looked up, confused. "Looking for Robin and Cam?"

"No. Doing capers and punishing bad guys."

Tom saw a flash in Hua's eyes that revealed he'd asked himself the same question. How long did they want to live secret lives? How long could they get away with it? What would it take to break up the Kidnap Gang?

Hua's answer was not really an answer. "We should focus on finding them right now. We can talk later about where the gang is headed."

When Tom took Bennett for a walk to do his business, he saw that one other campsite was taken. A Lincoln Town Car was parked on the far side of the knoll. The vehicle seemed an odd choice for camping, but he sniffed the air and concluded the campers had grilled steaks for dinner. Calling softly to Bennett, Tom backed away, hoping their neighbors wouldn't feel the need to socialize. Traveling with his parents as a kid, he'd learned that people were often friendlier in the open air of a campground. It wasn't unusual to invite complete strangers to a bonfire or even to supper. If the people in the Lincoln were that type, they'd be disappointed. He and Hua wouldn't be around much, wouldn't be sociable, and wouldn't stay long. He hoped.

Hua was arranging the cushions into bedding when Tom and Bennett returned. When they'd made their beds, taken off their shoes, and turned off the lantern, Tom couldn't relax and drift off to sleep. Hua's restless movements revealed he was awake as well. Only Bennett rested, snoring softly and pawing at Tom's back as he dreamed of chasing squirrels.

"I saw a diner that had an 'Open All Night' sign out front," Tom finally said. "We might wander down there and see if we can find out what's been happening in Brandell."

"Good idea." Putting on their shoes and coats, they left an unhappy Bennett in the van. Hua promised to bring him back a snack, though Jai would have disapproved.

"It's a small town," Tom said as they walked. "If something odd happened recently, people will be talking about it."

The diner was only eight or nine tables, watched over by a tired-looking older woman who perked up briefly to see two strangers in her doorway. Tom chuckled to himself at the "Please Wait to Be Seated" sign, and the waitress didn't take it all that seriously either. "Sit anywhere you like, guys. Coffee?"

Though neither wanted it, and the smell suggested the coffee had been on the warmer too long, they both said yes. As they passed a case of pies, Tom decided he could do with a slice of apple. He would eat alone, since Hua operated on the premise that the digestive system needed twelve hours' rest each day. He seldom ate after six p.m.

Two sheriff's deputies sat at a table by the front window, shoveling in the day's special, Swiss steak with mashed potatoes and green beans. Tom nodded to the one who looked up as they passed, a young man whose uniform bulged at the gut. The guy's gaze moved to Hua then back to Tom, but he didn't seem suspicious. Hua wore what was for him a drab outfit, khaki cargo pants with a flannel shirt and a cap that said “Yellowstone.” Tom kept the prosthetic hand in his coat pocket as he followed Hua to a table.

“How's the special?” he asked the officers.

“Good,” the skinny one answered. The other nodded agreement, his mouth full. “You guys here to do some hunting?”

“Hiking. We’re writing a blog on lesser-known trails.”

“Nice.”

Tom wished he could think of a way to ask if there'd been any unusual happenings in the last twenty-four hours, but nothing came to mind. Anticipating that they would be eavesdropping, Hua took the booth next to the officers, seating himself with his back to the heavy-set deputy.

At first they made a show of talking about their supposed hike the next morning. Hua waxed enthusiastic about the different birds they might see, and Tom tried to sound interested. As Tom pretended to study the menu, Hua leaned back and listened to the conversation at the next table. When the deputies left he reported, “Their only excitement this week was a local man who got drunk and shot out the windows of an empty building.”

Tom was disappointed. “Maybe Luca will find out something at the motel.”

She did not. When they returned to the campground, Luca was waiting in the van. "I could have called," she told them, "but it's kind of lonely in that room all by myself."

"We eavesdropped on the local cops," Tom said. "They've apparently had no unusual events lately."

"That's what I got from the motel owner too. She said a couple stayed last night, but other than them it's only me in the past week. They left this morning. She didn't see them go, but the key was in the room."

"Their stuff is gone?"

"She said the beds were made and the sink was wiped clean."

"Sounds like Robin," Hua said. "She never leaves a mess for someone else to clean up."

"So they left the motel, headed for home." Tom petted the dog absently. "As far as we can discover, they didn't have an accident along the way. No trouble with the local police either."

"Then where are they?" Luca seemed to be holding onto her cool only with determined effort.

Tom licked his lips before replying. "I think we need to speak with the mayor."

Hua frowned. "Do you think she's clever enough to have tracked them down?"

"Not really, but we need to make sure."

"If she did, she didn't turn them in," Hua said. "Those deputies would have been talking about it if they'd arrested a couple of out-of-town break-in artists."

“First thing tomorrow, I’ll find out what the mayor knows.” Luca zipped her coat. “What are you guys going to do?”

Tom sighed. “Wander the area and hope for a miracle, I suppose.”

Pulling her collar up, Luca asked, “How could they disappear like that?”

Hua’s expression was grave. “What if someone from a past caper caught up with them?” They were silent for a few seconds before he added, “If that is the case, we are all in danger.”

“And Robin and Cam—” Tom didn’t finish, but his meaning was clear. If a criminal they’d shamed, robbed, and humiliated had somehow chased them down, the two founding members of the Kidnap Gang might already be dead.

Chapter Nine

As Cam watched helplessly, Mark Parsons tied Robin to the other chair, using strips of cloth torn from an old sheet. “Don't want to leave any marks on your wrists,” he explained, “but I have to leave for a while, and we can’t have you scampering off.” Once she was secured, Parsons released Cam from his chair and retied his hands behind his back. He wrapped the remains of the sheet over Cam's head, which made him feel disoriented, unbalanced, and short of breath. Leading him to the car, Parsons ordered Cam to lie across the back seat on his stomach. When he obeyed, Parsons lashed his feet so tightly to the armrest he was unable to sit up or roll over. Parsons went back inside, and when he returned, he dumped several objects on the passenger seat up front.

The drive to their destination took perhaps fifteen minutes. “While I hung out around here for the last month,” Parsons said in a conversational tone as they bumped along primitive roads. “I did some exploring that's going to pay off now. Lots of cabins on this lake. Lots of interesting outbuildings.”

After a series of turns down bumpy roads, Parsons stopped the car and untied Cam's feet so he could get out. Directing the way with sharp commands, he finally ordered, “Stop.” Cam wanted desperately to make a break for freedom, but he had no chance with his hands tied and eyes covered.

There was a rattle of metal. “Walk forward slowly. In about twenty feet you'll come to a raised threshold.” When Cam's feet found the barrier, he stepped over it. He sensed a dimming of light outside his makeshift hood.

“This is your home for a while,” Parsons said. “As long as Robin cooperates, I’ll bring you food and water every few days.” There was a clunk as something landed on the plank floor. “If you work at it, you can get free of those ropes in a few hours’ time. There’s food in there for incentive.” A few seconds later something soft hit Cam's chest, followed by a second, similar missile. “Blankets. It will get chilly in here, but I don't think you'll freeze.” With that a door slammed, and Cam heard a padlock slide into a hasp and click closed. Soon the car backed away, and silence fell.

Using his teeth, Cam managed to pull the sheet off his head. At first he could see nothing, but in time his eyes adjusted to what little light there was. He was in a small wooden building, no more than six by six feet. The construction was tight, with walls, floor, and ceiling all lined with tongue-and-groove cedar. In a corner was a wood-burning stove like the one Cam's father had used to heat his workshop in winter, except this stove had large, smooth rocks set in a metal pan on its top. Along three sides were benches, also made of cedar. Pictures Cam had seen in magazines came to mind, people wrapped in towels or wearing bathing suits, chatting as they cleaned their pores with steam from the heated stones. It was a freestanding sauna, the kind some people build in their back yards. As his vision improved, he saw there was a bucket in one corner with a long-handled ladle for dipping water and pouring it on the heated stones. He could almost hear the sizzle of steam rising, but he knew he wouldn’t have the luxury of heat during his stay in this place.

Listening, Cam heard the faint slap of waves outside. He was near a lake, probably the same lake the other cabin was on. Parsons had no doubt raided empty cabins for food and supplies, and when he needed a temporary prison, this place had come to mind.

Cam had to get out, but it wouldn’t be easy. The whole idea of a sauna was to keep heat in, which meant it was tightly sealed. Still, difficult isn't impossible. The first order of business was to free his hands. Once he’d done that, he'd figure out the next step. Ignoring the chafing that resulted from movement, Cam began twisting his hands, flexing and releasing every chord and muscle in an attempt to stretch the ropes that held him.

Chapter Ten

"What have you done with Cam?" Robin demanded when her father returned to the cabin.

"He's safe," Mark replied. "As long as you cooperate, I feed him. If you run, if you call for help, if you cross me up in any way, you'll never find him. He'll either starve or die of thirst, and it will be your fault."

"No," she responded. "It will be *your* fault. You'll be a killer, Mark, and while I lay a lot of evil at your door, I never believed you could cold-bloodedly murder another human being."

He shrugged. "Desperate times. I'll keep my part of the bargain as long as you keep yours."

"This isn't a bargain. It's extortion." Feeling tears of frustration sting her eyes, Robin forced herself to focus. "Tell me what I have to do."

"Well, I'm sort of making this up as I go," Mark admitted, "but here's my idea. You approach Robeson, saying you recently learned that the couple who raised you aren't really your grandparents. Your mother..." He paused to come up with a name. "...Angela, I think, was born to Dolores Robeson shortly before she died." He made an airy gesture. "We need to add some details, but according to Lola, Dolores' body wasn't discovered right away. It's possible her neighbors didn't know she had a kid, so no one mentioned it to the cops."

"Who will believe that?"

"You'll have to sell it, but I know you can," he said confidently. "I'll come along later to help."

"Of course you will."

Ignoring her sarcastic tone, he went on. "Our little girl grew up happy and healthy. At nineteen she met a wonderful man. They got married and had a child of their own."

"Me."

"Right." He put a hand on his chest. "But sadly, Angela and...Bill—I like Bill for your dad, okay? Anyway, they were killed in a car accident when you were...oh, say two years old. Bill's parents were much older, so again my wife and I raised someone else's child."

"You don't look like my grandfather."

"We can make you look younger and me look older. It'll work."

Robin sighed. "Why does this matter now, after all these years?"

Mark's expression turned sad. "Recently and ever-so-tragically, my wife died. Going through her desk, you found your mother's real birth certificate. Her mother's name was listed as Dolores Robeson. Without telling me, you began looking for your biological family." He lowered his head in false humility. "I will of course understand your curiosity, though it will hurt me to know my little Daphne can't accept that we consider her our child, no matter what her blood says."

“What if Robeson doesn't care that he has a living descendant?”

“Oh, he'll care, Robbie. The older one gets, the more he wants to know he's made something—someone—that will remain when he's gone from this world.”

Robin blew upward to dislodge a strand of hair that had fallen over her eyes. “Okay. I'm supposed to convince this man I’m his heir so he'll hand over some portion of his fortune to me, which I then give to you.”

“I have an idea how to speed the process up. A week, two at the most, and you’ll be on your way and so will I.” With the air of sharing a wonderful secret he said, “When I took your phone, I messaged everyone in your call list to let them know you and…Cam, is it? –have decided to take some time off for a secluded, romantic vacation.”

The limited number of people on her contacts list wouldn’t believe that, but what could they do about it? No one, least of all Robin herself, could have predicted that returning to Brandell would mean a reunion with her long-lost father.

Not only were her friends unable to act, she was too, as long as Cam was in danger. She had to find out where he was and send help. After that she’d deal with what her father had in store for her. Taking a deep breath, she voiced a small rebellion. “I won’t be Daphne. That name sounds nothing like me.”

He seemed surprised. “Okay, you pick then.”

It didn’t matter, but then again, it did. He shouldn’t be in control of everything. “Serena.”

Victorious in the larger plan, Mark could afford to be generous in the details. “Lovely. It conjures happiness and peace.”

Chapter Eleven

Luca left Hua and Tom's campsite unsure how she was supposed to get the mayor of Brandell to talk to her about anything. The guys appeared to think Gessing would blab her secrets to the first woman who showed up on her doorstep willing to listen, but Luca figured a white, small-town, middle-aged divorcee wasn't likely to spill her guts to a stranger of a different race from a different world.

Having joined the gang only a few months ago, Luca often got a kick out of the personalities in the unlikely band of justice seekers. They had skills, she gave them that, but she figured it was only a matter of time until the eye of law enforcement turned on them. The result would be arrest, but oddly, the idea didn't scare her. It made her eager to protect them, to extend their glorious craziness. The Kidnap Gang was the best group of people Luca had ever met, and she intended to stick with them as long as they needed her.

Luca had been given her first solo assignment, and she wasn't about to fail. She toyed with the idea of pretending to be a beauty consultant, but door-to-door sales were uncommon these days. She might follow the mayor to work in the morning, say she was thinking of moving to the area, and then play it by ear, but that seemed weird too. No approach Luca could devise allowed her to bring up the subject of bribes and the intruders who'd shown up in the mayor's bedroom in the night.

If someone got in once, might it happen again? She'd heard the details of Gessing's house often enough when she helped Robin and Cam practice the caper. An older modular construction, the place had several possible entry points. Had Gessing burglar-proofed them all since yesterday? Doubtful. She'd probably done what she could and then made an appointment for professional assistance in the future.

Two hours later, Luca tried Helen Gessing's sliding glass door. It didn't budge, and her phone light revealed a broomstick in the track. Simple but effective. That sent her to the bathroom window, which had been Robin's second choice. "People open it to let the steam escape after a shower," she'd said, "and they often forget to relock it."

To Luca's great disappointment, the window was locked. She began checking other windows, testing each one with her fingers. Most had exterior screens screwed to the frame, so she couldn't even reach the windows themselves. Doggedly she kept going, and at the front she found a window with no screen. From its slightly bent frame she concluded it was where the air conditioner went in summer. Now it was her opportunity for entry.

Luca was no B&E expert, but she'd grown up in an area where it did no good to call for help when you locked yourself out of your apartment or when some kid thought it was funny to lock the laundry room doors and then climb out the transom window. You had to be a problem-solver, and that meant she'd picked a few simple locks and jimmied a few windows. It wasn't crime; it came with the territory.

Slipping the blade of her Swiss army knife between the two frames, Luca worked at the latch until it turned, freeing the lower section. The metallic clunk sounded loud in the night, but when she paused to listen, no dog barked and no door opened. Sliding the window up, she climbed through and stopped again, breathless with anxiety. The lights were out. The place was quiet. The occupant was asleep.

Opening the bag she'd brought along, Luca got herself ready. Her disguise was ad libbed, since she hadn't come prepared for a caper. She had black pants; that was easy, and a long, black sweater she now put on backwards. She'd been stymied for a while as to how to hide her face, but in an unlocked shed down a side street she found gloves and a fishing hat with black mosquito netting. Without a mirror she couldn't tell, but she was pretty sure that in a dark room, she'd be merely a voice and a silhouette.

Her main concern was whether Gessing had a weapon. Jai hadn't asked for details from Robin on how the caper had gone, but they'd discussed the possibility that a woman who lived alone would have a gun or some other weapon with her at night. After a break-in, that was even more likely.

She stopped in the doorway to decide how to proceed. Gessing was asleep, but a dark outline on the pillow beside her confirmed Luca's fears. A gun.

The prospect of having the weapon pointed at her froze Luca for a moment. She'd had some bad encounters in her life, but nobody had ever threatened to shoot her. Breathing in through her nose and out through her mouth, she tried to calm herself. Her best move was to creep to the bed and get the gun without waking Gessing, but for a while she couldn't make herself move. Going toward the gun seemed crazy. Moving away seemed the sane thing to do.

Listening to Gessing's regular breathing, Luca focused on Robin and Cam, missing and probably in danger. They'd been good to her, and she wanted to find them. With that in mind she stepped forward, reached over the sleeping mayor, and picked up the gun.

Stepping out of reach, she said in a low tone, "Hey, Helen. Wake up!"

She came awake at once, sitting straight up in bed and taking in the situation in an instant. Like other unprepared gun owners, her weapon was now more a threat than a protection, though Luca took care to aim away from Gessing. "I'm not here to hurt you."

Alarm turned to anger. "So what are you here for then? I did what you said, even though it cost me—" She stopped. "You're not—"

"I'm the follow-up," Luca interrupted. "Sort of like the Ghost of Christmas Yet to Come."

Gessing looked confused. "What?"

"I want to know if you sent someone to find the two people who came last night."

"Sent someone?" She was clearly lost. "I did what they said. I turned down the...you know. The money."

"That was good." Luca took a step forward. "Are you sure you didn't go looking for them or hire someone to track them down?"

She shook her head violently. "I don't want anyone to know about...you know…" Suddenly she seemed to wilt into the sheets. "I gotta tell you, it's hard. I agreed to be the mayor because nobody else wanted the job, but now that I'm in office, people criticize everything I do. If I put up new streetlights, I'm either wasting taxpayer money or I didn't put in enough of them. If I try to get developers in, half the people say, 'It's about time she did something,' and the other half scream that I'm ruining the pristine natural beauty of the area."

At the frustration in Gessing's voice, Luca let the gun fall to her side. "I hear you, girlfriend. People are never happy, no matter how much you do for them."

"It's not like I get paid a lot," she complained. "Running a small town is a part-time job, so I have to keep my realty business going too. And do you think that as mayor I can establish office hours that people will stick to?"

"I bet they expect you to be mayor all the time."

Gessing pointed a finger at Luca. "Exactly. People call all hours of the day and night, and I'm supposed to drop whatever I'm doing and go talk to the city plow guy who drives too fast. And I'd better make sure the Christmas decorations are up by December first, no matter who's sick or on vacation."

Luca took a seat at the bottom corner of Gessing's bed and laid the gun in her lap. "It sounds like you've got a tough job."

"Nobody knows." Gessing sniffed. "Nobody cares either."

Luca felt bad for her. "Listen, I bet you do it better than most people would."

Another sniff. "I try."

"That's good. But you can't take money from crooks. You're a public servant, so you have to do what's best for the public."

"I did the right thing." Gessing's voice was slightly defensive, so Luca didn't point out that without their intervention, she might not have. "I really do care about Brandell. I try to be a good mayor."

"That's wonderful." Patting the lump in the plush blanket where Gessing's foot stuck up, Luca stood. "I'll leave the gun in the mailbox. You should go back to sleep now."

Gessing put a hand on her chest. "After two nights of you guys and your midnight visits? I may never sleep again."

Chapter Twelve

Cam shouted for help every few minutes, calling loudly and for as long as his lungs could manage. No one came. At the same time, he continued working to free his hands. Though he couldn't see it, the rope had some give, and by turning and twisting, he loosened it enough to allow his fingers to reach the knots. After that it was a matter of picking at them until he found one that undid the outermost knot and allowed him to reach the next and the next. As he worked, Cam returned to a habit he'd had since he was a kid, talking aloud to help himself focus. "There's a bunch of them, but they're all granny knots. Parsons said, 'Scout's honor,' but if he ever was a Boy Scout, he must have skipped the knot-tying badge."

When he felt the last knot give, Cam's relief was tempered by pain as the blood began flowing freely into his hands. Rubbing his wrists until it no longer felt like he had wooden blocks at the ends of his arms, he shouted for help for a while. Same result, nothing.

If no one was around, he'd have to help himself. His immediate needs were food and warmth, since the temperature had dropped. Cam felt around until he found the blankets Parsons had tossed his way. Wrapping himself in both of them, he sat down on a bench and located the bundle he'd heard Parsons set on the floor. It was a knapsack, and inside it, the first thing he found was a small packet of Oreos. He ate all four of them, swigging between bites from the water bottle.

Once hunger wasn't an issue, Cam explored his prison cell. By running his hands over the walls and ceiling, he learned that the sauna had two outlets, the door and a hole where a stovepipe exited the structure. It was much too small to be used as an exit, but he pulled the pipe apart at a seam and looked out. The view he got of stars overhead pleased him, for no reason other than he liked outside better than inside. Cam stuck the section of sheet Parsons had used to blindfold him through the opening, pushing it up until it protruded through the roof. He replaced the pipe section he'd removed, catching one end of the fabric in the seam to hold it in place. Something white flapping on the roof of the sauna might draw notice, and someone might come to investigate. It was a faint hope, and Cam muttered, "He probably picked this spot because nobody can see it from the road." That reminded him to holler for a while, though his throat was getting raw and he doubted it would bring results.

Cam examined the door, his best hope for escape, testing every inch of it with his fingers. It rested firmly in its casing, and the hinges were on the outside. He tried ramming it with his shoulder, but the space was too small to build impetus and he merely bounced off. The tongue-and-groove cedar offered no breaks and was impossible to breach without tools. Cam dumped out the knapsack, hoping for a knife or fork he could use as a pry bar, but found only more cookies, four plastic-wrapped deli sandwiches, and a second bottle of water. Giving up on escape for the moment, he ate one of the sandwiches. "Weird," he commented after the last bite. "Could be turkey. It's hard to tell." Though he'd have liked a second sandwich, he decided it was best to be frugal. "Never know when Jerk-face will bring more food."

Daylight penetrated the sauna with no apparent entry point, as daylight does. Things went from black to deep gray, and Cam saw the place more clearly. Realizing he needed some sort of sanitation, he set the water bucket in one corner for use as a toilet. In the opposite corner he set his remaining food and water. He tore the nylon lining out of the knapsack to use as a makeshift cleaning cloth. "Not great," he said to the air around him, "but it's got to do."

Sitting back down on the bench, he gave in to a moment of despair. Parsons seemed perfectly willing to let Robin's "husband" die. Robin had no way of knowing where he was or if her dad kept his word about feeding him periodically. She would do what she could to keep Cam alive, but in the end, his life lay in the hands of a ruthless man. Cam didn't know enough about Mark Parsons to predict his reaction if Robin didn't do as he wanted. If she tried to contact Tom and the others, would he hurt her, even kill her? If she did as he said, would he kill her anyway when her usefulness to him was done? The tension between them was obvious. Even if he wasn't a killer, the scheme Parsons had cooked up could result in Robin's arrest. In that case, Cam figured he'd be left to starve in this place with no one to hear his final, weak cries.

"No." He stood, throwing off the blankets. "You can't get stuck thinking about bad stuff." Words his father had often said sounded in his head: *Worry steals today's joy with the fear of things that might never happen.*

Both he and Robin were in a bad spot, but he'd keep working on getting himself free, and she would figure out a way to get the better of the crook. That's what Robin always did.

Chapter Thirteen

Robin spent the night tied to a chair, which left her hurting in so many places she couldn't isolate a single sore spot. Pain shot up her arms, her back, and her legs. Her neck and shoulders ached. Her hands numbed even though she flexed them every few minutes. In addition, she was hungry, having last eaten at breakfast the day before. Her stomach sent pangs designed to tell her brain it was time for a meal, but her brain was unable to do anything about it.

She was in no mood for humor when Mark awoke, rose from the cot in the corner, and picked up her car keys. Dangling them in a smart aleck parody of parent-child relationships he asked, "Sweetie, can I borrow the car?"

"No. If I remember right, you're almost as horrible a driver as you are a person."

"Too bad, because it isn't up for discussion." Jutting his lower lip, he turned thoughtful. "I was caught off guard by the determination my former friends showed in pursuing me, so I'm presently without a vehicle. I thought I'd lost them in Miami, but I returned to my hotel and there they were, waiting in the lobby. I wandered the streets all night, not sure what to do, but the next morning I withdrew the modest amount of money I had in my bank account and hitched a ride to Atlanta with a trucker." Mark's face brightened. "He was a really nice guy. Helped me find a driver headed to Indianapolis, which brought me close. The trucker dropped me off at the Brandell exit, and I walked the rest of the way." He tilted his head. "I think that was a good thing. I mean, who'd expect to find me hoofing it down some two-lane state road?"

"No one who knows you," Robin admitted.

He grinned. "See? I'm adaptable." Gesturing at the cabin he went on, "No one's visited this place in a decade, and the whole area is mostly deserted this time of year, so I'm off the grid, as they say."

"Without a car, clothes, or funds."

"Yeah." He sighed. "I walked into town the first day and bought some things, but it took forever, and carrying four sacks of groceries back here almost killed me. I started looking for some form of mechanized transportation, and down the lakeshore a bit, I found a four-wheeler stored in a shed." He shook his head at the memory. "They left the key hanging on a hook near the door frame, can you believe that? Anyway, I borrowed it, and that's how I've been getting around."

"Then you don't need our car."

"But I do. The four-wheeler's back at the motel where I found you two." He paused, looking at the logo on her keychain. "You drive a Ford. Remember that Taurus we had in Terre Haute? Homely thing, but it ran like a top."

"All I remember of Terre Haute is that I had to leave school in the middle of the year—for either the fourth or fifth time—without saying goodbye to my friends or my teacher."

Mark made a dismissive gesture. "Experiences like that get a kid ready for the real world."

It felt like Robin's tongue wasn't under her brain's control. "What was real was the black eye Chris got when he said he didn't want to move again."

"I never hit any of you." Even Mark couldn't swallow that lie, and he added, "If I did, it was for good reason."

She shook her head angrily. "Like when Mom tried to tell you the phone had been shut off for non-payment, or the time Chris asked for a few bucks for baseball cleats? Whenever one of your schemes failed, we'd move somewhere new and then spend weeks walking on eggshells, afraid you'd punch one of us simply for entering the room."

Mark's lips grew tight, but he tried for a cool response. "You were a kid. You had no idea how much pressure I was under with the three of you dragging at my heels."

"I'm pretty sure the accepted way of dealing with pressure isn't knocking your family around." In a rush like a dam breaking, Robin allowed herself to voice the memory of years of abuse. "You hurt us—Chris worse than me or Mom, but we all got it when you felt like dishing it out."

"Life isn't easy or pretty or simple, Robbie. It's a father's job to teach his family that. I might not always have—"

"I recall that life wasn't easy," Robin interrupted, "when you got a big score and went on one of your 'holidays,' leaving us with no income for months at a time. I remember that life wasn't pretty when I didn't distract the woman at the gas station long enough for you to finish whatever petty theft you were committing. In fact, I got smacked in the mouth for it. And I know life wasn't simple when at five years old I had to pretend to have cancer so you could take advantage of some church group. If that was teaching me about life, great job, *Daddy*."

He sniffed once, his face tight. "So I wasn't the perfect father or the perfect husband. I admit that."

Mark's fake remorse seemed even worse to Robin than defense of his actions. Heat rose from her chest and colored her face. "You're a bully and a coward and a cheat. You're everything I despise in this world, everything I've dedicated myself to—"

She stopped herself, though it took effort. She couldn't reveal that she'd formed an organization to punish people like her father. Giving Mark Parsons that kind of information was dangerous, yet she was aware that every crook the Kidnap Gang punished was atonement on Robin's part for what this man had forced her to do all those years ago.

"You're the worst kind of father, husband…person. I have nothing but contempt for you."

For a moment Robin thought he'd strike her. The biggest sin of all, she knew from experience, was forcing Mark Parsons to face what he really was. She and Chris had learned young to say as little as possible when he was around. Their mother had practiced willful blindness and used flattery as protection from abuse. Her fawning manner had often made Robin feel sick. Now she'd dared to speak the truth, and she waited to feel the slap, the pinch, the closed fist, fighting the familiar dread of his anger. Terrified of her father as a child, she found it difficult to face him still. She forced herself to meet his gaze, aware that it had taken her years to come to the point where she felt strong enough to do so.

Though his hand rose in subconscious longing, in the end Mark walked away, slamming the cabin door behind him to underscore his unhappiness.

Once the car was gone, Robin began sawing at the rags that held her. No matter how she twisted, she was unable to free either hand.

Giving up on that, she rocked the chair from side to side in hopes of pulling it apart. Despite its age, it remained in one piece. She finally slumped in defeat, cursing the craftsmen of the 1900s who made furniture that was meant to last.

Chapter Fourteen

It was stressful to stay in the cramped van all night, especially when Bennett sensed their unease and began moving around. Tom would have liked to do some reconnaissance, a search for their car or simply a walk to orient himself, but he knew that strangers wandering the streets of Brandell after midnight would create suspicion. Out of conversation, he and Hua had covered the present situation extensively and weren't interested in other topics, they waited in silence. Bennett rested, contributing gaseous smells to the closed space with unwelcome frequency. Tom tried to doze. Hua consulted his tablet computer a dozen times, checking to see if there was news. They got neither rest nor results.

At eight o'clock, they put Bennett on his leash and began exploring. They looked at the only repair shop in town, hoping to see the car Robin and Cam had been driving. When the bays opened, they saw a blue panel van on one side and a vintage Mustang on the other. Tom sighed as he turned away. It had been a long shot. They had nowhere else to try. "This is not useful," Hua said. "They could be miles from here, and we're patrolling a town where nothing has happened, perhaps a town where nothing ever happens." His phone buzzed; he looked at the screen and said, "Luca." He put the phone on speaker so Tom could hear.

"The mayor isn't our girl."

Hua checked the time on his phone. "You spoke with her already this morning?"

Briefly Luca explained her decision to visit the woman's bedroom in the night rather than try to finesse information out of her. She ended with an assessment. "Gessing isn't the kind of person who'd hunt Robin down. She's actually pretty nice when you get to know her."

Tom and Hua exchanged looks of concern. The fact that Luca had taken it upon herself to plan and carry out a crime was unnerving. All their capers were discussed at length among the group, with every eventuality considered and planned for. What if the mayor reported her midnight visit? Now that Gessing had refused the bribe, she had no reason not to tell the police about the interlopers who broke into her home. Luca might have left fingerprints or a hair or skin cells behind, and though they'd never asked, she might be in a database somewhere. The whole gang might be compromised by her rash act, though she obviously considered it a success.

Hua shook his head, and Tom got the message. With Robin and Cam missing, it wasn't the time to chastise her. He kept his voice even as he said, "We've been all over Brandell and haven't found anything that points us in a direction."

"I'm not sure if it helps," Luca said, "but the motel owner is griping that somebody left a four-wheeler in her parking lot yesterday. If it's still there this afternoon, she's going to have it towed away."

"We'll swing by and have a look."

Ten minutes later, Tom and Hua stood staring at an older model Arctic Cat ATV as if willing it to tell them where it came from. The machine sat silent, its key missing and its headlights blank in the autumn sunlight. At the back was a small custom plate that said "Lost in the Pines."

"Machine break down?" asked a man who was walking his Yorkie.

As Bennett and the smaller dog began the sniffing process required to become friends, Tom answered, "No. I guess someone abandoned it here."

"Huh." The man walked around the ATV, and his little dog reluctantly left Bennett's side and trotted behind. "Lost in the Pines, eh?" he said conversationally. "I've heard of it."

Tom kept his tone casual as he asked, "Can you tell us about it? The motel owner would like to get the machine back to where it belongs."

He rubbed at his neck. "It was a resort out on the south end of Pitcher Lake. I think it's closed down now."

"Pitcher Lake. Where's that?"

"West of town maybe five miles. There's all kinds of cabins out there, most of 'em seasonal. A lot of the roads aren't even plowed in the wintertime."

When the man and his dog went on, Tom phoned Luca, who'd been watching out her window, and told her they planned to visit the old resort. "Whoever left the four-wheeler there might have seen Robin and Cam," Luca said. "Maybe it broke down and they gave him a ride home."

As Tom and Luca talked, Hua found an online listing for the resort. It hadn't been updated in years. When they returned to the van, he entered the address in the GPS and started for what they hoped was the four-wheeler's home.

The GPS got lost after about eight miles. The voice kept saying they'd arrived at their destination when there was nothing but forest in sight. “Keep going,” Tom suggested. “Maybe we’ll see something.”

A half mile farther on, Hua braked. “Look.” A faded sign with an arrow said, “Lost in the Pines, 1/2 mile.” Hua turned down a drive heavily coated with rust-colored pine needles.

When they reached the resort, they found playfully decorated cabins that were now ruins due to neglect. Some tilted crazily, and one had no door at all. The main building was larger, more modern, and appeared to be used occasionally. They walked around it and stopped at the lake, looking at the many cabins nestled along its shore. Most were small and primitive, but a few had been modernized and expanded. About a third of the way around was an attractive summer home with huge windows along the lakeside, all shuttered now in preparation for winter.

“What is that small building near the big house, the one that stands by itself?” Hua asked. “It looks like an outhouse with a smokestack.”

Tom looked where he was pointing and thought about it. “I’d guess that’s a sauna.”

“I don’t know that word.”

“It’s like a steam bath you set in your back yard. I think you’re supposed to sit in the heat for a while and then go roll in the snow.”

Hua shivered. “That does not sound attractive to me.”

“Me neither, but I guess you wouldn’t know until you try it.” He turned away. “There’s nothing out there we care about. Let’s see what else we can find here.”

On the other side of the lodge they found what they'd been looking for: a metal storage shed whose door gaped open, revealing emptiness. "Could have been a four-wheeler in there," Tom muttered.

When they looked closer, they found that the lock on the shed door had been smashed. "Someone stole himself a ride into town."

"And abandoned the machine at the motel," Hua said. "Where did the thief go?"

"With Cam and Robin, maybe," Tom answered. "The question is did they invite him along, or did he invite himself?"

Chapter Fifteen

Mark returned from his trip to Maple City, a large town about forty miles away, smelling of soap and in a good mood. “I worked out the details of the con on the drive, found a truck stop that let me clean up, and got everything I think we’re going to need,” he told Robin. “With a little practice, we’ll be ready to go this afternoon.”

“How is Cam?”

He gave her an admonishing look. “I’ll take care of him, Robbie. Concentrate on your part.” He set several shopping bags on the table. “I bought you clothes in a younger style. Honestly, Sweetheart, you dress like you’re forty.” Showing the various items he’d chosen for her, Mark chatted as if their relationship was normal and amicable. “I put this stuff on your credit card, since I don’t like using mine unless it’s absolutely necessary. You never know how good Ronnie’s minions are at tracking stuff like that.”

“He’s got people who can track your digital footprints?”

“He’s got people for everything. Ronnie’s one of those anal types, and when I went after his money, it was like I touched an exposed nerve.” He smiled. “I was lucky to get away, but I’m smart too. I don’t think they have any idea where I am.”

"I get it," Robin said tiredly. "You're smarter than everyone else on the planet. Now let's get down to what I'm supposed to do when I get to Robeson's place."

"Sweetly and sincerely, you're going to inform the old codger that you recently learned you're related to him. Here, I'll show you what I did." One by one he laid out documents he'd manufactured at a copy shop. As he talked, he folded some, rubbed others against the table edge to crease them, and darkened one by laying it flat on a pan and pouring tea over it. After he hung it up to dry, he showed Robin three photographs he'd filched from the library's local history section. "Doesn't this couple look like a great mom and dad for you?"

Better than what I had, she thought, but that made her feel bad. Her mom hadn't been bad, just…gullible. The couple in the photo did look like nice people, and she wondered how her life would have been different if she and Chris had had parents who paid their bills, stayed in one place, and thought of their children's welfare before their own. No sense wondering. Her aching arms reminded her that her father thought only of himself. Life is what it is. As Tom often said, "You take what you get and deal with it the best you can."

When he had the documents the way he wanted them, Mark untied Robin. "Move around a little," he ordered. "We don't want you to be too stiff." She rolled her eyes at his choice of pronoun. *"We" don't want any of this, Dad.* Still, she obeyed, gingerly moving her limbs until they began feeling normal again. As she regained control of her hands, she considered whacking Mark with something, perhaps a piece of wood from a stack next to the stove. If she acted quickly…Robin imagined the force of the blow she might aim at the man who'd made her so miserable so many times.

Cam's predicament made that impossible. Even if she was able to overpower him, Mark could simply refuse to tell her where Cam was. Robin wasn't the kind of person who could beat information out of anyone, much less her own father.

"Put on the outfit I laid out and pack the rest in your suitcase," he ordered. "I'm willing to bet you'll be invited to stay over at Robeson's house until the relationship question is settled."

Glaring until he turned his back, she changed into gray leggings and a tank top paired with a bright red pullover sweater that hung off one shoulder. Mark turned to inspect her, frowning. "The clothes are okay, but we need a little makeup, and..." He took Robin's chin in his hand. She shivered at his touch, but he appeared not to notice. Reaching up, he loosened her hair from the topknot she'd started with on Monday and fluffed it around her face. "Softer, younger. When he looks at you, we want him to see his little girl."

"She probably didn't look anything like me."

"We see what we want to, Robbie. Surely I taught you that much."

It was true. As a kid she'd watched him weave a spell for his victims, offering what he sensed they longed for: love, money, or simply someone who cared enough to listen to them. Like any good con man, Mark read his victims' tells, little actions that gave away their emotional state, and acted accordingly.

"You've spent a lot of time thinking about this."

He smiled as if she'd meant it as a compliment. "At first I listened to Nurse Lola just to be nice. But even after I was done with her, it tugged at my mind. A lost heir—what a great story." The smile became a wolfish grin. "What a great opportunity!"

For more than an hour, Mark made Robin go over the scenario he'd created. He questioned her closely, testing her ability to adapt to the situation and ad lib when necessary. When she rose to every challenge, he seemed pleased. Robin didn't let on that she lied for a living. She was like Mark in that way, but, she hoped, different in ways that mattered. Ignoring his praise, she focused on Cam. Once she freed him from whatever prison Mark had devised, she'd turn her skills to paying her father back for this latest betrayal of the parent-child bond.

Satisfied she was ready, Mark handed her the car keys. "Off we go, Serena. You'll drop me off in Maple City, where I'll get a vehicle for my own use." He pointed. "See? I found a Minnesota license plate for your car at a salvage yard. It's expired, but I doubt anyone will notice."

"You thought of everything," she said sarcastically.

He bowed as if she'd praised him. "All part of the job."

As she made her way outside, Robin was surprised to find the day bright and cheerful. Her mood was better matched to Uncle Tim's decaying cabin, dark and depressing. She squinted as her eyes adjusted, though the warmth felt good on her skin. Mark pointed toward the car, and Robin stumbled forward, her feet revealing her unwillingness to deceive an innocent man and steal his money. "Think of Cam," Mark warned. "He's waiting for you to come for him."

"It's the reason I'm doing this," she said. "For him. Not for you."

The ride to Maple City was mostly silent. Robin followed Mark's directions, which led back through Brandell and then along a well-maintained state road to the larger town. She pulled in at a small car dealership that advertised bargains on "Basic Transportation Vehicles." Nothing she saw in the lot would have met Cam's standards, but since Mark would be using her credit card, cheap was good.

"You're on your own." Mark got out of the car but leaned in through the window. Robin winced as he reached in and gripped her shoulder. "Remember, when I have what I want, you get your man back, and I get to board a plane to somewhere nice. You'll never see me again." Grinning, he held up three fingers as he backed away. "Scout's honor."

Leaving Maple City, Robin followed the directions Mark had given, continuing west about five miles before turning onto a county road that twisted and turned, leading in the end to a tiny jewel of a lake. Along its edge she saw no homes, either near the road or across the water. Did Harrison Robeson own the whole lake?

It seemed so, since the road ended at a paved driveway that sloped steeply upward. A wrought-iron gate stood open, and an arch above it said "Robeson." Robin turned in and drove up the hill. For most of the way she passed through thick pines, sturdy maples, and massive oaks, the latter two looking older and heavier now that fall had robbed them of color. Though it wasn't exactly warm outside, she rolled the window down and sniffed at the air, picking out smells of nature: pine, decaying leaves, and even a faint trace of skunk. Her mood lifted a little, though she bit her lip when she considered what she'd come there to do.

Periodically the lake glinted blue between the black trunks, growing farther and farther below. The last few gold leaves of autumn drifted onto the road and skittered to the side as she passed. After perhaps half a mile, Robin saw several outbuildings on her right. At her left the drop was steep, and she saw two different sets of stairs going down to the water. They were rough, simply logs set into the hillside, with hewn cedar posts as handrails.

The trees opened suddenly, and there was the house, as impressive as Mark had described. A combination of rough timber and smoky glass, it blended into the landscape like a really big tree house. Roofs slanted in all directions, and the cantilevered porch offered what had to be a stupendous view. Here a more formal set of stairs descended to the lake, treated timbers with manufactured railings and concrete footings. At one side a track ran downhill, and a weatherproof chair sat empty at the top. She guessed that since the old man could no longer manage the steep climb, he'd had a lift installed that allowed him to visit the lake when he chose to.

Leaving her car, Robin approached the wide plank door. She raised a hand to knock, but it opened with an abrupt jerk that implied her presence on the threshold was an inconvenience. Looking up, she met the gaze of a Scandinavian male as tall and broad as Cam. Where Cam was dark-haired and dark-eyed, this man was all Viking, with white-blond hair, fair skin, and ice-blue eyes. Robin's first thought was that a man so beautiful should have been modeling cologne. Judging from the damp towel slung over one shoulder, he'd been washing dishes.

The vision spoke in accented English. "Can I help you?"

"Um, yes. I mean, I hope so. I'm looking for Harrison Robeson."

The blond giant's brow furrowed. "Mr. Robeson doesn't see people he doesn't know."

"Oh." Robin feigned disappointment. "I wanted to..." Looking around, she seemed suddenly to change her mind. "I didn't expect…this." She gestured at the house. "I wanted to know where I...who I am."

The man folded arms the size of telephone poles across his chest. "What are you trying to say?"

“I think, I mean, I'm pretty sure Mr. Robeson is, um, a relative.”

The arms settled more tightly against his impressive pecs. “Mr. Robeson has no living family. I've been his personal assistant for five years, so I would know if he did.” His *v*’s came out as *f*’s, and final consonants were emphasized. *AssistanT. DiD.*

A soft whir behind the man caused him to turn, and Robin got her first glimpse of Harrison Robeson. Settled in a wheelchair that looked to have every bell and whistle available, the old man seemed too small for his skin, a collection of bones in an oversized sack. Still, his manner was bright. Squinting through thick glasses he asked, “Who have you got there, Svein?”

“I'm sorry your nap was interrupted,” Svein said.

“No problem,” his boss replied cheerfully. To Robin he said, “We don’t get much company.”

“This young woman came here by mistake.” Svein’s tone was cool.

Robeson laughed, revealing dentures too large for his shrunken face. “All the way out here by mistake? That's hard to believe.”

“The mistake isn't directions,” Svein said. “It’s her reason for coming.”

Stepping around the caregiver, Robin spoke directly to her host. “Mr. Robeson, I think my mother was your granddaughter, and her mother was your daughter Dolores.” She patted her purse. “I recently stumbled on some papers that convinced me I had to find you.”

The old man's face lit. “You knew Dolores?”

"No. She died long before I was born." Robin put on her most earnest expression, though her face burned red, as it always did when she lied. "If we could talk for a few minutes, I'll show you."

The pause that followed felt as if time had stopped. Svein glared at Robin, who tried to look honest. Robeson set his chin on a bony fist and considered. When she was on the verge of giving up, plotting the most dignified exit she could manage, he raised his face and spoke. "Svein, dig out some of those cookies you made this morning while I show this young woman the view from the deck."

Chapter Sixteen

When Tom's phone rang, he groaned. "What's wrong?" Hua asked.

"It's Chris."

"Oh."

After some hesitation, he answered the call. "What's up?"

"I've been trying to reach my sister since yesterday, but she isn't answering her phone. Then I got this weird message from her about taking time off. I thought I'd better check with you."

Tom sent Hua a helpless look. They'd all received the same message: *Won't be around for a week. We've decided to take some time for us*. "Is it some sort of code?" Luca had asked, "Cam's idea of a joke?"

"No," Hua had replied. "Cam doesn't joke—at least, not like that."

Nothing they could come up with explained it.

Neither of them wanted to lie to Chris, but they didn't want to worry him needlessly either. In the end Tom told the truth. "We lost contact yesterday. We're tracing their movements, but so far we haven't found any sign of where they've gone."

Chris sighed. "Tell me what you know."

Tom did, ending with, "If there's anything you can do, I'll let you know, but right now, we're flying blind."

"If they were able to tell us what's going on, they'd have done it by now," Chris said. "We should assume they're in trouble."

"Could someone in Brandell have recognized her?" Tom asked. "Some person who knew you as kids?"

"I doubt it, but even if that happened, it doesn't explain why they would go silent."

"Right. Listen, we're doing everything we can to find them."

"I know you are. Let me know if I can do something, please."

"You're only an hour or so from Brandell," Tom said. "If we need help, you'll be the first person we call."

Chapter Seventeen

As they ate cookies and sipped fragrant coffee, Robin told Harrison Robeson her story, showing photographs of strangers and false documents as she went. She tried to smile and look earnest, but the feeling that the whole thing was wrong wouldn't go away. Though not a natural liar, she'd been taught the tricks, the direct gaze, the shy smile, the doubtful phrase—"Oh no, that would be too much trouble"—as a way of leading the mark toward the goal of the con.

When she felt they deserved it, Robin could use those things to deceive people. This time was different, though. This wasn't a crooked businessman or a corrupt politician. He was a nice old man who watched her closely as she spoke, his manner eager and his eyes kind. It took her back to those childhood times when kind men and nice women had expressed sorrow for whatever tragedy her father told them she was enduring: the loss of her mother. The pain of illness. The pangs of hunger.

Though she felt like a rat and her stomach roiled with acid, Robin adopted a convincing manner. Until Cam was safe and Mark was gone from her life a second time—for good—she had to maintain the lie.

"I was raised by people I thought were my grandparents," she told Robeson as a disapproving Svein hovered nearby. "My parents were killed in a car accident when I was little." She laid one of the photographs Mark had taken from the library archives on a tray Svein had rotated into place on Harry's lap. Apparently his hands were so arthritic that holding things was difficult for him. The couple standing next to a one-story house had a young child, held in her father's arms. Their clothing said '90s, the mother in denim jeans and jacket, the father in a white, short-sleeved shirt that suggested middle management, perhaps at a chain store.

"My grandparents were great. When Gram died a few months ago, I tried to help Gramps figure out her system of paying bills and such. In a metal box at the back of a desk drawer, I found the real story of my life."

"And my name is part of that?"

"The one parent listed on my mother's birth certificate is Dolores Robeson. With a little research, I found her death certificate, which gave me her parents' names."

"Harrison and Stella Robeson."

"Yes. I learned that you moved from San Jose, California, to Maple City, Indiana, in 2012. I live in Minneapolis, which my computer said was a nine-hour trip. I wanted to meet you and talk about…family things." She glanced around. "I didn't expect this."

Robeson shrugged. "I have done well in life according to some measures." His brow knitted as he added, "Not so well in others."

"Then you did have a daughter named Dolores?"

He nodded. "Our only child. She ran away at seventeen."

"I'm sorry," Robin said sincerely. "I know she died in June of 1980."

He nodded. "Drug overdose."

She took a bite of her cookie, though nerves made it feel like she was nibbling cardboard. “No one told you she had a child?”

His gaze met hers. “No.”

Robin laid the copy of the birth certificate Mark had aged and folded on the tray before him. “My mother was born in May of that year. The father is listed as unknown.” She paused. Robeson stared at the fake certificate as if mesmerized. Mark was right; he wanted to believe what she was telling him.

Feeling like a cheat, Robin handed over her next piece of evidence. “Grandma wrote everything down. I'm not sure why, but it's all there if you want to read it.”

She laid several sheets of note paper atop the others, hand-written lines in purple ink. Fumbling for his glasses, Robeson put them on, adjusting until they sat near the end of his nose. The room fell silent as he frowned, moving his face close and then farther away. Finally he looked up at Robin. “Reading handwritten stuff is hard for me these days. You'll have to help me out.”

Clearing her throat, Robin took up the sheets and read aloud the story Mark had concocted and set down in the neat, Palmer Method script taught in elementary schools in the last century.

> *“My name is Gladys Bills, and I was a home health nurse, working mostly in San Francisco, in the summer of 1980. At that time, I had two clients in an apartment building in a bad neighborhood. One day as I left the place, I heard a baby crying. The child's voice was scratchy and hysterical, like it had been upset for a long time. I knocked on the door where the sound came from, but no one answered. Finding it unlocked, I stuck my head in and asked if everything was okay. On a rumpled, filthy bed lay a woman, a girl really, motionless and pale. Beside her the*

baby screamed, her little feet and fists waving in the air. I went inside to try to rouse the woman, but she was dead. I looked for a phone to call for help, but there was none.

What I did that day was a sin that some will condemn and some will understand. I picked up the child to calm her. She immediately stopped crying and turned her little face to my chest, looking for milk. She was starving. A dozen emotions flowed through me: pity, fear for her future, distress for a mother who cared so little for her child, and—I can't think of another word for it—-love. The child needed someone, and I confess I needed her almost as much. We carried canned formula we could give to needy mothers, and I took one from my bag, made up a bottle, and fed her. It might seem odd to others that I didn't go for help, but the mother was beyond anything I could do for her. The child was not.

As I held that little girl, walking up and down the room with her in my arms as she fed, I saw almost nothing in the place to indicate her presence: no tiny clothes, no baby supplies except two bottles in the sink with dried milk clinging to their insides. The infant wore a filthy, adult-sized t-shirt. Her diaper was a dish towel fastened with safety pins."

"Oh, Dolores." Robeson's comment revealed both pain and pity.

"I'm sure she wasn't herself at the end," Robin said soothingly.

"No." He nodded at the sheets Robin held. "Your grandmother took the child."

"Yes." Robin found her place and began reading again.

"I had always wanted children but was unable to conceive. Holding that orphaned, unwanted baby, watching her eat, I got an idea that wouldn't go away. It seemed God was providing what I wanted, and at the same time, offering the child a chance at a life she'd never have anywhere else.

Since no one had come to see about the little one, I guessed the mother was alone and unconnected to her neighbors. In such places people mind their own business, so if anyone knew the dead woman had a child, they'd assume the state would take the baby and see to its welfare."

Robeson seemed to agree with Gladys' contention. "I visited the building after Dolores died, and I doubt the residents would have volunteered information to the police." His voice grew bitter. "The drug addict who OD'd in 4C didn't even create much of a stir."

"I'm sorry," Robin said again.

He managed a wry grin. "Let me guess. Your grandmother took the baby and walked out of there like she had every right to her."

"Listen," Robin said, and she read on. "*Once the child finished eating, she fell asleep. I picked up the few things that suggested a baby's presence and left with her in my tote bag.*"

"No one could tell she'd taken the child."

"Right." Looking up, Robin told him, "She went to a pay phone and called in an anonymous tip about the body. She felt bad, but she was afraid they wouldn't let her keep Angela."

"That's what she named my granddaughter?"

"Angela had a good life, Mr. Robeson. She was loved, secure—" She smiled. "On my dresser at home I have a picture of her as Homecoming Queen. She married her high school sweetheart. A year later they had me."

Robeson looked embarrassed. "I forgot to ask your name."

"Serena. Serena Dykstra."

Reaching out, he touched her hand lightly. "Nice to meet you, Serena."

His eyes told her he was more than willing to believe her story, so it was time to pull back a little. "I didn't come here to upset you, Mr. Robeson. When Gram died, I found all this and—" She gestured toward the packet of documents and photos. "Suddenly the person I was my whole life is gone, and I'm someone else entirely. I want to know who my people are. I want to meet my cousins and aunts and uncles—"

"I'm sorry, my dear, but there's only me." At her surprised look he went on, "I had two brothers, but they're both gone now. Neither had grandchildren" He spread his mottled hands. "The Robesons are a dying vine—at least we were until today."

Svein cleared his throat. "Boss, you're going to need more than this woman's word that she's family."

A flash of irritation crossed the old man's face, but his voice remained calm. "I'm told it's a simple and painless process to test one's DNA these days."

Robin took on a nervous manner. "Mr. Robeson—"

He pointed a finger at her. "Call me Harry."

"Harry, I repeat, I didn't come here to upset you. I need—" She met his gaze earnestly. "You don't know what it's like to learn your family is made up of strangers."

"Would you be willing to have your DNA tested, to see if you're my great-granddaughter? It could make quite a difference to your future."

She let her voice go frosty. "All I came for is information about certain health matters. Believe me or don't, but if you answer a few questions, I'll leave you in peace."

Svein was standing behind the wheelchair, and Robin saw him roll his eyes. Svein wasn't going to be easy.

Ignoring them both Harry asked, "Will you do the test with me?"

Rising, Robin shook her head. "This was a mistake. I should go."

"Please, my dear." Now he took her hand and held it. "For me."

"You're thinking it's because you're well off financially, but that isn't why I came."

"Now that I've met you, I won't be able to rest until I know for certain if you're Dolores' grandchild." He still held her hand, and he squeezed it lightly and repeated, "Please?"

She let the silence drag for a few seconds before replying. "All right."

There was a tablet fastened to the arm of Robeson's wheelchair, and he asked it a question. When the answer came he said, "Svein, will you go into town and buy a DNA kit? They have them at Walgreens."

"Boss—"

"You claim I need proof, Svein. I accept your reasoning, though I believe I already know what we'll discover. Get what we need, and we'll get the proof you're looking for."

Though obviously unwilling, Svein took a set of car keys from a peg near the door. "I won't be long."

"We'll sit out here and chat until you return." Svein left, tossing a disgusted glance at Robin as he did. Harry seemed not to notice. "Have another cookie, Serena, and I'll tell you about your grandmother."

Chapter Eighteen

Luca's thoughts kept returning to the fact that Robin had spent time around Brandell in her childhood. Though she wasn't sure how it figured in, it felt like her disappearance had to do with that. She tried to recall what Robin said about the great uncle who'd owned a cabin in the area. His name was Tim, but neither Chris nor Robin had been able to recall his last name. "That's okay," Robin had told Luca. "I don't want to go anywhere near that awful cabin anyway. It was bad."

Since Luca had eaten at the town's only diner twice already, and since she was a naturally friendly type, she was welcomed at dinnertime like an old friend. The busman, an old guy with a voice like a foghorn and about five teeth on his bottom jaw, asked teasingly when she entered, "You again?"

"Is there anywhere else in town to eat?" she asked.

"No place that's any good. Set yourself down right there and Cara will be right with you."

She was the only customer, and as he refilled the condiments, they talked about the weather, which he said was exactly right for pumpkin pie; the Colts' chances for reaching the Super Bowl, which he said were fading fast; and the day's special, which he recommended if she liked onions. The fact that onions figured prominently in the dish had been clear from the moment she entered and sniffed the air.

When she got a chance to direct the conversation Luca asked, “Do you remember a man named Tim that had a cabin around here? I heard he liked to fish more than most.”

His face split with a grin. “You mean old Skelter. Now I ain't thought of him in a while. Man was dedicated, let me tell you. Serious as a heart attack about his bait and tackle.” He added, “Didn’t matter, bass, trout, walleye, or bluegill, Skelter could catch it and cook it too.”

“He’s probably dead by now.”

“He is, bless his soul, and I don’t think anybody’s been in that cabin since. They say his sister held onto it, thinking her son might want it someday, but according to what I heard, the man don’t even live in the USA.” His white brows rose, possibly indicating disapproval of a person who’d leave his native land for a foreign place.

“Where is this cabin?”

“On Pitcher Lake” He tapped a saltshaker on the table edge to settle the contents. “Pitcher is the smallest lake around here, but it’s got tons of cabins.” He scratched at his chin. “Skelter’s place isn’t much to look at, but he always said fish in the lake is what matters, not having a fancy place to sleep in.”

“Can you tell me how to get to it?”

He stopped working to look at her. “Why? Ain't nothing out there.”

“I heard the lake is pretty, and I'd like to take some pictures.”

Satisfied with that, he gave directions, pointing this way and that as he spoke. "You'd leave town going west and turn right at Gary's Outpost. Past the Bide-a-Wee Tavern, maybe two miles down, look for a two-track. There won't be no road sign, but nailed to a tree there should be a piece of wood that says 'Helter.'"

"I thought you said his name was Skelter?"

"Nope. I called him Skelter because of the song. You know, 'Helter Skelter'?"

When the busman returned to the kitchen, Luca called Tom. "The cabin Robin used to visit belonged to a man named Helter." She repeated the directions she'd been given.

"That's the lake where the four-wheeler came from."

"Since Robin knows about the cabin her uncle owned, she might have gone there if…if the car broke down or something." Knowing Robin or Cam would have called in that case, she added lamely, "I mean, we need to track down every lead, right?"

"Right," Tom said. "It's getting dark, but we'll drive back out to Pitcher Lake and explore."

Tom called an hour later to say that with deepening darkness and a largely unlit landscape, they'd given up trying to find the sign the old man mentioned. "We drove down a dozen driveways and found a dozen dark cabins. They all look alike."

"Get some rest," Luca advised. "You can try again in the morning."

"Yeah." Tom's frustration and fear made his tone sound angry. "As soon as it's light, we'll look until we find it." A second later he added, "Mostly because we don't know what else to do."

Chapter Nineteen

As Mark Parsons had predicted, Harry Robeson asked “Serena” to stay at his home while they waited for DNA results. “We've missed so many years,” he pleaded. “Give an old man a few days of your time.”

“I'll make some calls,” she replied. “I'm supposed to be back at work on Wednesday, but I think they'll let me have a few more days.”

Using Harry’s landline, she made a fake call to her supposed boss and then a second, real call. “Gramps, I'm going to be out of town for a few days,” she said to Mark Parsons’ voicemail. “I'll explain when I see you, but I didn't want you to worry.”

Ending the call, she told Harry, “It’s kind of good he didn't answer. I'm not sure he’ll understand why I came here.”

“I suppose it's hard for adoptive parents to learn they weren't enough.”

“But they were,” she protested. “My coming here has nothing to do with what they did or didn't do for me. It's more about—I don't know how to explain it. You want to know where you came from, what kind of people, what sort of background.”

“Old guys like me love talking about the past,” Harry said, “so I'll be glad to answer all your questions.”

As it wound down the day had turned cool, so they moved inside to wait for Svein to return with the DNA kit. The view was still stunning, since the north wall of the room was all glass. Robin explored the living room, browsing collections of things Harry Robeson found interesting: books, maps, science toys, and stones of many types, polished and displayed singly or in small groups. On one wall was a collage frame with dozens of photos, each of Harry with one other person. They were male, female, black, white, brown, plainly dressed, and formal. Every single one smiled as he or she hugged Harry. "Who are all these people?"

Harry seemed embarrassed. "They made that for my retirement party. It was very nice of them."

"Who is 'they'?"

He paused for a moment before answering, and she concluded he was framing his response. "I used to take people under my wing a little," he said modestly. "I tried to help them get on a good path."

"People who were headed in the wrong direction?"

He shrugged. "Sometimes somebody caring a little bit makes all the difference."

Robin was intrigued, so she pointed at a random photo. "Tell me about this person."

He squinted to identify the person pictured. "That's Ramona. She came to California illegally and got a job cleaning offices. I worked late one night, and we got to talking. She seemed careless about doing her job, and I noted the smell of marijuana wafting around her."

"What did you do?"

"After we'd talked for a while, I hired her."

"To clean your home?"

He chuckled. "No. As a lab assistant."

"You talked to someone for a few minutes and decided she was suited for research work?"

"I noticed three things about Ramona." Harry raised his fingers as he explained each point. "After just one year, her English was very good, which told me she listened and picked up nuances. She asked me about what I was working on, and though it wasn't easily explainable in layman's terms, she got the gist and asked intelligent questions. And finally, it was clear she'd come to the states wanting something better than what she had. I decided the pot-smoking was her way of blunting her ambition, so the disappointment didn't drive her crazy."

"I'm willing to bet that's not how most people would have seen it."

"Maybe. I had some leeway in staffing by that time, so I hired Ramona and worked with her until she got comfortable in the lab. It took a few months, but soon she was one of the best."

"What did the others think of having their cleaning woman working with them?"

"I doubt they noticed. Geeks don't care where you come from as long as you can do the work."

Harry was probably wrong about that, but they might have accepted that their boss was an eccentric genius and let it go at that. "Is Ramona still working at the lab?"

"She could be. It's been a while since I saw her."

"So each of these people is someone you singled out and helped in some way?"

"I tried to help where I could."

She was thinking that Harry Robeson was the kind of man she'd needed in her life. "Not everyone meets a person who looks for their strengths and helps develop them."

"I try to keep in mind that I started out with certain advantages simply by being born male, white, middle-class, and a U.S. citizen." He looked up at her. "I'm sure you've experienced the 'little girl' treatment often enough."

Recalling the law firm she'd once worked at where the men talked down to her and touched her butt any chance they got, Robin nodded. "I have, but not all men are like that."

"Of course not. Still, I always figured it didn't hurt me to use whatever influence I had to give a boost to someone struggling against prejudice or poverty."

She returned her gaze to the photo wall. "And these are all people you helped?"

"I did what I could. What individuals do with what they're offered is up to them."

Robin returned to the couch and sat down. "Tell me about yourself."

"Pour us each a glass of wine, and I will." As she obeyed Harry began, "My—our ancestors were Polish, named Wróblewski. Obviously, someone along the way Anglicized it." Taking the glass she offered with both hands, Harry took a sip and smacked his lips in appreciation. "I'm told they were of the aristocracy, but that's an easy claim to make. Whatever they were, during one of the many times Poland was overrun by its neighbors, they emigrated to the U.S. and settled in Pennsylvania. We were farmers for generations, my father and his father before him, but that life didn't appeal to me. I hated the back-breaking work, chafed at the isolation, and despaired at the unpredictability of success from one year to the next. Fortunately, I had a talent for science, and I received a scholarship to MIT. Once I had my bachelor's degree, I moved to California precisely at the right time to cash in on the technology boom. I made a bit of money there, and met a woman who was, as they say, my soul mate." His eyes misted. "We had Dolores, the prettiest child you can imagine. For a while we were completely happy."

"But Dolores became troubled."

"Yes. I'm not sure how we failed her."

"I'm sure it wasn't your fault," Robin objected. "She could have been bipolar or had some other condition that went undiagnosed. It was common back then."

He nodded. "We struggled with her moods and acting-out for months, and then one day she was gone. I hired detectives to look for her. I harassed her friends daily, hoping she would contact one of them. There was nothing."

He paused, his expression unbearably sad. Robin was tempted to confess the truth and leave the man to his grief, but she remembered Cam, trapped somewhere and dependent on Mark for sustenance. She remained silent, waiting for Harry to continue.

"Three years after she left, the police found Dolores in that horrible apartment your grandmother described in her journal. We brought her home and buried her, but the world hardly noticed her absence. A dead junkie didn't even rate an autopsy, which is why we had no idea she'd had a child."

“If Gram had known there was family that cared, I’m sure she'd never have taken Angela.”

“Of course she wouldn’t.” Harry ran a finger around the rim of his wineglass. “I’m grateful the child had a good home.”

The mood had become depressing, and Harry tried to lift it. “I think I should message Svein and tell him to bring home a pizza for dinner.” Robin agreed, though she guessed Svein would take it as an insult to his cooking and lay the crime at her door.

“Where did you find him?” she asked. “He seems very, um, loyal.”

“Yes, loyalty is definitely one of Svein’s traits. I needed someone who wouldn’t mind living out in the boondocks and being on call twenty-four-seven.” Harry gave a little chuckle. “Svein likes very few people and trusts even fewer. I’m fortunate he decided I’m worthy of his time.”

“I take it he’s Swedish?”

“Yes. He came to this country at fourteen, but things didn’t go well for him.” That seemed to be all Harry had to say on that subject. “Is meat-lover’s okay? That’s what Svein and I usually get.”

Whatever he thought of Harry’s decision to welcome a stranger into his home, Svein did as asked, returning with the DNA tests and a large pizza. While he plated slices for them, Harry and Robin followed the test instructions carefully and packaged their samples for mailing. Though the box said results took three to five business days, Harry paid an extra fee to expedite the process. “They’ll let us know by Thursday,” he announced.

They'd finished their first slices when the doorbell rang. The look Svein sent Robin's way as he rose to answer it hinted he'd arranged something she wouldn't like.

“Harry?” a female voice sounded from the entryway. “Har-ry, are you decent?”

A woman of about seventy appeared in the doorway, stopping with hands raised like a Broadway legend stepping onto the stage. Blond curls framed her face, and she apparently subscribed to the idea that makeup should be applied more liberally as one ages. Svein deftly caught the coat she shrugged off, revealing colorful clothing weighed down with jewelry and a long, even more colorful, scarf. Crossing to Harry, she kissed him on both cheeks in a theatrical manner. “I'm sorry I've neglected you,” she said. “I get busy with my projects and forget I have family obligations.”

“Natalie.” A world of forced cheerfulness sounded in the old man’s single utterance.

“I've been saying to myself, 'You need to get out and see poor old Harry.' And then I was driving back from Salem tonight and I said to myself, 'It isn't far out of the way. You could stop in right now.' So I did.”

“We're having pizza. Would you like a slice?”

“No, thank you.” Her tone implied she'd rather dine on maggots. “I had dinner with our state representative and a few of his closest friends.” Interlacing her fingers she crooned, “Such a lovely man.”

There was a brief silence, and no one seemed to know what should happen next. Finally Harry said, “Natalie, this is Serena Dykstra. Serena, my wife's niece, Natalie Finch.”

“Pleased to meet you,” Robin murmured.

"And what brings you to Harry's home, my dear?" Natalie's tone revealed she already knew.

Svein answered for Robin, his gaze cold. "Miss Dykstra believes she's Harry's great-granddaughter."

Natalie's carefully drawn brows rose. "That's not possible."

"At the moment, no one can say." Harry sounded defensive, as if an argument had already begun.

If his emphasis on *no one* was meant to shut Natalie up, the hint completely missed her. "Dolores died, Harry. We'd have been told if she'd had a child."

Harry's lips formed a tight line, and Natalie turned her attention to Robin. "What proof do you have, young lady? You can't just show up at a person's door and claim blood kinship with a stranger."

Harry tried to help, though his expression suggested he recognized the hopelessness of it. "We're in the process of examining the evidence."

"Har-ry!" She might have been speaking to a five-year-old. "Anyone who waltzes in after a wealthy man's ninetieth birthday and says, 'Oh, look! I'm a long-lost relative!' is definitely suspect."

"There's a lot here that you don't understand, Natalie."

"Well, you can't be thinking of including her in your…family. She's done nothing for you while…others have been both relative and friend." Her tone turned coquettish. "Who brightens your day with visits and those cranberry muffins you love?"

Harry's dentures seemed to have locked. "To be honest, Natalie, I'm not fond of cranberry muffins. You are, and in your mind, what you like must be what everyone likes."

She reeled a little at that, but a moment later she regrouped and tried again. “Muffins aside, I'm saying that family isn't necessarily blood. It's the people who've been with you for years.” Her lips pinched, and she inclined her head toward Robin. “She might have come here to bamboozle you out of your money.”

“Attempts to bamboozle me have been made before this,” Harry replied. “I seem to recall you wanting me to fund a community theater so you could play the star.”

Natalie recoiled, one hand clutching at her chest. “I wanted the town to have a little culture, Harry. I never said I'd be the star of anything.”

“Not out loud maybe, but that's what I heard.”

Her tone turned pleading. “Think what you like of me, but please, don't give in too easily to this...person. You're elderly and alone, a prime candidate for tricksters.”

Harry shifted impatiently in his chair. “Thanks for stopping by, Natalie, but we won't keep you. Serena and I have matters to discuss, and we don't want to bore you.”

Though her lips worked as she chose and rejected arguments, in the end Natalie saw no choice but retreat. Svein followed with her coat, his face tight. When she was gone Harry confided, “I try to be tolerant, but I've never been able to stand that woman.”

“I'm sorry to be the cause of a quarrel between you.”

He waved that away. “This isn’t the first time she’s huffed out of here all offended. Natalie is a bulldozer. She pushes at a person until he reaches his limit and tells her off. Then she stalks out in high dudgeon.” He grinned. “Her outrage never lasts long, because if she stayed mad, in a very short time she'd have no one left to talk to in the whole county.”

“I’ve met people like that.”

Pushing his empty plate away, Harry wiped up a crumb of pepperoni with a finger and ate it. “Unfortunately, my money always brings Natalie back. She forgives me, no matter what I say or do, because she hopes to be named in my will.” He sighed. “In a week, maybe two, she'll be back with more advice and a dozen more of those damned cranberry muffins.”

Natalie's visit unsettled Robin for a couple of reasons. First, she was sure Svein had arranged it, which meant he was taking an active role in opposing her. Second, for all her theatrics, Natalie Finch wasn't wrong about Serena Dykstra. In fact, she was one hundred percent correct.

Chapter Twenty

Though he tried everything, Cam couldn't stop thinking about food. It wasn't like he was starving in his little cell. The bag Parsons had left contained prepackaged items he'd had on hand at the cabin, apparently bought at a gas station or convenience store. Cam couldn't help thinking about real food, the things he'd ask for if a genie or other magical being appeared and offered to conjure whatever he asked for.

He might order a meal like those he'd had at home on the farm in Georgia. Though his parents weren't rich, they'd never gone hungry. In a muttering tone, Cam listed items he'd have liked to be eating, and he pictured his mother setting each one on a table covered with her blue-and-white holiday tablecloth. "Fried chicken, black-eyed peas with bacon, collard greens, mashed taters, and corn bread. Sweet tea, and for dessert, pecan pie with vanilla ice cream." The image lasted only until he bit into the deli sandwich that was his actual main course. The dry bun, skimpy meat, and tasteless cheese erased any pretense that he was having a home-cooked dinner.

As he took a second bite, Cam switched pictures. Once he was on his own, he'd developed a taste for fast food, and he loved all the places: Wendy's, McDonald's, KFC, Arby's, it didn't matter. He had his favorites on every menu, and while Hua shook his head, Cam wolfed down whatever super-sized meal-deal was offered. He tried to imagine he was eating a Beef N Cheddar with curly fries and a large Coke. Taking a swig of water, he washed down a second unsatisfying bite.

With intermittent sips, he finished the sandwich. As he set the wrapper aside, an image came to mind of the last meal they'd shared together in Kansas. Hua influenced the eating habits of the household, being both an excellent cook and one who loved spending time in the kitchen. Unimpressed by diets or cleanses or fasting, Hua encouraged what he called "nutritionally responsible eating," reasonable portions prepared with good ingredients and minimal amounts of fat and sugar.

Cam pictured the gang, seated around their rectangular table, Robin at one end and Tom at the other. Cam and Mai had helped Hua carry the dishes from stove to table, and he vividly recalled how each one looked and smelled: a big yellow bowl filled with shrimp stir-fry, a platter of spring rolls, and chunks of cantaloupe set in bowls on either end of the table. There'd been low-fat cheesecake for dessert, and through Hua's personal magic, it didn't taste low-fat at all.

Taking a last sip of water, Cam set the food aside. It would probably do a guy good to eat lighter for a few days. But if that genie set a Whopper with Cheese in front of him at that moment, Cam would have scarfed it down in a heartbeat and asked for a Dutch Apple Pie to chase it.

Chapter Twenty-One

Wednesday morning, Robin and Harry lingered over a breakfast of scrambled eggs, crisp bacon, and perfectly browned toast. After setting the meal out, Svein had donned a jacket and retreated to the back yard to rake leaves. They could see him outside the breakfast nook, his stiff, choppy movements telegraphing irritation. Ignoring him, Harry spoke to Robin of his younger days, when he and his wife had met.

"The firm I worked for in California used to arrange events to help its young techies and geeks meet possible mates. They called it the Nerd's Picnic, though we didn't know that at the time. The company execs invited students from local community colleges, hoping each of their employees would meet a nice girl, marry her, and establish ties that kept them from moving on to other companies. Stella came with a cousin she was visiting, and I noticed her right away." He grinned. "I was too shy to approach her, but she noticed me gawping and came right over."

"Good for her."

The doorbell rang, and Robin's spine tensed, knowing who stood on the porch, his disarming smile ready. Until now this had been an exercise, but this gentle old man would soon be hooked like a fish on a line. Though Harry's guest room was designed for comfort, she'd slept badly. Over and over she asked herself how she'd go through with it. She liked Harry, and he didn't deserve to be lied to and fleeced of his money. Over and over she'd asked herself how she could do such a thing to him. The answer was inescapable. She could because she had to. Cam's life depended on it.

"Shall I see who's there?" she asked.

Harry set down his fork. "Please."

Dreading the face she would see, Robin opened the door and put the right amount of surprise into her voice. "Gramps!"

Mark was already in character, looking conflicted about being there. He wore faded, clean jeans, a zippered hoodie, and cap that said, "Proud American." He'd dyed the hair at his temples gray and drawn tiny lines around his eyes. He added to the idea of age with a slight stoop and a frown, as if his vision were fading. He smelled like bargain after shave and looked like a movie star a little past his prime.

Harry, who'd followed her to the entry, looked from Mark to Robin in confusion. "Harry, this is my grandfather, Reuben Bills. Gramps, this is Harrison Robeson. I think you know that he's my great-grandfather."

Stepping forward, Mark shook Harry's hand. "Mr. Robeson." A hint of sadness in his tone conveyed the fears an adoptive grandparent might have when meeting his child's real family.

"How did you find me?" Robin asked.

"Checked the search history on your laptop." Mark spoke directly to Harry, but he set a hand heavily on Robin's shoulder. "I'm no computer whiz, but this little girl taught me a few things."

"Serena and I have been getting to know each other," Harry said.

"I suppose it was time." Straightening a little, he made what sounded like a formal statement. "I ask your forgiveness for keeping her past a secret all these years. My wife and I did what we felt was best, first for Angela and then for Serena."

"You knew she had family?"

Mark shook his head. "Not at first. Angela's birth certificate gave us the family name, Robeson. I tried to convince my wife we should find her relatives, but she said if someone was looking for the baby, we'd hear it on the news. When nothing was said, she insisted no one wanted Angela. She begged me not to risk losing her by going to the police." His smile was sad. "I loved her so much that I couldn't go against her wishes."

"How did you explain the child?"

Mark seemed eager to share that part of the story. "We moved away from everyone we knew. I worked for a national chain grocery, so I simply asked for a transfer. The store in St. Paul, Minnesota, had an opening for a manager, and I took it. Since Gladys was a nurse, she could get a job anywhere. After we'd been in Minnesota for a while, we told our families we'd adopted a little girl." He turned to Robin. "We had a pretty good life there, right, Serena?"

"We did, Gramps."

"Losing Angela almost killed us, but having her little girl to care for kept us going." Mark's eyes misted, and he turned his face away slightly, as if to recover control. "Since Gladys died, Serena has kept me going. She's one great girl."

"I've already seen that," Harry acknowledged.

Mark must have decided he'd set the scene adequately, for he said, "Serena, do you mind if I speak to Mr. Robeson alone for a few minutes?"

"Gramps—"

"You haven't been down to the lakeshore yet," Harry said. "I guarantee it's worth the trip."

"I—"

"Walk on the beach." Mark took up the sweater she'd draped over the chair back and handed it to her. "Let two old men talk for a while."

"But—"

"We won't say anything bad about you, I promise." Opening the slider, Mark shooed her outside. "We won't get many more days like this."

Feigning reluctance, Robin obeyed, turning back to wave at Harry before descending the steps. The decline was steep, but evenly spaced landings allowed time to rest and take in the view. The sun was indeed warm, and there was no hint of breeze. Remnants of fall color remained at the edge of the lake, but dull yellows and faded browns had replaced the bright golds and scarlets of days before. The water was even bluer today than it had been before, almost exactly matching the bright sky. Behind her Robin heard the rustle of leaves and Svein's measured movements as he worked. At the bottom of the staircase was a bench where she sat down, imagining what was going on at the house.

Mark, playing the part of Reuben/Gramps, would tell Harry the real reason for "Serena's" visit. She's been having some health problems, he'd confide, and her doctors recommended finding biological family in order to diagnose and treat her illness. From there his information would be a mix of medical terms and lies. He would explain that her problem was believed to be a hereditary condition that could spell disaster if untreated.

Harry would immediately be concerned at the possibility that his genes were to blame for Serena's medical problems. "It'll add to his feeling of responsibility," Mark had predicted.

He would explain the possibility of a brain aneurism called Ehlers-Danlos syndrome, a weak spot in the brain prone to burst unexpectedly, often causing death within seconds. He would pause and ask Harry, "Have you by chance had a close relative who died of a stroke?"

With rising dread, Harry would recall that his older brother died of a stroke at fifty-two and his only nephew did the same at thirty.

Mark would sigh deeply. "That's what the specialist predicted. If Serena has Ehlers-Danlos, she needs to make some decisions about her future."

She imagined Harry asking, "Can they fix this…Ehlers-whatever problem?"

"First they need to know that's what she's experiencing," Mark would explain. "The tests they ran were inconclusive, possibly because the aneurism-prone spot is deep in her brain. Two surgeons at Mayo Clinic believe it's too risky to attempt to reach it." He would leave it at that for a moment, letting the hopelessness of the situation sink in before going on. "Serena tries to be optimistic, but it's like living with a time bomb inside her. When she has a headache or her vision gets fuzzy, she's afraid the stroke is on its way."

Robin guessed Harry would say something like, "But she's so young!" and Mark would let his head sink to his chest. "They can't predict when such spots will give way. One doc told me privately that if it does, nothing they can do will save her."

Robin pictured Harry's face when he heard that. He'd learned only a day ago that he had a great-grandchild. Now he had to face the fact that her time on earth might be dreadfully short.

Mark would sell the story; that was what he excelled at. He would accept the latest blow bravely, claiming he and Serena would stand together and face whatever future tragedy they must.

He'd let Harry fret on it a little, and then he'd toss out the bait. "There's a surgeon we heard about who can do the operation Serena needs, but he's unavailable."

Harry's eyes would meet Reuben's. "What does that mean?"

"For one thing, he lives in Spain. For another, he's in such demand that he can afford to be selective about his patients."

"Selective?"

Mark would chuckle grimly. "Like so many things in this world, it comes down to money. A surgeon's time is limited, so the ability to pay becomes a way of prioritizing the use of his talents."

Harry would be aghast at first, but being a man of the world, he'd recognize that life, like most things, is for sale. How long before he offered to pay for her surgery?

Robin guessed it would be a matter of minutes. Svein would suggest as strongly as he dared that his employer should wait to see if Serena was actually the relative she claimed to be. Harry would consider that unimportant. He liked her—liked Serena—and he'd insist that whatever the DNA tests said, the money would be spent on a good cause. While she listened to the birds overhead call, "Shame! Shame!" Mark's plan was halfway to completion.

Watching him spin his web was like returning to her childhood. Mark loved figuring the angles, anticipating possible snags, and doing end runs around anyone in his way. That was good, because he might let Cam live if things worked out the way he planned. If they didn't, he would turn angry. That would be bad.

What stood in their way? Svein was already doubtful and would oppose them at every step. Mark was probably already figuring how to either get him on their side or neutralize him. She felt a stab of fear. Would he hurt Svein?

No, she decided. Mark's arrogance would demand he outwit Svein rather than harming him.

When she returned to the house, Mark and Harry had moved to the deck. Each had a mug of coffee, and they appeared to be at ease with each other. Svein had come inside, and she saw him through the slider, dust mop in hand, his face a mask of disapproval. She heard a muted crash as he knocked over a knick-knack in his carelessness.

"Was the climb down and back up worth the effort?" Harry asked.

"Oh, yes," she replied. "How did you find such a beautiful place to build a home?"

"My wife never forgot Indiana, and more than once she mentioned this bluff." He chuckled. "Apparently it was a popular 'make-out spot' for the locals. When we decided to retire here, the land was for sale. I bought as much acreage as I could get, and the rest of the lakeshore is state land. That means we have no neighbors, only the occasional fishing boat or hunters and hikers on the opposite shore."

"The house is perfect for its setting."

Harry tilted his head, acknowledging the compliment. "I was lucky to find a very talented young woman who turned my notions into reality. But enough about wood and metal. Your grandfather has something to tell you, so I'm going to leave you two alone for a while." Turning the chair, he wheeled himself up the ramp that led inside. Svein was there, and he closed the slider behind Harry, bending down to speak urgently. Harry waved a hand, sending Svein's concerns into the air.

Mark rose from his chair, took Robin's arm, and led her to the railing. With their backs to the house, he murmured, "Make sure your body language sends the correct messages, Robbie."

She nodded, aware that she was supposed to be hearing both bad and good news. "Reuben" would tell her that her genetic inheritance might well include Ehlers-Danlos, but her surgery would be paid for. Her reaction should be mixed: anxiety, relief, and, at the last, distress at burdening the great-grandfather she'd recently found.

She did her part, shaking her head as if to say she couldn't let Harry pay, crying a little, and swaying into her supposed grandfather's arms as he patted her back reassuringly.

When their little play was over, she went inside and spoke to Harry directly. "I can't let you do this. You hardly know me, and I would never have asked—"

"I know that, which is why I'm glad Reuben here did." Harry stretched his hands toward her, and after a moment, she took them in hers. "I have nothing left in this life except a large amount of money, my dear. I don't need a single thing, so if I can help you live a better, longer life, I'll be happy." He sobered. "I can't stand the thought of you having a stroke that can be prevented."

She drew in a ragged breath. "I'll admit that it's scary, having the threat of it hanging over me."

“Then let me fix it. When you're well, I promise I won't make demands. I want you to have a life, a chance to live longer than my Dolores did, or your poor mother, for that matter.”

“I can hardly believe this is happening,” Robin said. “I wish I could do something to repay you.”

Harry chuckled. “Svein takes good care of me, so there's nothing I need. But you'd be welcome to stay here, if you don’t mind living out in the sticks. You wouldn't need to work for anything.” He gestured at Mark. “And Reuben can visit anytime.”

“I don't know what to say.”

“Simple,” Harry urged. “Say you'll let Reuben make the arrangements.”

This time Robin's tears weren't fake. The man's kindness was amazing, and she wanted to sob out a confession. It wasn’t right, taking advantage of his loneliness. Mark Parsons wasn’t worth Harry Robeson’s little finger, and yet she was aligned with him against Harry’s best interests.

Only the thought of Cam stopped her from blurting out a confession. Instead she faked gratitude. “Then yes. Thank you, thank you, and yes.”

After adding his thanks to Robin’s, “Reuben” went outside to make the necessary calls. An hour later he returned with a long face. “Dr. Alvarro is on vacation until Monday, but his nurse says he’s booked solid until the first of the year. Late January is the first possible date, and she warned me that can’t be guaranteed.”

Harry looked concerned, but Robin said, “I'll be okay until then.”

“What about the dizzy spells?” Mark asked. “Aren't they getting worse?”

“No,” she replied, but it was clear she was lying.

“I assume you have her medical records?” Harry asked. “We could get my brother’s sent to us today, so this doctor can see the precise location of the aneurism that killed him.”

“That would be helpful. Dr. Alvarro has already reviewed Serena’s records. He’s certain he could help, but first in line are those who can pay what he asks.”

After a brief silence Harry said, “This doctor is on vacation?”

“Yes. Until Monday.”

“Might he cut his vacation short if the price was right?”

“I—I don't know. His fee is already high.”

“See if he'll fly here and do the surgery this weekend. If we set it up correctly, it will only require a day or so of his free time.”

Mark seemed unable to comprehend. “How could we—?”

Harry held up a crooked finger. “Let's give the man some incentive. We'll pay all expenses and double his fee if he gets here as soon as possible.” Harry turned to Robin. “Are you ready to do this, Serena?”

“So soon?”

“Is there any reason to wait?”

“Well, no...”

“And every day brings a chance of disaster. Let's get it done.”

Robin felt a wave of warmth wash over her. “I'm so grateful, Mr. Robeson. May I hug you?”

“Sure.” He grinned. “And stop with the Mr. Robeson. What’s wrong with plain old Harry?”

Chapter Twenty-Two

Even in daylight, Tom and Hua had trouble finding the Helter cabin. After repeatedly following roads that dead ended on the shores of Pitcher Lake, they decided the directions they'd been given were wrong. The road that circled the lake bristled with tertiary trails and driveways, and following each one to its end was time-consuming and pointless in many cases, since there was no marking to tell who a cabin belonged to. It was also uncomfortable, due to uneven and primitive roads. Tom had to slow to a crawl to navigate them, and clods of mud slapped against the van's sides as they crossed through wide, deep puddles. Bennett, who'd been excited at the outset of the adventure, finally curled up on the passenger side at Hua's feet and napped, groaning softly in objection when they hit an especially large bump.

After several fruitless tries, Hua made a suggestion. "If Robin and Cam came here, they'd have had the car, yes? That means we only need to investigate roads with tire tracks, and only those indicating a car, not a truck or other vehicle."

"Right," Tom agreed. "That will eliminate a lot of time spent turning this beast around."

Even then they had no success for some time. Finally Hua pointed to a driveway that disappeared into a grove of trees.

"Someone has been in and out of that one several times since it last rained."

Turning, Tom followed the drive toward the lake, though the van lurched and groaned. Holding onto the armrest, Hua craned his neck to see ahead. "There. A cabin."

"And there's the sign." Tom pointed to a board less than a foot long that said" HE T R" in hand-painted, faded, letters. "We'd never have seen that in the dark."

Steering around a mud-hole the size of a major-league infield, Tom parked a few yards back from the log structure. Even for a cabin, it was on the low end of suitability. The place seemed to be sinking into the ground. Its walls were stained dark with damp at the base, and its roof sagged in the center and had a thick coat of lichen on the edges.

When they got out, Hua pointed to wide, fat marks a four-wheeler's tires had made on the soft ground near the door. Tracks showed that the ATV had gone in several directions, along the driveway, down the lake shore, and onto the adjoining properties. "If someone took this from that old resort, he's been using it as transportation," Hua said. "Since he left it at the motel, he must have found another way to travel."

"Maybe our car." Tom stared at the woebegone cabin. "We need to know who's been staying here. Let's see if we can get inside."

The door facing the drive was padlocked shut, but on the lake side they found a second door with an ancient lock that required a skeleton key. Apparently picking up a scent he recognized, Bennett danced around them and huffed excitedly as they examined the lock. Tom pounded on the door, but there was no answer.

“Maybe I can pick it,” Hua said, but Tom held up a hand to signal he should wait. Going to the eaves, he ran his hand along the wooden under-ledge and after a few seconds made a grunt of satisfaction. “Here.” He handed Hua a metal key. “People usually leave a spare somewhere. Don't want to drive a hundred miles to fish camp and then realize you left your key at home.”

Opening the door, Hua peered cautiously inside. Pushing past, Bennett sniffed at various spots, happy with the smells but disappointed not to find the people he associated with them.

The single room contained only the basics of life. In the center of the wall nearest them was a small metal stove. The corner beyond it had a cot-like bed with two folded army cots stored above it on a rough shelf. A second corner was the kitchen area: a dry sink, some battered coolers, and an airtight metal cabinet meant to keep food away from mice, squirrels, and other local wildlife. Beside it sat a wooden table with two chairs. Hung on pegs nearby were two more of the folding kind, apparently available for company. The last corner held two battered armchairs with a small stand between them. On the table was a stack of reading material Tom's dad would have called “girlie magazines.” At the center of the room, a kerosene lantern hung from the rafter. A shelf held a couple of flashlights, the old type with fat metal handles that required DD batteries. Tom tried one then the other. Neither worked. Tom sniffed the lantern and recoiled. “This has been used recently.”

“They were here.” Hua had been examining the dining area. “There's a bag of trash in this cooler, and it looks like someone was tied to this chair.” He pointed to fresh marks where the finish had been rubbed away by friction. Opening the trash bag, he took out several lengths of clothesline rope and some grayish flannel, torn into strips. Looking up at Tom he said softly, “Robin and Cam were prisoners here.”

“That explains why they haven't contacted us.”

Hua sifted through the trash in the bag. “This stuff is from the last day or so. Their captors fed them, so they must want them alive.”

“For how long?” An ex-soldier, Tom was used to facing hard truths. “Do they need both of them or just one?” He looked around the gloomy cabin before finishing the thought. “Even if they have something in mind for both of them, their usefulness won’t last.”

Hua’s eyes darkened. No stranger to tragedy either, he understood from Tom’s words that one or both of them might already have lost the person he loved. “What do we do?”

“I don't know,” Tom’s single hand worked as if closing around some unknown person’s neck. “We need to search this place until we find some kind of clue to where they are right now.”

Chapter Twenty-Three

As a city girl, Luca found the ways of small towns odd but kind of nice. Once she'd been at the motel for two nights, the owner, Fran, seemed to regard her as an old friend. It helped that Luca brought coffee and some sort of treat each time she returned from the diner, and they chatted as they sipped and nibbled. Believing there had to be a connection between Robin's childhood visits and her recent disappearance, Luca asked Fran about old-timers who'd know the history of the area. "Your best bet for that is Mrs. Greenwood at the library," Fran said. "She's older than dirt, but I swear she never forgets a single thing she's seen or heard."

Luca was waiting when the library opened at ten a.m. Mrs. Greenwood was not what she'd expected: no crepe-soled shoes or tight bun for this librarian. She wore black leggings under a loose, bright red top, black ballerina flats, and her white hair floated around her face like spider webs. She was still hanging up her coat and scarf when Luca entered, and she turned with a smile that faded slightly when she saw her. For the first few minutes, the librarian was polite but standoffish. Luca sensed discomfort with her looks, maybe with her race, and she hurried to explain that she'd been sent from the state's tourism office to assess the need for local funding.

The woman's attitude changed in an instant. "Lord knows this area could use some refreshing." Her voice was sibilant, like a cartoon snake, probably due to ill-fitting dentures. "For decades this place buzzed with tourists, but the numbers have declined a great deal for the last few decades." She sniffed disapprovingly. "We face a lot of competition from bigger towns with bigger lakes."

Luca let her go on for a while, making sympathetic noises at the idea that other towns sank to such tactics as dredging their harbors and constructing marinas. When the lady's complaints ran out Luca asked, "Do you remember a guy named Helter who used to come here to fish?"

The woman's eyes narrowed. "What are you asking about him for?"

"I know the family," Luca said. "The kids who used to come here."

"You mean Robin and…what was the boy's name?"

It was a test, and Luca provided the answer. "Chris."

Greenwood nodded. "Yes. I never met Mr. Helter, but I did get to know those two a little. This was…oh, at least a decade ago, maybe longer. The first time they came in, I told them I couldn't give them library cards, since they weren't permanent residents. The next day their mother came in with them and explained they were staying at their uncle's place for at least a month. That was Mr. Helter. They needed to keep up with schoolwork. She seemed very responsible, and I arranged to get them textbooks as well as what they wanted for leisure reading." She added approvingly, "They were very conscientious about returning the materials on time."

"You remember the kids from that one month?"

"Oh, no. They came back, maybe three more times. Each time they had me order books for them so they could keep up with their grade levels." She raised salt-and-pepper eyebrows. "From what I gathered, the father's job required them to move often, so they used the cabin as a sort of waystation while he looked for a house to rent." Her nose twitched disapprovingly. "One would suppose the parents wouldn't leave one place until they'd made arrangements for another, but that was apparently their way."

Luca imagined Chris and Robin staying at a cabin that had no cable—maybe not even a TV. Had they fished with their dad during the day and read by the fire at night? It seemed a kind of Abe Lincoln existence, and she wondered if they found the breaks from school restful. She was enjoying the image and almost missed the librarian's comment. "—odd that someone else mentioned the place recently."

"You mean the Helter cabin?"

"A new patron." A half-smile touched her lips. "He's very nice. Good-looking too."

Could she mean Cam? "Was he looking for directions?"

"Oh, no. He's apparently staying out there and has been for some time." Greenwood tilted her chin to one side. "You can always tell when someone's been living the rustic life. He smells of wood smoke and, well, sweat. Like he hasn't showered in a while." She smiled. "Still, he's a very charming man."

"Do you know his name?"

"Mark Something. He came in to use our computer, but he didn't have a library card, so I made him show ID before I let him use the PC." Her nose came up. "He was disappointed when I told him he could only have an hour at a time, but that's what everybody gets."

"Do you know what this Mark is doing in Brandell?"

"I gathered he's got some sort of development in mind. He researched a man from Maple City who's quite wealthy, so I concluded he's looking for investors."

"He told you that?"

"No, but he didn't delete his search history." Greenwood's manner turned pedantic. "When using a public computer, one always should."

Being part of a gang of kidnappers made Luca consider other possibilities one might have for researching wealthy people. "This man with lots of money lives in the area?"

Realizing she'd shared information she shouldn't have, Greenwood pressed her lips together and raised a hand as if to say she was done.

"If this Mark is looking at developing Brandell's resources, I'd like to meet him," Luca said. "Do you think he's still around?"

"I haven't seen him lately." She nodded at the single PC on a table near her desk. "He was a little frustrated with our old equipment, so he might have gone to a bigger library that has better technology."

Leaving the library, Luca texted Hua: *Man frm cbn vstd lib 2 resrch rch local. Cnxton?*

Seconds later she got a response. *Psbl. Not here tho.*

Chapter Twenty-Four

Tom and Hua's search of the Helter cabin turned up two of Robin's blouses, a sweater, and a pair of pants folded neatly on a shelf in the tin cupboard. "Like she needed to make room in her suitcase for something," Hua commented. "But what?"

Tom shrugged, unable to explain it. "It doesn't look to me like they'll be back."

As they left the gloomy cabin and went out into the bright blue day, Tom took a breath of fresh air. The lake smelled a little fishy, but it was ten times better than the moldy air inside.

Bennett went into a crouch, growling a threat. Turning, they saw a man standing at the cabin's grimy side window, obviously watching them. Eyeing Bennett warily, he said, "Hang onto that dog. I'm not bothering anybody."

Tom made a quick assessment of the stranger. Sturdily built and well-muscled, though not as tall as Tom. Tough, with eyes like closed doors. Not a local, judging by his clothing. Over a turquoise shirt and slightly dirty white pants he wore a red-plaid flannel with the out-of-the-package fold marks still visible and a corduroy jacket with a fleece-lined hood. Tom concluded the man had started somewhere warm and added layers of clothing as he traveled north.

“We're visiting from Michigan,” he offered. “Where are you from?”

“Florida,” he replied. “Staying at a friend's to do a little fishing.”

Everything about the man, his overly-wide grin, his tropical-plus-tundra outfit, and the tell-tale bulge of a pistol under his jacket, set off Tom’s inner alarms. “Catching anything?” he asked. “Sturgeon, maybe?”

The guy hesitated. “Got a couple nice ones, around eighteen inches.”

Tom felt Hua's eyes flash toward him. Though Hua knew nothing of fishing, he sensed the clueless lie. The guy was all wrong.

“My buddy said this place is abandoned,” the man said, “so when I saw you two going inside, I wondered if he made a mistake.”

Tom made his reply casual. “It’s up for sale, and some friends of ours were supposed to meet us out here to look it over. Either we missed them or one of us got the day wrong.” Turning his gaze back to the man he asked, “Maybe you saw them? A couple in their twenties. The woman is dark-haired and pretty. The guy is dark-haired too, and built like a Titan.” Seeing confusion in the man’s eyes, Tom added, “He’s big.”

“Haven't seen them.”

Tom gave an exaggerated sigh. “Missed communication, I guess.” He moved to the van, and Hua followed, letting Bennett in first. “Good luck with the fishing.”

“I’m looking out for a friend too,” the man said. “You seen a skinny guy about fifty, a real pretty boy with black, curly hair?”

“Sorry, no.”

“He’s supposed to fish with us.”

The tone was so false that Tom had trouble hiding his doubt. “We haven’t seen him, but we just got here.”

As they drove away Hua said, “That was no fisherman.”

“Right. He's here for something, but it isn't sturgeon.”

“Could he be part of Robin and Cam's disappearance?”

Tom shook his head. “He seemed to know less about the cabin than we do. I don't think he's been inside.”

“I'd bet he will be, as soon as we're out of sight.”

As if to accentuate their suspicions, Bennett growled at the side window. Turning, Hua said, “There's a car parked in the trees.”

Tom slowed and tried to see, but they'd passed the point where it was visible. “What kind?”

“A Lincoln, I think. Gray.”

Recalling the one he’d seen at the campground, Tom drew some conclusions. Two men, poorly prepared for late fall in Indiana, sleeping in their car and prowling the area. It meant trouble for someone.

“The man behind the steering wheel looks even bigger than the one we just met,” Hua commented.

“It looks to me like some citizen of Brandell is in trouble with a Miami drug lord.”

Hua patted Bennett’s sleek head. “We can’t worry about that. We have enough concerns already.”

Chapter Twenty-Five

Mark left Robeson's place after lunch, claiming that since he hadn't come to Maple City intending to stay, he needed to pick up a few things. He had a call in to Alvarro's hotel in Majorca, he told Harry and Robin, and when the doctor called back, Reuben would convince him to agree to do Serena's surgery or "die trying."

Robin watched him drive away in the ancient Chevy pickup he'd chosen to match his persona of a retiree with limited resources. His real purpose in leaving was to arrange the next part of the scheme, getting fake DNA results delivered to Harry Robeson's email inbox.

Mark had obtained Harry's email address and password using Remote Administration Tools. "You gotta move with the times, Robbie," he'd crowed when she expressed surprise that he knew about such things. She was vaguely aware of the possibilities of RAT because Hua talked about them, but Hua spoke fluent geek, and she usually merely nodded when he explained the marvels that technology could uncover.

The Walgreens in Maple City carried only one brand of DNA test. Mark had bought one and submitted samples for himself and Robin, giving Harry's email address as where the results should be sent. Now he would wait at an internet café in Maple City, checking Harry's email every half hour or so. When it came, he'd delete the message giving results of Harry and Robin's test. Harry would see only the other message, results that showed a familial match between Test Subject A and Test Subject B.

Robin had to admire her father's capacity for duplicity, and she admitted that she'd used what she learned at his knee in various capers the Kidnap Gang had carried out. She was trying to figure out if she had to be grateful to him for that when the doorbell rang. She jumped, and Harry commented, "More company in the last few days than I've had since Christmas."

The man Svein ushered into the room was tall and thin, with an earnest demeanor. "Mr. Robeson, I hope I haven't come at a bad time. I haven't been by in a while, so I thought I'd visit."

Harry cleared his throat before answering. "Of course not, Pastor. You're welcome anytime."

Robin got a glimpse of Svein's smirk as he left the room: another attempt on his part to block her progress with Harry. Svein wasn't giving up easily. If only Cam's life didn't depend on her thwarting Svein's all too correct instincts.

"It's good of you to stop by." Harry made the introductions. "Serena, this is Pastor Dan Carroll, from Brandell Presbyterian. Pastor, Serena Dykstra."

They shook hands, and it felt like she'd touched a dry maple leaf. "So nice to meet you."

"Are you visiting from California, Ms. Dykstra?"

"No," she replied. "I'm from St. Paul."

"Minnesota!" His enthusiasm was about as real as his flat-black, spray-on hair color. "I didn't know Harry knew anyone from there."

Harry apparently decided to take the matter head on. “Serena and I might be related. We're looking into the possibility.”

“Related? How nice for you.” Pastor Dan spoke to Serena, and his meaning was clear. Despite his milk-toast manner, she sensed hostility. What had Svein told him about her?

Perhaps to avoid questions, Harry turned the conversation to church matters. He asked about the building fund, which Pastor Dan claimed was progressing slowly but steadily. “Our people don’t have a lot of extra money to give,” he said, “but they know the work is worthwhile, so they give what they can.” After a pause he added, “We all give what we can.”

Robin got it. The man might truly be worried for Harry’s sake, he was his pastor after all, but he also hoped his church would benefit from Harry’s money, either now or after his death. “Serena” was a double threat: a liar come to cheat a parishioner, and an heir who might inherit Harry’s wealth. Goodbye to the new fellowship hall.

His next question was delivered in an ingenuous tone, but Robin guessed he knew the answer. “How does one go about proving kinship these days?”

Harry seemed eager to demonstrate he wasn't a foolish old man. “We sent in our DNA. The results will be back this afternoon.”

Pastor Dan’s response confirmed Robin’s suspicions. “I'm sure you opted for the more secure test, so there's no possibility of someone tampering with the results.”

There was a pause before Harry asked, “Who would do that, Pastor?”

Realizing he'd stepped too far, the man backtracked. "No one would, I'm sure, but it seems wise to take the most responsible method before making any...long-term decisions."

Harry's expression turned from pleasant to something else, and Robin got a glimpse of the businessman who'd carved a place for himself in the complicated, cut-throat world of technology development. "Serena, will you excuse Pastor Dan and me for a few minutes? Our talk about the goings-on at church will only bore you."

"Of course." Rising, she took her sweater from the back of her chair and went to the slider. Every part of her felt ready to betray her fears: her knees felt wobbly, her face warmed with embarrassment, and her shoulders longed to hunch defensively. In order to appear calm she turned her face away, steadied her knees, and forced her shoulders to drop to their natural position. "Nice to meet you, Pastor."

Stepping onto the deck, she started down the stairs, wishing the breeze could sweep away the guilt she felt. Harry was about to tell his pastor to mind his own business, probably in no uncertain terms. The tragedy of that was that whatever his motives, the man was right. She was a charlatan. She was after Harry's money. And there was nothing she could do to avoid hurting him when the charade was over. She sat shivering on the bench, though the sun was warm and the hill blocked the wind.

"Miss Dykstra?"

She turned to find Svein on the steps above her. "Mr. Robeson wanted me to ask if you'd prefer beef or chicken for dinner."

"Either is fine."

"He likes beef better."

"Then let's have that."

Svein's mouth worked as if he fought to either say something or say nothing. He didn't seem able to walk away. "Is there something else?"

"I looked up Dr. Alvarro. And Ehlers-Danlos Syndrome."

"Then you know they're both real."

He licked his lips. "I want you to know that I'm paying attention."

Meeting his gaze, Robin said, "I know you don't trust me, Svein." His head bobbed in what was probably an involuntary movement. "I can appreciate that you're trying to protect Mr. Robeson."

"I consider it my most important purpose," Svein said. "All the other things, the shots, the monitoring, the cooking, someone else could do. But no one cares for his welfare as much as I do."

Hearing the sincerity in his voice she asked, "Why is that, Svein? What did Harry do for you?"

At first he leaned back, as if dodging the question. But after a moment Svein's gaze moved up, over her head, and he spoke to the view, to the lake, the trees, and the sky. "I came to this country with my father when I was fourteen, after my mother died. He got a job in a factory in New Albany and an apartment so dull and empty it made me want to jump off the balcony. When he wasn't working, my dad was drinking. He'd never much cared for me, and he got farther and farther away as liquor took the place of everything in his life.

"At school I was considered odd. My English was different and I wasn't—I'm not—comfortable around a lot of people. I did enough work to make the teachers leave me alone and tried to ignore my schoolmates."

"You must have had girlfriends." Robin hadn't meant to interrupt, but someone with looks as striking as Svein's had to have stirred interest.

"There were girls, but they were…silly." That wasn't the word he wanted, but he apparently couldn't come up with a better one.

"Superficial?"

"I suppose." He shrugged. "It went on like that until I was seventeen. That year a girl came to our school who was different, and I—I fell into what I thought was love. She and I would skip school and spend the days doing as we liked." His face shifted subtly. "I liked being with her. It turned out what she liked was stealing cars." Robin gave no reaction to that, waiting in silence until Svein finally went on.

"Janine could get into a car, start it up, and be gone in no time. I had to hurry if I wanted to ride with her, because she thought it was great fun to leave me standing on the sidewalk."

"And when you were quick enough, what did the two of you do?"

"We rode around for a few hours, usually in the city but sometimes out in the country. I liked the trees, the rivers, and the feeling of openness. Janine liked to go fast, and I will admit, there is a thrill to it: the roar of the engine, the wind striking you in the face, the pull of gravity when you take a corner at a ridiculous speed. It was especially pleasing for a kid who has no hope of owning anything as nice as what we stole."

"And when the ride was over?"

"We'd leave the car somewhere, wipe away our prints, and walk to a bus stop."

"How many times did you get away with it?"

He shrugged. "Maybe a dozen."

"But eventually you got caught."

"Yes." Svein took a breath. "Janine blamed it on me. The police showed me the video where she cried and said I'd done everything. She'd been foolish to go along, she said, but she loved me and couldn't say no to me." Svein's smile was bitter. "The truth was exactly the opposite. I was the one who said no at first. I was the one who told her it was too risky. I was the one who suffered guilt when we left someone with a damaged fender or a blown engine."

"But the police believed her."

"Yes."

"How does Harry come into this?"

Svein almost smiled. "In the strangest way possible. His lawyer was assigned my case as part of his pro bono work. He's a storyteller, and he told Harry about this dumb kid who let his…passion for a girl lead him into trouble. One day Harry showed up at the detention facility and asked if I would tell him about myself. At first I said he should get lost, but he repeated that he wanted to know about me. I learned later that he has helped others like me over his lifetime, people who needed a break no one else would give them. He's an excellent judge of character."

Not really, Robin thought, but she didn't argue.

"In the end," Svein said, "I told him my story, thinking he would dismiss me as a liar, as the police had. Instead Harry said,

'I'm thinking of hiring a caregiver. If I go to the judge and tell him I would like it to be you, do you think you can live in a lonely place out in the woods with no one but me for company?'" Svein chuckled softly. "I said I could, and we have been together ever since."

"Do you ever miss your old life?"

He sniffed derisively. "What would I miss? My father snoring in his bed? The schoolmates who didn't care if I lived or died? Or the girlfriend who threw me to the wolves at the first opportunity?"

"But someday you'll want more than this solitary, lonely life."

"Harry was very practical when he made his offer." Svein shifted his feet. "I was young, barely eighteen, and he put the bargain to me clearly. 'I won't live forever,' he told me, 'if things work out between us, I will leave you a large bequest in my will, so you'll be able to do whatever you want when I'm gone.'"

"Sounds like he has a death wish. Who invites a juvenile delinquent he's never met to become his caregiver, promises him a large inheritance, and lives in his home out in the sticks with only him for company?"

Svein made an impatient gesture. "I told you, Harry is a good judge of people. I would never hurt him, and he understood that I needed time to grow into who I wanted to be and away from what I was becoming."

"Then you're happy here?"

"Harry taught me more in the last five years than I could have imagined. More than my father for sure. More than school ever could. And more about goodness than anyone I've ever met." He turned to look Robin in the eye. "The money is a consideration, of course, but it is not the main one. I am content to be what Harry needs now, because he was what I needed then."

"I'm glad you told me, Svein."

"I told you so you will understand that I won't let you or anyone else hurt Harry."

Robin shook her head. "I mean him no harm, Svein. I'll—" She didn't know how to say it without giving herself away. "I'll always treat him as well as I possibly can."

When he merely looked at her, she admitted to herself it was the weakest of assurances.

"Dinner will be at six." Turning, he went back up the steps, his wide, rigid back signaling that she hadn't done anything to convince him of her innocence.

Chapter Twenty-Six

"Someone used Robin's credit card, the Lynn Taylor ID she was carrying," Hua said. They'd stopped at a gas station and Tom had gone in for food while Hua checked his tablet. The van filled with the smell of overdone hot dogs, which interested Bennett and made Hua's nose twitch disapprovingly. Tom handed him his fruit cup, which he set aside temporarily. "Copy shop, car rental, clothing store." Gently shoving the dog's big head out of the way, Tom leaned toward the passenger seat to see the screen. "The last two are in a town an hour away," Hua said, "but the copy shop is here in Brandell."

"Where? Haven't we been down every street in this burg?"

"It's in the back of a real estate office," Hua said. "The one run by Mayor Helen Gessing."

"Great." The comment was more groan than anything else. "We'll have to follow up. We sure can't send Luca to do it."

"How do we ask about a credit card used in her store?"

Tom considered. "I have the fake FBI badge and ID you made for me in my backpack."

Hua regarded him critically. "Sorry, Tom, but you look like a guy who's been camping, not a federal officer."

Glancing in the rear view mirror, Tom nodded. “I’ll get a razor and stuff from the dollar store. Then we’ll go to that second-hand place on Main Street and see if they have something less casual that will fit me.”

An hour later Tom was freshly shaved and dressed in a suit he was sure had belonged to someone’s now-dead grandfather. Shoes had been a problem, since he had wide feet, but he’d stuffed them into narrow wing-tips and left the laces loosely tied. He could stand the pain for twenty minutes. Leaving Hua with his head bowed over his tablet again, he went into the Windy Woods Real Estate office, noting a smaller sign in the window that said, “Copies: While U Wait or Make Ur Own.”

The office held two desks, a large map of the area, and a rack of brochures offering services for both buyers and sellers. The air was scented with pumpkin spice, and Tom saw a reed diffuser on a shelf near the door.

The smaller desk was empty. In the larger one sat a petite, dark-haired woman of about forty with eyes that sized Tom up both professionally and personally. Mayor Helen Gessing seemed to reach a positive result in both cases, and her greeting was silky with promise. “Can I help you?”

Using his flesh-and-blood hand, he showed her the badge and ID. “Gary DeYoung, ma’am. FBI.”

Her eyes widened. “What can I do for the Feds?”

“We understand you offer copy services.”

“Yes. In there.” She gestured toward a door at the back of the office. “Would you like to see?”

When Tom nodded, she led him into a room with three different copy machines, two computer terminals, and two tables, one empty, for patron's use, and one stacked with samples. Gessing seemed proud of the possibilities she offered customers. "I needed all these machines to compete in the real estate business, but I figured I might as well make a little money off them on the side." She rolled her eyes. "In a town this small, you do what you can to keep your head above water."

"Impressive. We're interested in a client who used your equipment recently, Lynn Taylor."

"Sure. I remember him."

Tom frowned. "Him?"

"Yeah. Tall guy, dark hair. A real charmer." She raised her brows. "Is he on the Most Wanted list, like a Mafia guy or something?"

Chapter Twenty-Seven

Dinner that evening brought yet another unexpected—and unwelcome—guest, at least in Robin's view. She'd been napping in the bedroom assigned to her, exhausted from the strain of the caper and lack of sleep, and hadn't heard the man's arrival.

"This is my attorney, Anthony Biers," Harry said when she entered the dining room. "He's going to handle the arrangements for our...adventure. Because he's able to make himself useful, Anthony often stays over for a day or two. He's endeared himself to the point of having his own room and a parking spot in the garage. Anthony, my great-granddaughter, Serena Dykstra."

Rising to shake Robin's hand, Biers waited until she was seated before taking his chair again. In his mid-thirties, he had the build of a basketball player and a grin that said he never took himself too seriously. "Harry pretends he doesn't like my company," he said in a confiding tone, "but secretly, he craves my sparkling wit."

"I see." Robin was trying to decide how to handle this new player. Unlike Natalie and the pastor, Biers showed no sign of mistrust or dislike. Not very lawyer-like.

Helping herself to the dish nearest her, broccoli with cheese sauce, she passed it across the table. "Where are you from, Mr. Biers?"

“Anthony, please. I live in Salem, about fifty miles from here.”

“Oh, yes. I came through it on my way.”

His brows rose, though his tone remained even. “Coming from Minnesota, isn’t it faster to take 65 straight down to the Scottsburg exit?”

In her head, Robin heard a voice asking sternly, *What did I tell you?* Emily Kane, a retired FBI agent now also retired from the Kidnap Gang, had often warned them to give as few details as possible in casual conversation. She'd screwed up, revealing a lie and possibly damaging her credibility.

She reached for a sip of water to cover her need for time, but she had to focus on not spilling it into her lap. Finally she said, “I get tired of the freeway, so I took secondary roads and enjoyed the countryside.”

“Some pretty spots around here.” Harry helped himself to the broccoli.

Robin nodded, grateful for the unintended help. Turning to Biers, she said, “I'll bet you see a lot of interesting drama in your work.”

“I do.” He looked to Harry. “Remember that who-stole-the-pig case I told you about a while back? Wait till you hear what the judge’s ruling was on that one.”

As they ate Svein’s excellent meal of roast beef and sweet potatoes, Robin encouraged Anthony Biers to continue talking about himself. The few times he asked about her background, she answered briefly and then asked another question about his work. Harry often entered the conversation, prompting Biers to, “Tell her about the man who thinks he's Bram Stoker reborn,” or “Remember the client you dragged into the shower to get him clean and sober for court?" Biers always obliged, telling anecdotes with humorous asides and a natural storytelling talent.

When the meal was over Biers asked, "Should I show Serena the boat, Harry?" Turning to her he said, "He's got an antique sailboat that's a real beauty. When I win the lottery, I plan to buy it from him."

"I've been saving it for you," Harry said teasingly. "But if Serena takes a liking to it, you're out of luck."

The comment caused Robin a stab of distress. Harry assumed far too much. That she actually was his great-granddaughter. That she'd someday be his heir. That she'd want all the things he'd collected over his life. She dismissed the idea of keeping a boat Biers obviously coveted. "I'm no sailor. I don't know port from...whatever the opposite of port is."

"Starboard," Biers supplied. "I'll show you the boat tonight, and if you like the looks of it, I can take you out for a sail tomorrow. We won't have many more good days for it this year."

Other than a ferry or two, Robin had never been on a boat in her life. Noticing Svein practically listing toward her as he waited for her answer, and she guessed he'd had a word with the lawyer. Harry's caregiver was desperate to stop her plans, and she understood. Who wouldn't try to stop an elderly man from spending a large amount of money on a woman he'd met a few days ago? Still, Robin felt like one of those tennis-ball launchers had been aimed in her direction. How many more people had Svein contacted in his attempts to discredit her?

Instinct said to refuse Biers' offer, since he'd no doubt try to trick her into admitting she was a phony. As an attorney, he was trained to ask questions that might reveal lies and evasions. She could say she had a headache. Surely people with brain issues were allowed such weaknesses. But that would put Svein on guard even more than he already was. Cam's predicament, never far from her mind, returned with full force. This was a test she needed to pass. "Sounds nice."

The boathouse sat a few hundred yards down the beach from the main staircase. The sun was long gone, but the pathway had solar-powered lights along it that turned the pines from green to a golden glow. At the neat, cedar-walled building, Anthony took a key from under the eaves and unlocked the door. Stepping in ahead of Robin, he turned on the lights. "Come in."

The place was large, airy, and clean, though the faint smell of fish and aquatic plants lingered. It held four watercraft, an aluminum rowboat painted green, a speedboat that appeared faster than most, a pontoon for lazy trips on the water, and the sailboat they'd come to see, which sat in a hoist above the water. It was beautiful, even to someone who didn't know what an antique boat was supposed to look like. The wood was highly polished, as were the brass fittings. Along the deck, ropes lay coiled neatly, ready to be useful.

She made appropriate noises of appreciation as Anthony described the craft's attributes. His eager manner revealed his love of sailing and this boat in particular. "Have you sailed all your life, Mr. Biers?"

"Anthony," he corrected. "And yes, since I was a kid. We lived near Patoka Lake, and my dad had a 22-footer." He grinned sheepishly. "When Harry found out I like to sail, he said I can take the *Dolores* out any time. I don't get up here often, but when I can, I drive down in the afternoon, stay overnight, go for a sail in the morning, and then head back to Salem." He tilted his head. "How about it? Are you up for a couple of hours on the lake tomorrow?"

She tried an excuse. "I didn't bring any warm clothes."

Biers waved the objection away. “There are coats and scarves at the house. Harry’s always ready for guests, though he seldom has any.”

“I know he has no family left, but doesn’t he have friends?”

“Harry’s wife got sick soon after they moved here from California, so he never got to know many people.” Biers led the way to the boathouse door. “The friends he did have are either dead or mostly house-bound, much like Harry.” He clicked the padlock closed. “These days it's usually just Harry and Svein.”

“Svein is very…dedicated.”

“And a little territorial. I’m the one that introduced them, but I never dreamed he and Harry would click like they did. Svein has become Harry’s everything: cook, nurse, property manager, and house mother.” After a pause he said, “There was a home care nurse for a while, but Svein learned to give Harry’s injections, check his oxygen levels, and do whatever else he needs done. When the nurse left for good, Svein was a lot happier.” Anthony’s teeth flashed white in the darkness. “Not that Svein is ever happy. He tends to think everyone is out to get everyone else.”

“I think he'd prefer it if I disappeared.”

Biers chuckled aloud. “To be honest, that’s pretty obvious.”

They’d started up the stairs, and Robin stopped. “Anthony, I didn't come to Brandell to become Harry's long-lost heir.” That part was true, and she chose the rest of her words carefully. “If a person has one blood connection left in the world, it's natural she'd want to get to know him and find out what her background is.”

“I understand that,” Biers said, “and it’s clear Harry likes you. For years he's had no one, and now here you are, a replacement for his lost Dolores.” They moved out of the spill of light at the landing, and she could no longer see his face. “Your appearance could be good for a lot of people.”

Was he hinting he'd support her claim to Harry's money? In return for what?

The greedy in-law. The hopeful pastor. The doubtful caregiver. Had she now met the duplicitous lawyer? How was Robin supposed to navigate the traps that lay in her path, reach a goal she had no desire to achieve, and escape her father’s clutches?

She chose a neutral comment. “I hope so.” It was hard to know what she hoped. Getting Cam back meant helping Mark get the money he badly needed. Once that was done, she would disappear from Harry’s life. She hated knowing how betrayed he’d feel when that happened. All she could do, Robin decided, was not deceive the poor man any longer than she had to.

Chapter Twenty-Eight

Hua found the bath house at the campground acceptable, though by no means luxurious. There were private stalls with doors that locked, and though the pressure was pathetic, there was plenty of hot water.

As he left the building, shivering a little since his hair was damp, he stopped to notice the stars. They seemed close, and the blue-black sky behind them seemed impenetrable. It was—

Grabbed from behind, he was jerked off his feet and dragged into a clump of trees. Unkind hands twisted him around and slammed him against a trunk, taking his breath away for a few seconds.

"What are you guys doing here?" a voice demanded.

Hua experienced a flash of sympathy for people the gang had kidnapped over the last few years. They no doubt feared pain, even death, when they realized they were at the mercy of unknown attackers, as he did at that moment.

When his head stopped spinning, Hua saw the face of the man they'd seen at the cabin that afternoon. Bringing his face so close to Hua's that he felt the heat of his breath, the man repeated the question.

"We were supposed to meet some friends," Hua said. "As we told you, they never showed up."

“And who are these friends?”

“Their name is Taylor.”

He muttered the name as if it meant nothing to him. Leaning in again he demanded, “Where's Mark?”

“I don't know anyone named Mark.”

“I think you do.” Grabbing Hua’s arm, the man twisted it until he turned against the tree trunk, gasping in pain. “His real name is Mark Parsons,” the guy said in Hua’s ear, “and he’s a low-life conman. A couple days ago we found out some relative of his owns the cabin you were at today. From the looks of the place, he’s been staying there with a woman.” The man released Hua’s arm and spun him around so he faced him again. “Since you and your buddy showed up there, we got a little suspicious. Then like magic, I see you here in the park, and I think, ‘The little creep is spying on us.’” He pinched Hua’s shoulder. “Now where is Mark? And don’t lie to me, or I swear I’ll give you a beat-down like you never imagined.”

“I don’t know Mark. I'm not lying,” Hua gasped “We came here to find our friends.”

The man grabbed a handful of Hua’s hair. “Come with me, little man.” Dragging Hua down the hill, he opened the back door of a large, black car and shoved him inside. As he did, a guy who’d been lying across the front seat sat up, his puzzled expression revealed by the dome lights. The shift of his body was reminiscent of an earthquake Hua had once experienced, shaking everything around it. His voice was croaky and cranky at being disturbed. “What the hell are you up to, Ernie?”

“I saw this guy coming out of the bath house. He’s one of the guys that was at the cabin this afternoon, so I decided to see what he knows.”

"You decided, did you? You dumb—" The man couldn't think of a word that was insulting enough. "We were supposed to be discreet up here, so what do you do? You go and kidnap a guy."

"We got a job to do," Ernie shot back, "and if I remember right, we was told to be quick about it."

"You don't know what the boss said. You weren't even there."

"No, I wasn't." Ernie's tone was aggrieved. "I get to be the silent partner, bein' that I ain't married to Ronnie's niece."

"It ain't who I'm screwing that puts me in charge. It's because I've got a brain in my head." Before Ernie could reply his companion went on. "So what's this guy got to say?"

"The same as he said this afternoon. They're looking for friends that didn't show up when they was supposed to."

The big man turned his gaze on Hua. "Who are these friends?"

"Lynn and Richard Taylor. They're wildlife photographers."

"And they disappeared?" Hua nodded, and the big man rubbed at his whiskers, putting the information together with what he knew. "What if our guy snatched these people? We know he needs transportation, but he'll be scared to use his own credit card. He finds a couple that's passing through this burg, kills them, and takes their car. He might even use the guy's ID to get out of the country before anybody finds out he's dead."

That scenario caused Hua an involuntary shiver. "Who is this Mark?"

The larger man's narrow eyes slid over Hua's face disinterestedly. "Nobody you need to know about."

Ernie gave Hua an impromptu lecture, like a kindergarten teacher drawing lessons from life experience. "Just remember: it ain't a good idea to cheat a guy that's got a long memory and resources like me and Mr. Gerald Perkins here."

"Jeez, you're using my name now? Why don't you let the guy have a look at our drivers' licenses while you're at it? He should know all about us so he can run to the cops and spill his guts."

Ernie made a rude noise. "He won't say nothing about us to anybody, will you, little man? He knows what would happen if he did." He turned to Hua. "Am I right?"

"I solemnly swear that I will never speak of tonight's events outside this campground," Hua replied.

"We're supposed to take your word for that?" Gerald asked scornfully.

"My word is very good."

The big man sighed. "Okay, get out." Hua obeyed, though he wasn't sure they'd actually let him go. Once he was outside the car, they could easily kill him with a blow to the head or a knife between his ribs.

He never learned what the men had in mind, because several things happened in quick succession. As he exited the car, Ernie took hold of Hua's collar. At the same moment, a threatening growl sounded from the pathway to the bath house, and Tom ordered, "Let him go."

Surprisingly, Ernie obeyed. Tom stepped out of the shadows, holding Bennett by his collar. Bennett wasn't happy about it. "Where's your friend?" Tom asked.

"I'm here." Gerald leaned out of the car, and in his hand was a pistol. Light from the bathhouse glinted faintly off the silvery barrel.

Tom's lips tightened, but he didn't back down. "What do you want with us?"

"We told you. We're looking for a guy. We were asking your friend again if he knows where Mark is."

"We don't. We're strangers here."

Gerald made a decision. "If that's true, we got no beef with you."

Tom actually took a step forward, though Hua didn't know how he made himself do it. "We think our friends were at that cabin at some point, but they aren't there now. If you think this Mark had something to do with their disappearance, we'd like to know what you know."

"You don't need to know nothing." Gerald moved toward Tom, so they stood only a few feet apart. Bennett lowered his head and made a noise deep in his throat, but the big man ignored him. "Here's what you're gonna do. You're gonna get in your van with your dog and your friend and go someplace else."

From behind Hua, Ernie put in his two cents' worth. "Otherwise, things won't go good for you."

Tom licked his lips. "Fine. That's what we'll do."

The muzzle of the pistol in Gerald's hand dipped, and a second later the gun disappeared from sight. "Smart boy."

"Tell us one thing. Is this Mark a charming type?"

"I s'pose the ladies would say that. What's it to you?"

"A woman I met today mentioned a stranger in town who's like that."

"What woman?"

Tom didn't expose Mayor Gessing to another, possibly more violent, questioning. "We stopped to ask for directions to the cabin, and she said something about another man who'd asked the way out there. She used the word *charming* to describe him." He shifted his feet. "Listen. We don't want any trouble over this Mark guy. To prove we mean it, we'll leave Brandell right now."

"Good decision," Gerald said. "We'll make sure you do."

Pulling at Bennett's leash, Tom led him away. Hua fell in behind them. Ernie and Gerald followed to the top of the knoll and stopped, waiting expectantly while they got into the van. As Tom started the engine, Hua crawled into the back and secured the gear they'd been using at the campsite. Frowning at the smell emanating from a bag of pork rinds Tom had been snacking on, he asked, "Where are we going?"

"Anywhere but here. We'll come back for Luca in the morning."

"What if they see us?"

He managed a grin. "I doubt they'll shoot us on the main street of town in broad daylight."

"I will text her, in case she visits the campground and finds us gone."

"Tell her to meet us at the diner at seven." Driving off the campsite, Tom turned toward the exit. "Don't mention what happened here. No sense having her worry all night."

"I promised those men I would not tell anyone outside this campground what we discussed," Hua said. "You will have to tell Luca the story, so I can continue to be a man of my word."

Chapter Twenty-Nine

Obeying the text Hua had sent, Luca started for the diner a few minutes before seven Thursday morning. She'd spent Wednesday afternoon on a series of disappointing interviews, hoping to find information about the couple who'd stayed overnight in Brandell. Luca covered her questions by saying the strangers' car had a "For Sale" sign in the window, and she hoped to find out more about it. "My sister needs reliable transportation for work," she said each time she asked if someone had seen them.

Her approach had resulted in blank looks and one offer of a substitute, a "real gem if you don't mind a little rust." Few of the townspeople even remembered seeing Robin and Cam, since they'd come late one day and left early the next. No one who recalled seeing them could report anything unusual. "The guy came in for some cheese curls," a woman at a convenience store told her. "He's pretty cute, but he didn't say much."

"He seldom does." Realizing she'd given herself away, Luca had rephrased. "Guys that cute are always the strong, silent type, right?"

As she entered the restaurant, leaving the cool morning air for the dry heat of a forced air furnace, she almost ran into a stocky, fireplug of a man coming out. He wore several layers of clothing, an orange-ish, tropical-print polyester shirt covered by a red and blue flannel topped with a pink camo jacket. He looked like a flamingo with an identity crisis.

The guy ogled her a little, perhaps impressed by her look for the day, mulberry-colored leggings with a lavender top and a magenta turban. Holding the door he said, "Sorry, Miss. I didn't mean to get in your way."

"No problem."

Looking over her shoulder he asked, "You ain't eating breakfast all by yourself, are you?"

In Tulsa, she'd have asked the big jerk what possible business it was of his who she ate breakfast with. In Brandell, she was more discreet. "I'm meeting someone."

His mouth drooped with disappointment. "That's me. Always a day late and a dollar short."

A second, even larger, man came along, stuffing bills into his wallet. "What are you doing now, Ernie?"

His gaze remained on Luca. "Talking to this lovely lady here."

"Well, let the lovely lady go get her breakfast. You and me got things to do, remember?"

With an attempt at a courtly bow, the first man left. The other paused to ask, "You from around here?"

"No. I'm staying at the motel down the street."

He nodded as if he could have guessed. "Have a nice day."

The waitress had come along in time to hear his question, and as she led Luca to a table she said, "They was asking if we had a tall, dark stranger come in here lately. I told 'em, 'Honey, if that happened, I'd run off with him and there'd be nobody to bring you your pancakes.'"

Ten minutes later Hua and Tom arrived, joined Luca, and ordered from the menu. "Why aren't we pretending we don't know each other anymore?" she asked when the waitress went into the kitchen.

Tom reported the night's events at the campground. When he described the two men, Luca gasped in surprise. "They were leaving here when I came in. You just missed them." As Hua glanced nervously at the parking lot, she added, "The waitress mentioned they asked her about some guy. Does he have anything to do with Robin and Cam?"

"We don't know," Hua told her, "but he used Robin's credit card. We think he might be holding them prisoner."

"But not at the cabin, at least not anymore," Tom put in.

The waitress brought their meals, and they made appropriate answers to her questions. They didn't need ketchup. There was nothing else she could get for them. They thought everything smelled yummy.

When she was gone again Tom told Luca, "Hua and I plan to stay at the Helter cabin tonight. It's doubtful those goons will go back out there now that whoever was there has gone somewhere else."

"Who do you think they are?"

"Hired muscle. I think this Mark guy owes money to a loan shark or some other scary type. He came to Brandell to escape them, but somehow they figured out where he was. He must have seen them coming and bolted again."

“Maybe with Cam and Robin’s car.”

Tom finished a forkful of hash browns before speaking. “There was no sign that anyone was…hurt at the old cabin. Robin left behind some clothes, neatly folded. They’d been tied up. I think if this guy had meant to kill them, he’d have done it right away. He’s keeping them for some reason.”

Hua finished his omelet and wiped his mouth with a napkin. “If we go back out there, we can perhaps find clues to where they’ve gone.”

“Okay,” Luca sipped at her juice. “You’re going to stay at the cabin. What should I do?”

“If you think you can learn anything more at the motel,” Tom replied, "you should stay there. If not, you’re welcome to join us at Pitcher Lake.” Smiling he added, “But I warn you, there are mice.”

“Let me ponder on that.” Luca raised her hands like a balance scale. “My current motel dwelling place, with a shower and electricity, or a creepy cabin, with a lantern and crawling creatures.” She grinned as one hand dropped below the table edge. “I believe I’ll stay where I am.”

Chapter Thirty

Sailing with Anthony Biers was the last thing Robin wanted to do on Thursday morning, but she saw no way to get out of it. She reminded herself that she'd been through similar experiences, pretending to be someone she wasn't, presenting a calm demeanor when her mind boiled with fears, and dealing with the unwanted companionship of romance-minded males. She'd learned from each past experience, and that should prevent her from saying the wrong thing, breaking into tears, or fainting in the man's arms, as she'd once done with Tom.

At 10:00 a.m. she came to the lake shore to find the boat ready at the dock and Anthony fussing with ropes—he called them lines—while he waited for her to arrive. "I see you found outerwear," he said, indicating the bright green raincoat and neck scarf Svein had grudgingly provided. Robin wore navy pants and a long-sleeved jersey top from the clothes Mark had bought for her. Luckily, she always took running shoes with her on a caper. It was impossible to predict when they might have to make a quick getaway, and she never wanted to emulate the goofy females in action movies who slowed everyone else down with easy-to-lose slip-ons, or worse, impossible-to-run-in high heels.

The day was gorgeous. With a cool-but-not-cold breeze, the boat slipped through the water like a dream. Biers was an amiable companion. It should have been a wonderful experience, but Robin was thoroughly miserable. Her stomach roiled, though she'd limited herself to toast and milk for breakfast. Her pretend smile hurt her face. Her heart ached with fear for Cam, who had now been locked in somewhere for days with limited food and water. She analyzed every remark the lawyer made, trying to avoid traps he might set for her. The combination made her weak and dizzy, and she suddenly felt like she was going to vomit.

"I need to sit down."

Ironically, her nausea fed the story they'd created about her having blockage in her brain. Biers helped her to a seat at the stern. "Sit in the center, where there's less motion. We can go back in."

"I'll be fine," she said. "It's lovely out here."

"It is." His gaze swept the vista before them. "Sailing is like medicine for whatever ails me." He sat down on the bench beside Robin, and she resisted the urge to move away. After a minute she made a show of resettling her clothes and put a bit of distance between them.

"Tell me about life in Minnesota," Biers said.

She shrugged. "Not much to tell. I'm a bookkeeper for a small company. I follow the Vikings in the fall and the Twins in summer. I volunteer at the library, reading to preschoolers."

He gave her a sideways look. "I bet the little boys love that."

"You couldn't tell from the way they behave—or don't," she joked.

"If I were in your reading group, I'd be completely absorbed."

Signals came loud and strong, and Robin met them head on. “Anthony, I'm dealing with a lot right now. Can we keep this casual?”

“Of course. It's just that you're very attractive.” He wiped a spray of mist off the seat with the sleeve of his jacket. “A guy sees possibilities.”

Did this “guy” see possibilities for romance or financial gain? Was Biers rushing in to make a claim before anyone else realized that Serena Dykstra might inherit millions? He obviously admired Harry’s gorgeous house, numerous boats, and other possessions. He probably counted on some sort of gift from the estate, but that would be nothing compared to marrying Harry's only blood heir.

Instead of commenting on what he’d said, Robin turned her eyes to the bow. “Let’s enjoy today and let tomorrow take care of itself.”

Chapter Thirty-One

Though Cam tried to keep his morale up, he finally admitted he was miserable. One of the things he wanted in life—no, needed—was being outside. Even when the weather was bad, Cam found things to do that took him outdoors. He raked the yard. He fixed the porch, walked the dog, anything that put him where sun, rain, or even snow hit his face. He was okay inside if he had work to do or an array of video games, but given a choice, he chose outside.

That made it hard to be locked up. The tiny patch of sky he could see when he took the stovepipe out was hardly enough to keep him sane, though it helped. Stars twinkled above, three of them. In the daytime he let the sun hit his face and sniffed the rotting-leaf smell that floated in on the breeze. It wasn't much, but it was all he had.

On some TV show he'd seen, they said prisoners of war made it through captivity by imagining their homes and loved ones. Cam tried to imagine what his friends were doing. Robin was trying to rescue him, of course, but having only a rough idea what Parsons had in mind, he couldn't picture her in action. He turned to the people he could imagine. "Hua is working in the garden," he said aloud. "He'll clear out the dead plants and collect the last of the squash and pumpkins. Tom is teaching Mai to speak English better and helping Jai learn to read and write it. Luca's probably doing chores around the house. She likes organizing and cleaning, but she does it kind of funny. She has all kinds of tools to protect her fancy nails, so she looks like she's on the bomb squad." After a moment he added, "Bennett the dog is stretched out wherever there's sunshine, in the kitchen doorway or in front of the slider at the east end of the house."

Picturing his friends doing home-type tasks helped to lessen Cam's anxiety, but when he finished that, he had to find new things to think about. He began going over their past capers, playing them like TV shows in his mind. He was able to put himself into the picture and at the same time stand outside it, watching the action. The names of the crooks they'd dealt with didn't come to him, only their defiant, angry faces. The divorce lawyer who cheated his clients by making deals with soon-to-be ex-husbands. The pill manufacturer who fell to his death while trying to kill Robin. The televangelist who spent donations for overseas relief on himself. And the original caper target, the man who'd cheated Cam's mother out of her property as she lay dying.

They'd done a lot of good, though Cam knew his parents wouldn't approve. Becoming a criminal wasn't what he'd imagined for himself, but if he and Robin hadn't teamed up, crooks would still be cheating people, and he'd never have met Hua. "When good things come from breaking the law," Cam asked aloud, "is it okay?" He couldn't decide on an answer.

Cam and Hua had speculated a few times about what they'd do if they weren't crime-fighters. It was idle talk, but they'd discussed having a truck garden and selling the produce. Listening to the farmers who sat around at the local hardware store when it was too cold or too wet to work, Cam had learned a lot about which crops grew well locally.

The men had been unsure what to think of him at first, but Cam knew farming and farm equipment. After he asked a couple of questions that revealed he was no amateur, one of them suggested he pull up a chair and join them. He did, and while he didn't say much, he listened. They spoke of how to manage fruit trees after years of neglect. They talked about what vegetables grew best in which months. And they mentioned the farm-to-table movement, gardeners providing food to restaurants in Kansas City. When Cam had told Hua what they said, he'd found more information online.

The idea of growing food excited both men, but in the end they agreed it was only a dream. They owed their allegiance to the gang, which meant they had to be ready at any time to leave on a caper. That didn't work well with planting season, harvest time, and a large garden's need for regular weeding and watering. It was best to stick with the small plot they tended to provide vegetables for their own use.

"Someday, maybe" Hua had said not long ago. "We won't always chase bad guys, will we?"

Cam had no answer to that, and he didn't know who might.

Chapter Thirty-Two

Harry was pleased when the email with test results arrived. Scowling the whole time, Svein increased the font size, printed the results, and handed the sheets over. Scanning the page, Harry announced what Robin already knew he'd find. "We're a match, Serena."

Robin glanced at Svein, whose expression clearly showed he wasn't convinced. Since he couldn't argue with science, he contented himself with glaring at her.

Trying to look pleased but not smug, she said, "I'm glad we were able to prove it."

"Now we have to focus on getting you well."

She shook her head. "Do you really think Dr. Alvarro will give up his free time to come here and operate on me?"

Harry raised a gnarled finger. "Because Reuben cares for you, I believe he's going to make it happen."

Robin winced, knowing how quickly Mark would be gone once he got his hands on Harry's money.

Sliding the DNA results into a pocket at the side of his wheelchair, Harry asked, "Have you spoken to him since he left?"

"No," Robin replied. She had no phone, but she didn't mention it, since it would seem odd. What twenty-year-old left home for an overnight trip without a cell?

"I'm sure we'll hear from him soon."

An hour later Robin came back from a walk to find Harry replacing the phone in its cradle. "That was Reuben. He'll be here soon with details, but the doctor has agreed to do the surgery in Indianapolis tomorrow. That's a two-hour trip, so we'll have to be on the road early."

"We?" Mark had planned to whisk Robin away and return in a few days with her head bandaged and the doctor's "bill" in hand. Apparently it wasn't going to be that easy.

"I made a suggestion, and after some discussion, Reuben agreed that it makes sense. Indy has excellent facilities, and it's not far from here, so your surgery will be done there, and I'm coming with you."

"You're coming to my surgery." It was something she'd never considered.

"Svein suggested it. I want to meet this Doctor Alvarro before I let him touch one hair on my great-granddaughter's head."

Svein appeared pleased, as well he should, since he'd made the con much harder for them. Now they needed a real hospital. How was Mark going to make that happen?

When he arrived, Mark put a good face on the changes Harry had demanded, though Robin could tell he was unhappy. Suggesting that "Serena" show him the lake, he led the way down the long staircase, voicing his anger as soon as they were away from the house. "I knew that Svein guy would be trouble."

"Let's leave," Robin urged. "If we go, I doubt they'll look for us."

"You forget, Robbie. I need money to get to Dubai—" He caught himself. "Or somewhere."

She wanted to scream that he didn't "need" anything. The threat of arrest and imprisonment grew stronger by the minute. While Harry had been easy to convince, Svein was not, and he was marshalling every resource and tossing every impediment possible in their path.

"How many times have you had to start over with nothing when one of your cons went wrong?"

Mark turned to her, and she saw fear in his eyes. "I've never had anything like this hanging over my head, Robbie. This guy isn't going to stop coming after me until I'm dead."

Though that chilled her, Robin kept her voice calm. "I get that you're desperate, but I don't see a way forward for this. Let's give up on Harry and think of some other way to get you the cash you need."

The Kidnap Gang had a little money. Could she buy Mark off with a plane ticket and a few thousand dollars? Was it right to spend the gang's money to extricate herself from Mark's clutches? She decided it would be if it meant Cam was set free.

Mark's reply told her he wasn't yet ready to give up. "Harry's prepared to hand over $250,000. If we can't do the con, we'll take the old coot hostage and make Pretty Boy Svein pay it as ransom."

She couldn't have that. Harry was ninety. Being abducted and held captive, probably at that awful old cabin, was likely to kill him. "That's kidnapping, and you'd be in a lot more trouble." They fell silent, listening to the chatter of squirrels in the trees behind them. Robin searched her mind for possibilities and found none. Finally she said, “Mark, we simply can’t fake this with Harry along. We don't have a waiting area for him to sit in. We don’t have a surgeon, an operating room, medical staffers, or a hospital to go through the motions of brain surgery.”

Mark nodded, his expression troubled. “If I had help, I could pull it off, but right now I can't trust any of my old pals. The reward Ronnie offered for my head is big enough to turn almost anyone against me.”

“That’s because all your friends are crooks.”

He shrugged, allowing her the point. “It would have been fun to make it work, you know?”

As he spoke, an idea entered Robin's mind. As Mark stared at the water, imagining how things might have gone, Robin considered. She didn't know if her idea was good or bad in the long run. Mark would get his way, steal Harry’s money, and escape trouble. That wasn’t how she wanted things to be, but a successful con was required to save Cam’s life. “I have some people.”

Mark turned to her with a sardonic smile. “You have people.”

“Yes. We...um, we've done a few scams.” She looked down at her hands, curled tightly around the railing. “In one of them we sort of infiltrated a hospital. We might be able to do it again.”

After a long silence, Mark made an odd noise. At first she was baffled, but then she realized her father was laughing. When he could breathe again he chortled, “Robbie, Robbie, Robbie. Like they say, the apple doesn't fall far from the tree.”

"Don't you dare think I'm anything like you," she ordered, jabbing a finger at him. "My friends and I con people who break the law and get away with it. We make them agree to go straight, and we watch to see they do."

"Really? My little girl created her own Justice League?"

"It's better than anything you ever taught me. And my friends can be trusted. They'd never rat me out, for any reason."

"Do you take money from these law-breakers?"

"Well, yes. It has to cost something, or they wouldn't learn from it."

"So you make your living on the con."

"We give half the money we collect to charity."

"Nice sop to your conscience, little girl," he said in a mocking tone. "I don't suppose you use any of the tricks I taught you when you punish the bad kids of the world."

She refused to confess to it out loud. At his feet she'd learned basic cons, scams that worked more times than not by appealing to the targets' vanity, greed, and lust. And sadly, it was Mark's voice that came into her head in times of stress, reminding her to stick to the plan and things would work out.

Robin refused to give him the satisfaction of admitting that, so she went back to practical matters. "I can get three people to Indianapolis by tonight. They could fill the roles we need."

"Four would be better. We need a doctor, a nurse, some sort of intake clerk, and an orderly, though I think nowadays they're called transporters." He thought about it. "I met a guy in Brandell who can probably handle that."

“Or we could use Cam. He's a very convincing actor.” Cam’s acting skills weren’t exactly smooth, but why shouldn't she lie to Mark, whose whole life was one big falsehood?

“Your hubby is great right where he is,” Mark replied. “He keeps you honest...or dishonest, in this case. My guy will be okay with a haircut, a shave, and scrubs. I’ll speak to him. You can get the others in place.”

“Don't go off to Indianapolis and leave Cam without food and water. If this goes sour—”

“No worries, Robbie.” Taking a phone from his pocket, Mark held it out to her. “Get your friends on the road. Once they arrive, have them text me their motel name and a room number. We'll have a little meet-up to figure out who'll do what.”

Taking the phone, Robin stared at it for a few seconds. The only number she could remember was Tom's, since it was only one digit different from hers. When she tried it, she got his voice mail recording: “Leave a message.” She had a moment of unreasoning anger. Where are you when I need you?

It wasn't Tom's fault. Robin’s anxiety seemed to double every minute, and having Mark standing beside her, eavesdropping on the call, made her snappish. Taking a deep breath, she left a message. “I need you, Bubbles, and Lily to go to Indianapolis right away. Get rooms at the Comfort Inn on the west side and text a room number to this phone. A man named Mark will contact you. Do exactly as he says.”

“That's my girl,” Mark patted her arm, and she recoiled as if bitten. “I have to go. I’m going to take your car. You’re not using it, and that pickup rides like a tank.” He slid the phone from her hand. “We'll keep in touch through Harry, so you won't need this.”

As she heard the car start, turn, and head down the drive, Robin stared at the lake, feeling as alone as she'd ever felt. She'd involved her friends in a problem that should have been hers to solve. She was responsible for Cam's abduction and the duping of an old man who wanted nothing more than a connection to his lost daughter. She didn't trust Mark for a second, but she had no way to change things. She needed to warn Tom, Hua, and Luca, so they knew how slippery, self-centered, and diabolical her father was.

Chapter Thirty-Three

As the stovepipe hole showed the beginnings of dawn, Cam heard a vehicle outside his prison. He wasn't sure what day it was about to be. Thursday? Friday? Had he been there for two days or three? It seemed like forever. Hurriedly he set the pipe back in place, covering his little chunk of sky.

The sound of the padlock snapping open announced Parsons' presence. "Get back," he called. Cam obeyed, knowing the gun would be aimed at him when the door opened.

The beam of a flashlight blinded him temporarily, and Cam raised a hand to shield his eyes. When Parsons lowered the light, Cam saw the Ford in the grayness over his shoulder. It was parked in the driveway of a modern cabin that belonged to whoever had built the sauna.

"How you doing, big guy?" Parsons asked.

"I'm okay. Where's Robin?"

"She's doing her part to get you out of here. She and I have to go up north, so I brought you enough food for a couple of days." As he spoke, Parsons shrugged off a backpack. To free one hand, he set the flashlight he'd brought along on the bench nearest the door.

"Why are you doing this to her?" Cam asked. "She's your daughter. She could get arrested for what you're making her do."

"Only chumps get arrested, my friend. Robin is trained in the con, and I know she's good because I'm the one who trained her." Cam said nothing, and Parsons asked, "Are you part of this gang she says she's got? You go around kidnapping people and making them confess what they've done wrong?"

Cam didn't know how to respond. It sounded like Robin had told him about their activities.

Em, the eighty-plus woman who helped them get the gang started, had always insisted they keep quiet. *If you get arrested, the cops will pretend they know more than they do,* she'd claimed. *They toss out bits of information and let the suspect incriminate himself. Admit nothing.*

Mark Parsons wasn't a cop, but Cam figured Em's advice worked in this instance too. "I don't know what you're talking about."

"I'll bet you don't." Parsons paused before asking, "Robin never told you about me?"

"She talks about her mom sometimes. Not you."

"'How like a serpent's tooth is an ungrateful child.'"

Cam frowned. "What?"

"A line I heard somewhere. I gave my kids every opportunity to get ahead in the world, and as soon as they were old enough, they turned on me." Parsons had closed the door, so it was dark again, but Cam heard bitterness in his voice. "Tossed me out of my own home. Turned my wife against me."

"If Robin and Chris were mad at you, it was because you did bad stuff."

"I wouldn't expect you to understand." Parsons slid the backpack toward Cam with his foot. "I need to go back for your water." He stepped outside, closed the door, and replaced the padlock. Leaning forward, Cam pushed the flashlight into a shadowed corner. Sitting back, he waited until Parsons returned and set a gallon jug of water down. "That should keep you for a while. If all goes well, Robin will be here to let you out sometime tomorrow afternoon, Sunday morning at the latest. I doubt you and I will ever see each other again, so I'll say goodbye now. You've been very useful to me, and for that I'm grateful." Allowing a touch of humanity to show he added, "Be good to my little girl."

"I bet I treat her better than you ever did."

His comment erased the softening in Parsons' eyes. Keeping the gun trained on Cam, he opened the door and stepped backward over the threshold. Behind him daylight gained rapidly on the darkness of a few minutes earlier.

When the padlock clicked on the outside, Cam let out the breath he'd been holding. With the breaking dawn, Parsons had forgotten about the flashlight he'd set on the bench.

Groping until his hand found it, Cam gave a little grunt of pleasure. He'd bought the tool himself, a bright LED light kept in the car for emergencies. It had tools attached to its handle: screwdriver heads, a belt cutter, and a glass breaker.

Cam had considered every escape possibility his prison offered and felt every crack and crevice, but any attempt to get out required tools. He figured the stove door could be used as a hammer if removed from the firebox, but his probing fingers had found no way to release the screws that held it in place. Now, Cam felt the tips of the various tools attached to the flashlight. "Okay," he said when he located what he sought. "Phillips it is."

Chapter Thirty-Four

Though it was a risk, Robin felt she had to warn Tom of the danger he and the others were in. To do that she needed access to a phone. She shadowed Anthony Biers for an hour, hoping he'd set his cell down and walk away, but his phone seemed almost a part of his hand. Svein wore his in a holster at his hip, so she had no way to get at it. Harry claimed he had no use for a cell. That left the land line, kept because the house was far enough from the nearest tower that cells sometimes didn't work.

When Harry went to his room to nap, she took up a spot near the phone table and pretended to read. Svein lingered in the room, straightening the bookshelf with an air that suggested she'd left it a mess, though she'd only removed a single volume. When he finished that, Svein got a broom and swept the tile floor, stopping pointedly before her until she lifted her feet and allowed him to clean where they'd rested. Next he got a dust cloth and wiped all the surfaces in the room, humming in a tuneless way she felt sure was meant to irritate her. Gritting her teeth, Robin pretended to be absorbed in the book, though she couldn't have said what the title or the topic was. Svein painstakingly cleaned every item on the end table beside her, the lamp on the wall over her head, and the figurines on a shelf above it. His rear bumped her chair several times, but he didn't bother to pretend he was sorry. Nothing like being shown that you're in the way.

Having made his point, Svein put on a jacket and toque and went outside. By turning her head, Robin could see him through the window, taking logs from a loose pile and stacking them neatly onto a rack. Once he was absorbed in the work, she stood and started toward the desk where the phone sat.

"Did I leave my glasses in here?" It was Anthony Biers, his brow knitted with either frustration or myopia. He'd been included in the plan to go to Indianapolis on Saturday, so he'd stayed on. "I had them at lunch, but after that…" He wandered the room, checking tables and shelves where he might have left them. Setting the book aside, Robin helped him look. After a short search she said, "Here." The glasses hung on the telescope Harry kept set up for bird and game watching.

"Right. I put them there when I looked at some geese." As he took the glasses from Robin, his hand brushed hers in a deliberate way. "Thank you, Serena."

She kept her voice neutral. "You're welcome."

He seemed unwilling to leave, and for once Robin missed Svein's presence. No one was likely to try to romance her when he was in the room. Biers cleared his throat before speaking again. "When you've recuperated from your surgery, maybe we can see a show together. I can get tickets to something good in Indianapolis."

Which would require an overnight stay, no doubt. "Sounds nice."

"There are some decent restaurants in Maple City too. I could show you the good ones."

"Anthony, I can't think past tomorrow. I'm sure you understand."

"Right, right." He made a calming gesture with both hands. "I'm—I—you'll make it through okay. I know it. And then we can see—" He stopped, unable to find the right words.

Still unsure whether he was smitten with her (in which case he would be disappointed) or hoping for easy money (in which case he would deserve his fate), she showed no emotion. "Yes. Then we can see."

Deflated by her lack of response, Biers went back to Harry's office, where he was working remotely. He'd received a box by courier, and he and Harry had conferred briefly before he disappeared into the office and closed the door. Now it closed behind him a second time, and Robin again reached for the phone, only to be halted again.

"Serena," Harry called from his room, "Can you help for a minute?"

"Sure." In Harry's room, obviously decorated in his wife's taste, she found him lying on the bed with a light blanket spread over his legs. "I need a glass of water so I can take my pill," he said. "Svein usually leaves one on the nightstand, but he forgot."

She went to the kitchen and got the water. As Harry took a pill so large that she winced as he swallowed she said, "My presence upsets Svein."

"Yes."

Surprised that he didn't say more, Robin waited until she was sure the pill had gone where it was supposed to go. "Do you need anything else?"

"No, thank you." Harry laid back on the pillow. "You're a good person, Serena."

No, I'm not. I'm here to cheat you out of your money, and I frequently break multiple laws. She thought of the photos on the wall in the den, all the people Harry had helped in his lifetime. How many times had he been wrong about them? Biting her lip, she said only, "Thanks, Harry. I like you too."

When she returned to the living room, all was quiet. Biers was apparently hard at work. Svein moved around outside, his muscled arms flexing as he lifted logs from the ground and stacked them precisely the way he wanted them. Harry would nap for at least an hour. Picking up the phone, she dialed Tom's number.

Chapter Thirty-Five

The stove door made a clumsy hammer, but it was better than nothing. Standing on the bench, Cam went to work on the stovepipe hole, prying at the aluminum cap with his screwdriver until it popped loose, rolled down the roof, and hit the ground with a tinny thud. He still looked out at a four-inch circle of blue, but between him and the sky was only wood. Wood can be broken. It wouldn't be easy, but it was what he had to do.

Wedging the screwdriver blade into the seam between two boards, Cam whacked the bottom of the handle with the cast-iron door. Each blow sent shudders of impact up his arms, but after about twenty blows, he heard the wood split. Moving the screwdriver farther down, he hammered again and was rewarded with a pleasing *crack*! The board split, and he ducked out of the way as a piece fell to the floor. He went to work on the other half, which soon joined its mate below.

"It's a start," Cam said aloud. As an accompaniment to labor, he'd always found his dad's poetry helpful. None of it was high-class stuff, but it helped him focus on the task at hand. He recited aloud, "It was early in September last October in July—" On the last syllable he struck the board he'd chosen a hard blow, and it cracked with a loud protest. "The sun was thick upon the ground, the mud shone in the sky." A second blow splintered the board, and he reached up with his free hand, pulled the pieces out, and tossed them out through the hole.

"The flowers were singing sweetly and the birds were full of bloom…" His screwdriver blade bit into the next board, and on "bloom" he struck the handle hard. "I went down in the basement to clean an upstairs room." The second board gave way and followed its predecessor to the ground.

"I glanced backwards out the window; the day was dark as night…" *Whack!* Split. Toss. "I looked a thousand miles away, a house just out of sight." *Whack! Whack!* Split. Toss. "Its walls were erected backwards and the front was round the back." *Whack*! Split. Toss. "It stood alone with others, and the fence was whitewashed black."

The job took all the poems he could remember: the one about the two dead boys who got up to fight and the one that started, "Just as I looked up, around the corner came Elmer…" He even said the one about the little dog named Jack that had caused his mother to shush his father if she heard him telling it. The rhymes passed the time and kept him from thinking about the strain in his shoulders from holding the heavy stove door overhead. Dad had learned most of them, he said, in the army, where he'd gone to ranger school and jumped out of perfectly good airplanes. That was all he'd say about his time in the military, and Cam figured that meant the rest of it wasn't as much fun as learning songs and funny rhymes.

When he finally sat down to rest, Cam's arms shook and he had a gash where he'd missed the screwdriver and hit his own fist. Still, he'd made progress. The hole was twice its original size, and the larger section of light streaming in made him feel hopeful. Eating one of his sandwiches and drinking one of the sodas Parsons had left in his latest delivery, Cam climbed back onto the bench and went to work on the next board.

Chapter Thirty-Six

When his phone pulsed, Tom almost didn't answer. The caller ID showed a number he didn't recognize, and it wasn't the one Robin's earlier message had come from. Still, the situation was unusual lately, so after a second he answered with a terse, "Who is it?"

"It's me, Homey."

He almost fainted with relief. "Are you all right, Clarabelle?"

"Yes, but I need to let you know what's going on. I don't have a lot of time, because someone might come along any minute."

"Okay. Tell me."

"Bozo's locked up somewhere with limited food and water. To get him back, I have to cheat a man out of a lot of money. That's why I need you in Indianapolis."

"We're on our way." He didn't explain they were an hour or so south of the city, not a few states west.

"I don't have much time, but watch your back. Mark's loyalty is to Mark, and he'll sell any one of us out if it benefits him."

"Who is Mark? Do you think he'd really let Bozo starve to death?"

“I don't know.” There was a sob buried in her words. “Mark is—he's—my dad.”

“Oh.” Tom knew a little of Robin's unhappy childhood, just as she knew a little about the struggles he faced daily to forget being blown to pieces in Afghanistan.

Apparently recalling that Tom and her brother shared the bond of being wounded combat vets, Robin added a further warning. “Ronald can't hear about this, Tom. If he knew Dad was making me do this, he'd hunt him down and strangle him. Though I’d love to tell Mark to go to hell, getting Bozo back is the most important thing. Once he’s okay, I’ll decide what to do about the trouble with Dad.”

“Is there any chance of us finding Bozo ourselves?”

“There are a dozen lakes and hundreds of cabins in the Brandell area, and he could be in any one of them.” She sighed before adding, “We have to get Mark what he wants and hope he has enough decency left in his twisted soul to hold up his end of the bargain.”

“All right, then. We do as he says until you decide differently.”

When he ended the call, Tom waited for Hua and Luca, who'd gone into a Subway attached to the gas station for food. He reported the situation, ending with, “Robin's dad is crooked, but I’m pretty sure he's also really good at manipulating her.”

Luca's comment was telling. Rearranging the ingredients on her chicken teriyaki foot-long she said, “It's hard to face down your own daddy, even when you know he's bad.”

“Exactly. We're going to do what Parsons wants, but let’s watch him every second. If there's a way to rescue Cam and get Robin out of his clutches, we'll take it. She hopes he'll do the right thing once the con succeeds, but I'm not as optimistic about that as she is.”

"Nor am I," Hua agreed. "One who cheats for a living seldom cares who gets hurt in the process." He wrapped half of Tom's meatball sandwich in a napkin so he could drive as he ate. "Can we assume this Mark is the same one the two large men are hunting?"

Tom spoke around a bite. "I think we can."

Hua opened the container with his salad inside, took the pepper on the side and bit into it, his face pinching slightly at the pickle-y taste. "I wonder if he knows they are presently so close to him."

"I don't know, but at least we do."

"If they show up," Luca said, "the plan might have to change. Should we warn Mark they're close, or let him find out for himself?"

"They're his problem," Tom said. "Ours is to find Cam and get Robin through this." After a moment he went on, "Con men think they're smarter than everyone else, so let's play dumb. Let Parsons think he's got us cowed."

"And we must play our roles well," Hua warned. "If the target discovers the deception, he might call in the authorities. Robin could be arrested."

"We all could," Luca corrected.

Hua gave Bennett a bit of chicken from his salad. "We must ask ourselves this: If Robin's father is aware of either the police or his pursuers, what will he do?"

"From the little I know, I'd say he'll will toss anyone, even his own daughter, to the wolves to make his escape."

"If he does, we have to be there," Luca waved her sandwich as she spoke. "Once Cam is okay, we'll scoop her up first chance we get and haul her butt out of trouble."

Chapter Thirty-Seven

Luca decided early on that she didn't like Mark Parsons. She admitted she'd been prepared not to, knowing what she did about him, but her dislike was personal as well as situational. If they'd met at some social event, she might have found his shallow charm entertaining, but she'd met too many like him, men who thought they were God's gift to this world. Beneath Mark's boyish manner, she saw a selfish egoist who liked duping others almost as much as he enjoyed spending their money afterward.

Parsons entered Luca's hotel room like a glad-handing politician, acting as if they were there to accomplish a task cooperatively. "I'm Mark. Robin says you can help with our little project."

Tom's eyes had turned steely-gray. "Robin says you'll let our friend die if we don't."

Though surprised by that, he recovered quickly. "I should have known she'd find a way to contact you again." Waving away Cam's predicament as if it were nothing, he assured, "Your friend will be fine as long as you each do your part." Moving to the desk in the corner, he swiveled the chair toward them and sat. Luca had her back against the headboard of the bed, one foot on the floor. Hua perched lightly on the opposite side, eyes trained on Mark like a laser. Tom paced like an angry lynx in a cage.

"We've convinced a certain very rich old man that Robin is his great-granddaughter. Once he accepted that, I confided—as her adoptive grandfather—that she needs very delicate brain surgery. We convinced him that Doctor Gael Alvarro, a famous Spanish surgeon, is flying into Indianapolis tomorrow to perform the operation."

"For a substantial fee."

Mark nodded. "In cash. Our talented doctor is no humanitarian."

"It's an old con," Tom commented.

"The old ones work best," Mark replied. "A lot of the guys have gone to internet scams, which is okay if that's your thing. Me, I like the personal approach. Smile in their faces while you empty their pockets."

"Tell us how the situation got complicated."

"We had it going," Mark's voice betrayed how much fun he'd had with that. "The snag came up when the old man, whose name is Harrison Robeson, decided he wants to be with—we named her Serena—for the surgery. That means to pull off the con, I need a hospital and a medical team." He paused to look at each one of them. "Robin says you people can arrange a setting for our little production." He bit at his mustache. "Any ideas?"

After a brief silence Hua said, "I can get us a hospital."

Mark turned his chair toward him, making it squeak. "How?"

"I will locate a small, private facility." Hua spoke slowly, figuring out the details as he went. "Posing as an inspector, I will inform them that their operating room is contaminated with some dreaded bacteria—C diff, perhaps. I will order the immediate isolation of the unit, and we will block it off from the rest of the building with biohazard signs and plastic sheeting."

"And we come in as the clean-up crew," Tom guessed.

Mark gave them a crooked smile. "Perfect. Nobody wants to deal with C-diff, so the staff will avoid the area like it's radioactive."

"I will locate a suitable facility and notify them of their problem," Hua said. "Your task will be to bring Mr. Robeson to a specific entrance at precisely the right time. Our window of opportunity will not last long. Once he is inside, we will close the entrance to other visitors."

"I can handle that," Mark said confidently. "Who'll be the surgeon?"

"I will," Tom replied.

Gesturing at his prosthetic hand Mark asked, "How's that going to work for a surgeon?"

"I'll manage. Bubbles doesn't look like a Spaniard, and no one would mistake Lily for a man."

"Those aren't your real names, I assume."

Tom shrugged. "Better if we maintain distance. I'm Homey."

"Okay, Homey. I hired a guy named Ned who'll help out where we need him. Once Bubbles there gives me an address, I'll tell Ned to meet us at the hospital tomorrow morning."

For an hour they worked on their plan. Beginning with what they hoped would happen, they then moved on to possible snags and how things might have to change. Mark didn't mention his reason for the con or the men who were looking for him. Luca hoped they were no longer a factor now that they'd changed locations.

As Tom had suggested, Luca asked some patently dumb questions, pretending she had trouble understanding how it was all going to work. Hua appeared to be fixated on Robin, asking over and over why she hadn't come to help with the planning. He came across as timid; Luca seemed clueless. Tom remained mostly silent, though he was unable to hide his antipathy toward Parsons.

Mark seemed to be okay with all of it. He reassured Hua that Robin would be there "when it counts." He was patient with Luca's inane questions and seemed willing to go over the plan again and again until she was sure of her role. Tom he ignored. Knowing a little about scammers from her days on the street, Luca guessed he was used to working with weak-minded crooks who responded to a strong leader and did as they were told. Mark probably figured he had Tom in a corner. He could be as mad as he wanted to be; he still had to do as Mark ordered in order to get Robin and Cam back.

Tom turned away with an impatient snort. After a moment Hua said, "You taught her tricks and schemes, sir, but Robin is a person of integrity. Your treatment of her in this matter demonstrates you had nothing to do with that."

Chapter Thirty-Eight

The more Tom thought about Robin's warning not to involve Chris, the more it seemed to him that she was wrong. Before a caper, they studied the target's personality and background, trying to predict how he or she would react in certain situations. Chris Parsons excelled at objective analysis, looking at a situation and identifying problems that might arise. This time Tom and the others were going in blind, controlled by a man they knew nothing about. Robin couldn't help, but Chris was available to them, and being the older sibling, he knew Mark Parsons better than Robin herself did. Chris would be angry to learn of his father's interference in Robin's life, but Tom believed he could set aside his anger and provide the information they needed to save Robin and Cam.

Tom called using FaceTime, hoping that his friend's reaction would tell him his assessment was correct. "Hey, what's up?" Chris asked when he appeared on the screen. His brow furrowed as he listened, and when Tom finished he said, "I never thought I'd see that dirt-bag again."

"I need you to tell me how he thinks."

"Never in a straight line. Mark is always figuring the angles."

"You're saying if there's trouble, he'll leave us hanging."

"No doubt about it. When we were kids, if something went wrong and he got caught in a lie, he'd find some way to blame it on us. More than once I had to apologize for things I never did." Chris made an anguished sound. "I don't doubt Mark's gotten even better at sliding out of trouble with all these years of practice."

"From what I sensed at our first meeting, the guy gets off on fleecing unsuspecting victims." As he said it, Tom's conscience gave him two little stabs. First, Tom enjoyed planning capers too, which meant he and Parsons had something in common. Second, he'd described Chris' father in very unflattering terms.

Chris didn't seem bothered. "I need to help with this, Tom."

"We're not sure how it's going to go, buddy. No sense putting yourself in danger without good reason."

"Let me help. I'll take care of the dog while you play doctor. I'll sit in the parking lot and keep watch in case somebody calls the cops. I need to feel like I'm doing something to stop him."

"Okay. I'll get back to you on that."

"Did Robin ever tell you about why Dad left when we were kids?"

"No. She seldom mentions him."

A moment of silence preceded the telling, as if Chris were marshalling memories, or maybe overcoming them. "When I was about fifteen, Mark made a few thousand dollars on a con, and he disappeared for a month, no doubt spending what he'd stolen on his latest side woman. With him gone, we were almost happy, at least Robin and I were. We didn't have much money, but we got by. Mom became a licensed Realtor, which wasn't a steady income but was something. I stocked grocery shelves early in the mornings, before I went to school, and Robin baby sat every weekend for a couple with two kids. Our grandfather, Mark's dad, sent us money quite often. I think he knew what an ass his son was, though he never admitted it out loud. So we were paying the bills, not always on time, but doing okay. Mom moaned a lot about how much she missed her man, but even she seemed less stressed with Mark gone.

"Then one day we came home from school and there he was." Chris cleared his throat before continuing. "After his little absences, Mark always acted like he'd never left, and we knew better than to ask where he'd been. I went directly to my room, and so did Robin. We weren't there ten minutes when it started, Dad swearing, Mom crying, and then the sound of fists, broken dishes, and pain.

"I'd been thinking a lot while he was gone. I wasn't Hercules by any stretch, but I'm built bigger than Mark, like the men on my Mom's side. I promised myself the next time he swatted one of us around, I'd stop him."

Chris chewed at his mustache, as he often did when stressed. Tom said, "You stood up for your mother."

"She had a big old fat lip, but as soon as she saw the look on my face, she started in. 'It was an accident, Chris. I'm fine, really.'" He shook his head. "I couldn't believe she was defending him. Accident—yeah, right."

"You went at him."

"Mom kept talking, but I didn't even slow down. I got in his face and told him he was done knocking us around. I said we didn't need him there—didn't want him there. I told him to get out."

"What did he say?"

"He laughed, but it wasn't a good kind of laugh." Chris' tone was bitter. "He said, 'Son, you'd better ask your mother about that.' I knew if I did, she'd side with him."

Tom remained silent, sensing there was nothing a guy who had two loving parents and no experience with domestic violence could add to the story.

After a moment Chris went on. “Mark said something about teaching me to respect my father, and I knew I was about to get a beating. I’d promised myself I’d fight back, but…it’s hard to overcome sixteen years of conditioning, you know? I wasn’t sure I had the courage, and Mom was whining, ‘He’s your father, Chris. He’s the head of the family.’” Chris muttered something unintelligible. “I almost backed off. They stood together against me, and I felt like I had to, to keep peace in the house.”

“But—”

“But then Robin came up beside me. I turned, and there she was, holding my softball bat like she knew what she wanted to do with it. ‘Get out!’ she told Mark. ‘We don’t want you here anymore. Ever.’ Dad started trying to smooth things over, calling her Robbie and telling her she was too young to understand what the world of grownups is like. Do you know what she did? She raised that bat even higher and said, ‘If you aren’t gone in ten minutes, Chris and I will beat the shit out of you.’”

“Wow.”

“Yeah, wow.” Chris finished the story. “I could see by his expression that Mark believed she’d do it, and between the two of us, he caved. Cussing under his breath the whole time, he packed his bags and left. Mom sat on the couch, sobbing. Robin stood there with the bat resting on her shoulder, ready to do what she’d threatened.”

“He left for good?”

"I don't think he intended it to be that way. He'd probably have slunk away for a while and then started calling Mom and stopping in while we were at school to sweet-talk her into taking him back. But as soon as he was gone, Robin said we had to move. She said we should leave the state so he'd never find us again. We started planning—by *we* I mean Robin and me. Mom was a mess, bawling and saying we'd ruined everything. Robin ignored her and sort of guided me to some decisions. She asked where we might go where Mark would never find us. 'Not to friends or relatives,' she said. 'If anyone close to us knows where we are, he'll worm it out of them.'

"At first I didn't have a clue, but then I remembered a guy at school who'd moved north from Cedar, Georgia. He missed his old home a lot, and he'd told me all about it. When I passed on the picture he painted of a peaceful city with lots of live oaks and a small-town feel, Robin said, 'That's where we'll go.' She hustled Mom around, got our things packed, and we took off in the middle of the night. We arrived in Cedar the next day with no idea what to do next. We didn't know a soul there, and we didn't have a lot of money. But there were 'Help Wanted' signs at several businesses, and by the end of the day Mom and I had jobs at a little restaurant. We had Mom use her middle name, Linda, figuring there had to be thousands of women in the U.S. named Linda Parsons.

"While we were interviewing, Robin bought a local paper and found an apartment we could almost afford. It wasn't very big, but the woman managing the building was nice, and I think she got an inkling what was going on. She offered to lower the rent fifty bucks a month if Robin and I kept the yard mowed and picked up."

Chris stopped, and Tom said, "You haven't seen your father since?"

"We told Mom if she contacted Mark, she'd never see either of us again." He sniffed. "It was harsh, making her choose between the guy she was crazy about and her own kids, but Mom never understood how much danger she was in. Every time he'd say, 'It's going to be different from now on, Babe. Scout's honor.' And Mom always dried her tears, hid her bruises, and said, 'That's great, Mark.'"

"I understand that's often the case."

"Yeah." Chris' tone changed. "Robin and I didn't think Mark would look all that hard for us, and apparently he didn't." He chuckled. "For some reason Mom blamed me for the whole thing. Robin became her favorite child, and I was the boy who didn't respect his father." He shrugged. "That was okay with me as long as we were free of him."

Tom sensed the story was ended, but not the moral. "Why are you telling me this?"

"First, to let you know why Robin is ambivalent about our dad. In some corner of her brain, she feels guilty about what we did. I think she also feels bad that Mom blamed me for what the two of us did to get rid of him. Second, I'm letting you know that I can be your secret weapon in all this. If I show up on the scene, Mark is sure to react." His brows quirked. "The problem is I'm not sure what form that reaction will take."

"You're saying your appearance might shock him into bolting, but it might also incite him to commit worse mischief." Tom gave a huffy half-laugh. "Not sure that's a selling point, bro."

Chris sighed heavily. "Mark is full of surprises. I'll be the first to admit they don't usually turn out well for his victims."

Chapter Thirty-Nine

Cam was different from most people, and he knew it. He was never witty and seldom funny, at least not intentionally. But Robin often reminded him that he had plenty of strengths, one of which was perseverance. Cam didn't mind hard work, and once he started a project, he stayed at it until he got the result he wanted. His progress on the hole in the roof was slow, and his arm muscles got shaky from being extended above his head for so long. Still, he kept going, starting over with his dad's poems when he couldn't think of a new one.

Destroying a building that someone had painstakingly, even lovingly, pieced together was mean of him, but he had to. Inch by inch the hole got bigger, the broken chunks of cedar became easier to extract simply because he had room to work at them, wiggling and jiggling until they came loose. When Cam could finally lift himself up through the hole to look outside, the ground around the sauna looked like angry beavers had been at work. "I'll find out the owner's name and send money for damages," Cam told the air around him. The air didn't answer, of course, but he sensed approval in the little breeze that cooled his face.

Once the jagged hole was big enough to get his shoulders through, Cam lifted himself up and onto what remained of the sauna roof. Choosing a clear landing spot, he jumped, rolling when he hit the ground to ease the jolt. Unhurt, Cam regained his feet, realizing too late that he should have tossed the remaining food and water out first. That wasn't important right now, he decided. He had to let Robin know he was free so she could tell her dad to go fly a kite.

The sauna sat behind an attractive cabin perhaps a hundred yards off a two-track road. Cam left the property, finding that the primitive road led to a gravel one. Once there, he had to decide which direction to take to find Brandell. He turned west but soon came to a gated driveway that disappeared into the trees. At one side was a signpost with a dozen names painted on wooden slats. A community of seasonal cottages, most likely empty this time of year. Turning around, Cam went back to the east. A half mile down was an intersection, and a sign pointing left said, "Brandell, 2 Mi." With a grunt of satisfaction, he started walking.

A few minutes later, Cam heard a car coming up behind him. Should he flag it down and ask for help? He might get a ride to town, or at least be allowed to use the driver's phone. But who would he call? Anyone who might help him was back in Kansas. Cam had to find Robin by himself, but he figured he'd be okay on his own. For one thing, Parsons didn't know Cam was free. For another, the guy thought he was dealing with amateurs. All Cam had to do was show up somewhere public, where Parsons couldn't pull out his gun and threaten them. He wouldn't be able to do anything to stop Cam and Robin from walking away. Cam decided he'd even let the guy keep their car if it meant he'd leave them alone.

"You lost?" The voice brought Cam back to the moment, and he turned to find a sheriff's deputy leaning out the window of his cruiser.

"No. No, officer, I'm...walking."

After three days trapped in a box, Cam didn't look like an upstanding citizen. His clothes were rumpled. He'd torn his shirt on a projecting splinter as he struggled through the hole. His hair was no doubt standing up all over his head, since he tended to run his hands through it when he had to think about stuff. What would this man conclude about the odd-looking stranger wandering among empty cabins and lake homes?

He hoped the deputy hadn't seen him come out the cabin driveway, because there'd be questions if the mess he'd left behind was discovered. Telling the truth—that he'd been imprisoned by a criminal—would only make matters worse. How many times would he have to re-tell the story to the sheriff, and maybe the state police? Even if they eventually accepted it as truth, what would that mean for Robin?

Usually Cam let Robin or Hua or Tom talk when there were lies to be told, but in their absence, it was up to him to allay any suspicions the cop might have. Why would a man be walking down a deserted road in this rumpled condition? A scene from an old private eye TV show came to mind—was it *Mannix*? *The Rockford Files*? It didn't matter. Caught in a similar situation, the detective had quieted suspicion with a story most men understood. "I got a little drunk last night," he said. "When I got home, my wife was mad. She said I should walk it off."

"Where were you drinking?"

Cam wracked his brain for the name of the bar he'd seen in Brandell. He remembered what it looked like, but what was it called? He tried a trick Em had taught him. *Pull the image of what you saw into your mind like a photograph,* she'd said. *Then focus on what you need to recall*. Picturing the sign, Cam remembered it was shaped like a clover. It had green lettering with gold edging. The main word started with a B. Brandell? No. Something foreign. The image cleared, and he saw the words. "The Belfast Pub."

The cop nodded, and Cam knew he'd got it right. "Would you like a ride home?"

He shook his head. "I better walk. Don't think it will help if I get dropped off by a policeman."

"Probably not," the deputy said. "But you're a ways from Brandell."

"Yeah, but walking is good. I'm starting to feel like myself again." A line from the TV show popped into his head, and he passed it along. "By the time I get home, I should be able to say whatever it takes to make her let me live in my own house again."

"Women," the man commiserated. "Ya gotta love 'em, but it's sure hard to live with 'em."

With a wave, the deputy went on, and Cam breathed a sigh of relief. He'd have to remember to tell the others about the encounter, so they'd have to admit that watching old TV shows pays off, at least sometimes.

Chapter Forty

Reuben returned to Harry's late Friday night so they could make the trip north together for Serena's supposed surgery. At five a.m. Saturday morning, he knocked softly on Robin's bedroom door. "I brought you a little breakfast," he said when she let him in. "You can't be seen eating before your operation, but you'll be sharper with some fuel in your tank."

Though her stomach roiled with nerves, Robin saw the wisdom in that. He'd brought a Danish and a carton of chocolate milk, and nostalgia hit when she saw the little container of waxed cardboard. Did her father remember how much she'd loved chocolate milk as a kid? She didn't ask. They were too far into the con to stroll down memory lane.

While she ate, Mark moved around the room, obviously antsy about upcoming events. "Your guy is good. He got us into the Schalk Doctor's Hospital, a private facility on the southwest side of the city. The little guy, Bubbles, convinced them they have a contagion problem."

"Posing as a health inspector."

"Yes. He informed them he'd found possible…" He paused to call the correct term to mind. "…the Clostridium difficile bacteria, commonly known as C diff, in their surgical theater. The manager was horrified, but Bubbles said he'd keep mention of the infection out of his report as long as they immediately hired a crew to do a deep cleaning. They rescheduled all of today's surgeries." Mark chuckled. "The kid has a gift for the con. He told the guy they could do the cleanup themselves, but he'd have to shut them down for two days and then do a second inspection."

"They agreed to let him send in the crew he recommended, because he said they could get it done today and he'd re-inspect this afternoon."

"Yup. Within an hour the black girl and my guy—his name is Ned—were posting signs saying no one could enter the area. The tall guy—Homey, right?—set a pan of bleach and a fan on the floor by the doors that lead into the rest of the hospital. Anybody who gets close will smell the fumes and be convinced the cleanup is underway."

Her gang had done it. They had control of a hospital's operating wing for the whole morning.

"Now we have to deal with Harry's support team," Mark said.

A slurping noise indicated she'd reached the end of the chocolate milk, and she swallowed before ordering, "Do *not* hurt anyone."

He shook his head in warning. "First rule of the con, Robbie, don't become attached to the marks." When she opened her mouth to argue he said, "I'm not some crazed murderer, but we do need to scale down the number of people attending your miraculous rebirth." He looked at her from under his brows. "You know we're better off without Svein. And who needs a lawyer around, ever?"

"You can't get rid of them both," she said. "In fact, I can't see Harry leaving home without them."

"He's going to have to do without one or the other. Who is more dangerous to our cause?"

Robin was torn, as she'd been many times over the last few days. She didn't want to help Mark succeed, but she had to. "The lawyer is sweet on me, or possibly on the idea of getting close to a possible heiress. I can handle him."

"Great. You deal with him. I have a plan for Svein."

She stuck a finger under his nose. "No violence, do you hear me?"

Mark bowed like an old-fashioned dandy. "Your wish is my command, Madame."

At six a.m., Anthony Biers pulled up at the front door, driving Harry's Cadillac CT6. Mark escorted Harry outside and helped him into the back seat, tucking pillows around his hips to soften the bumps and turns in the road.

"Svein isn't feeling well this morning," Harry told Robin as she climbed into the back seat with him. "Some sort of bug he's apparently terrified he'll pass on to you as you face surgery. I've asked Anthony to act as chauffeur."

"I hope he isn't too ill." Robin glanced at her father, who seemed busy adjusting the front seat. A metallic grind followed by a clunk said he'd found just the right level of comfort.

"Reuben spoke to him, at a distance, of course. Svein insists it's one of those twenty-four-hour things, and he'll be fine tomorrow." Harry thanked Biers, who had folded his travel wheelchair and stashed it in the trunk.

The ride was mostly silent, which was a relief for Robin. Mark glanced over the seat at her periodically, and she resisted the urge to slap the "caring" expression off his face. Harry and Biers no doubt believed her constant shifting in the seat and white knuckles represented worry about the upcoming surgery, so they limited themselves to needful utterances. In fact, Robin was second-guessing every decision she'd made for the last few years. While she'd convinced herself the gang's capers were done for good, she now saw it differently. Cam was imprisoned, the way they'd imprisoned others. She was being forced to do things she didn't want to do by someone who'd seized power over her, as they had often done. Worst of all, she'd come to realize that people like her father weren't easily changed. Mark thought like a crook. Mark believed he deserved other people's money if he was clever enough to get it from them. Nothing would alter the way he looked at life, and that was true for every person they'd kidnapped over the last few years. Had their capers really changed anything?

She'd convinced herself they were turning criminals into honest citizens, but how long would it be before each of them went back to their old ways? A year? Two? They couldn't watch them all, and the gang's oversight was merely another barrier to climb over, like the laws of the land and the objections of their victims. She let out a sigh, and Harry reached over to pat her arm comfortingly.

When they entered the hospital, Luca sat behind a reception counter to their left. She wore pink scrubs and a long-sleeved sweater that covered her ink, and she murmured, "Good morning. I'll be right with you." Behind the counter was office space containing copy machines, file cabinets, and stations where staff members kept up with their paperwork, or more probably in this age, their computer work. The machines hummed and beeped, though Robin guessed their current operations were only for show.

Directly ahead of Robin wide double doors announced: "Operating Theater: No Unauthorized Entry." A sensor pad near the frame indicated they opened electronically, probably with a badge employees swiped when going in and out. To the right of the doors was a waiting area with magazines, a TV tuned to a twenty-four-hour news station, and a few dozen chairs.

Treating Robin with professional politeness, Luca asked for her medical information, insurance and ID cards, and her preference for spiritual guidance, if any. When they finished, Luca told her to take a seat in the waiting area. Harry rolled his wheelchair close and said, "Anything her insurance won't pay, I'll take care of."

"Harry, you don't have to—"

"No, I don't," he replied. "But I want you well, both physically and fiscally. Since you're now part of my family, you have no choice in the matter." Behind him Robin saw Mark smirk, sure that Harry was well and truly hooked.

The double doors opened, and Tom appeared, wearing a lab coat. He kept his prosthetic hand in the pocket. "Miss Dykstra?" he said in a passable Spanish accent. "I am Dr. Alvarro."

"Pleased to meet you." The sight of Tom restored Robin's hopes they might get out of this together and with no one under arrest. "This is my great-grandfather, Harry Robeson." Tom bowed slightly toward the old man. "And his attorney, Anthony Biers." Reluctantly she turned to Mark. "And you've spoken to my grandfather, Reuben Bills, on the phone."

"Ah, yes. The man who does not believe I merit vacation time."

"I'm sorry, Dr. Alvarro," Mark said humbly, "but Serena is dear to us, and her condition is serious, as you know."

"But not beyond my talents." Robin suppressed a smile as Tom perfectly captured the attitude of a world-renowned brain surgeon.

One had to be confident, she supposed, to go poking around in other people's brains. “You followed the instructions I gave?” Tom asked her.

“I have.” Robin resisted the urge to reach out and touch him, seeking the reassurance of his strength.

“Then someone will be out soon to prep you for surgery.” To the others he said, “It will be several hours.”

“We're prepared to wait,” Harry replied.

“All right.” Tom turned as if to leave but then stopped, asking, “The...arrangements we discussed?”

“First, I have a question,” Harry said. “What happens when the surgery is done and you return to Spain?”

“I've called in an excellent local man,” Tom replied. “He will see to the aftercare. I can assure you, once the aneurism is removed, Ms. Dykstra will recover quickly and completely.”

Harry nodded. “My attorney here has three hundred thousand dollars in cash, as you specified. He will give it to you when Serena wakes up without brain damage.”

Tom bowed again in a Continental manner. “That is acceptable.”

When Tom had been gone only a few seconds, a young man—Ned, Robin assumed—appeared with a wheelchair. On the seat was a small tray with two paper cups, one filled with water and a smaller one containing two red pills. “A little medicine to relax you,” he said. Robin hesitated, unsure what part this played in their charade, but she couldn’t very well refuse. She glanced at Mark, who nodded slightly to indicate it was okay. Window dressing, she supposed, to convince Harry and Anthony that this was a real pre-surgical situation. Taking the pills, which were bitter on her tongue, she washed them down with water.

The attendant tossed the remains in a nearby wastebasket and returned to stand behind the wheelchair. “Hop in, and I'll take you back and get you ready for the big show.”

Though she sensed a young woman facing brain surgery would have something to say to those close to her, Robin couldn't think of anything that didn't sound like it came from a *Days of Our Lives* script. Bending down, she hugged Harry briefly. He felt insubstantial, like a breath of Old Spice, and she thought again that he’d have made a wonderful grandfather. An image of Harry holding an infant in his arms and making faces at her came to mind. Whose child would it be? She dismissed the thought that it might be hers, but she guessed he’d be thrilled if it were.

When she stepped back, Mark was waiting, arms lifted, and she had to hug him too. She'd rather have embraced a pufferfish at that moment, but she managed to get through it. It felt good to sit down, and she realized she was exhausted. How much had she actually slept since Monday? Stress was getting to her, and she no longer had the energy to resent Mark’s fussing as he played the loving relative.

“You're going to be fine,” he said cheerily, which was of course true. The attendant pulled the chair backward, and the little crowd of well-wishers retreated. It felt weird and theatrical, because it was. It also felt like she was viewing them through the wrong end of a telescope.

Ned swiped his badge, and the double doors opened with a hiss, revealing a corridor with several entrances, each marked with its purpose. “Pre-op.” “Operating Room #1.” “Post-Op.” “Surgical Ready Room.” Robin felt the turn her chair made into Pre-op, but it was hard to sit upright. *Keep your head on straight*, she ordered. She wasn't sure if she said it aloud or not, but she heard herself laugh at what seemed like a good joke.

After that, she remembered nothing for some time.

Chapter Forty-One

Luca sat at the desk, trying to appear busy. Her first job upon arriving had been to find the badges that opened the doors into the surgical unit. Tom, Hua, Chris, and the extra guy each got one, and she'd kept one for herself. Calls to the unit had been rerouted by the hospital's real staff, but she figured out how to call from one phone in the surgery wing to another. Periodically she'd move to another phone, call the main desk number and hurry to "answer" a call, speaking to no one. A few cars came close to the building, slowed as the occupants read the sign Hua had posted: "Biohazard Threat—Please Use Next Entrance," and drove on.

Surreptitiously watching the three men in the waiting area, Luca assessed their personalities. Mark was easy; since she already knew what he was. He did a good job of appearing nervous, shifting his crossed legs every few minutes and taking up a magazine only to toss it aside seconds later. The old guy, Harry, seemed content to sit calmly in his wheelchair, hands in his lap and gaze unfocused. She got no sense he was worried, but she supposed when a person had lived ninety years, he accepted that things would either turn out well or not. Worry makes no difference, one way or the other.

The third guy, a lawyer whose name she hadn't caught, was the only one who seemed truly stressed by the brain surgery supposedly going on behind the double doors. He'd sit in a chair for a while then get up and pace, squinting out the windows at the bright October sunshine and then turning to glare at the doors to the surgical theater. A couple of times he glanced at her as if wanting to ask what was taking so long, but he didn't.

Luca's job was to handle whatever happened out front without alarming Robeson or his attorney. Once Robin's party was inside, she'd turned off the electric eye for the exterior doors. If one of them tried to go outside, she'd invented a story about how the doors often got stuck due to dirt in the mechanism. She'd make a fake call for a repairman and announce that he'd be along when he could.

No one tried to leave the waiting room, so no one noticed.

The lawyer went to the window for the umpteenth time and stood staring out at the decidedly ugly view: the patient parking lot, largely empty of cars but not of trash and blowing dirt. Looking past him, Luca saw a gray car pull into a space near the street, far enough away that she couldn't see the occupants. She watched the car for a while, hoping whoever was out there wouldn't ignore the biohazard sign and try to come in. If they came to the door, looked in, and saw three men sitting calmly in the waiting area, what would she do to convince them to leave?

This, she realized, was why the Kidnap Gang practiced so much. The hastily-concocted plan they'd made the night before had great big holes in it. Luca felt sweat breaking out on her forehead and upper lip. Robeson thought the operating room was in use. Outsiders were notified it was not. How could Luca reconcile the two stories if the need arose?

To her relief, whoever was in the car stayed there. Probably waiting for an employee to get off shift or a friend to be released from the hospital. As she pretended to take another call Luca thought, *One less thing to stress over.*

Chapter Forty-Two

By the time Cam reached Brandell, he'd decided against calling Tom or Hua. He didn't have time to wait around for the others to arrive, and it would only upset everyone to hear about the trouble with Robin's dad. Cam didn't trust Parsons as far as he could throw him, so any delay in getting to Robin increased the chances she'd be arrested, hurt, or even killed. Besides, the problem was pretty much solved. Once she knew he was free, Robin could simply walk away—or drive away, if Cam managed to find a vehicle. What could Parsons do about it? Call the police and tell them the two people he'd captured and abused had left him unable to steal some old man's money?

Though their friends were surely concerned after not hearing from them for days, Cam decided he'd call once he and Robin were safe.

Cam remembered the name of the town where Parsons had taken Robin and the name of the target, Harrison Robeson. When he reached Brandell, he went directly to the gas station and asked where he might rent a car. The kid behind the counter acted like he'd asked for a ride to Venus. "We ain't got no Hertz around here."

"Do you have a car?"

That got a snuffly laugh. "I wish."

"Anybody you know got one I could use for a day?" Cam had removed the wad of cash he kept in the waistband of his underwear. "I can pay three hundred dollars."

The kid shook his head. "My mom needs her car for work, and my friends all drive junkers."

"I'll take a junker." Cam waved the money at him. "Three hundred. Split it any way you want."

After sucking at his teeth for a second the clerk said, "Let me call Pooper."

Pooper was a freckled beanpole with a 2004 Corolla that had been sideswiped on the driver's side. The accident was far enough in the past that rust had bloomed like evil flowers along the side panels. The passenger side was inaccessible. The engine sounded like there were gnomes inside hammering at the pistons. Cam handed over the money and made the promise Pooper demanded "on a stack of Bibles," that he'd return the car without further damage the next day.

Pooper and the attendant gave him directions to Maple City, and Cam had no trouble getting there. More difficult was finding someone to direct him to Robeson's home. He tried a gas station and then the post office. At the first, a young woman looked blank and shook her head; at the second, he was regarded with suspicion. "Why do you need to know?" the clerk asked. He explained he'd had the address in his phone, which had been stolen. Glancing at his dirty clothes and battered hands she said, "In that case, you should talk to the police."

Cam left the building frustrated, and he stopped on the sidewalk to think. Hua would come up with some clever way to trick someone into telling him what he wanted to know, but Cam didn't think he could do that. As he looked around for ideas, he noticed a flower shop across the street and a few doors down. Florists made deliveries, and they had GPS to help them find where they needed to go. Entering, Cam spent forty of his remaining dollars on a ready-made arrangement. "I haven't got her address," he told the woman behind the counter. "But she's staying with a guy named Harrison Robeson."

"That's not a problem," she replied, stripping dead leaves from a fragrant plant. "We can look it up online."

"Can you get it out there right away?" When she frowned he added, "I got a real important question to ask this girl, you know?"

The woman's face softened. "Real important, huh? You should have gone with roses." Leaning back, she looked out a window to see the parking space behind the store. "Looks like Harold's back from morning deliveries, so yeah, he can do it. Give him fifteen minutes for a potty break, and it'll be on its way."

Getting in his junker, Cam waited near the flower shop and followed the van carrying his basket of asters and chrysanthemums when it emerged from the alley and turned onto the highway. Cam was pleased with himself. Watching Robin and the others get what they needed by roundabout methods was starting to rub off on him. His parents wouldn't approve of their son being good at lying to people, but if they weren't dead he'd have explained that the members of the Kidnap Gang lied only with the best of intentions.

Cam hung back so as not to alert the deliveryman, and when the van turned up a long driveway with an arched gate that said "Robeson," he parked on the lakeshore as if to enjoy the view. After perhaps ten minutes the van left. Once it was out of sight, Cam got into the Corolla and climbed the hill. It wasn't that steep, but the little car's engine ground like a coffee mill. Cam wished he had time to give it a tune-up before returning it to Pooper, who seemed like a pretty nice guy.

As he neared the house, Cam's mouth got dry and his hands got wet. How was he going to do this? Ask the people outright if they'd seen Robin? Give some made-up reason for being there? He wished Hua were there.

Smacking the steering wheel in irritation, Cam told himself to stop being a baby. Hua was far away, and Robin was in trouble. He had to help her, which meant taking stock of whatever he found at Robeson's place and going from there. When he reached the house, Cam took in its impressive proportions, the view of the lake it overlooked, and a rusty pickup truck parked on the grass along the driveway. The floral arrangement he'd sent sat on the porch. Apparently no one had come to the door to receive it.

Cam rang the bell, but no one answered. He went all the way around the house, knocking at the back door, the garage door, and a slider that opened onto the deck. No one answered at any of those places. He circled the house again, this time peering through the windows. The place was silent and deserted, but through the garage window he saw the Ford he and Robin had been driving. She'd been here. An empty spot in the garage made Cam decide she must have gone somewhere with the owner of the place. He returned to Pooper's car, wondering what his next move should be. Wait for them to come home, he decided. He'd hide the junker somewhere and walk back up the hill, so Parsons wouldn't know Cam had escaped until it was too late.

As he was about to get in the car, a faint sound reached his ears. Cam paused, trying to decide what it was and where it came from. When it stopped for a few seconds, he almost concluded it was nothing, but then it started again. Someone was yelling, but the words were incomprehensible. In fact, they didn't seem to be English words.

He circled the area, trying to home in on the sound. Gradually he realized it came from a shed some distance down the hill. Cam approached the door, which was padlocked. "Is somebody in there?"

A very excited man commanded, "*Hjalp! Hjalp mig*!" A few seconds later: "Help! Let me out!"

Cam felt an immediate kinship with the prisoner, having so recently been one himself. "Give me a minute. I'll find something to pry with." Trotting off, he entered an unlocked, smaller shed that held gardening tools. Choosing a pair of clippers, he returned to the shed, inserted one blade behind the hasp, and pulled until the screws came loose from the wooden frame. The impetus of their release sent him staggering backward, and the door flew open. A guy every bit as big as Cam himself stood in the doorway, his face a mask of anger.

"Where is he? I will strangle him with my bare hands."

"Who?"

"Reuben Bills. He said he needed a gauge to check the air in his tires, and when I came in here to get it for him, he locked me inside."

"I don't know anyone named Reuben," Cam said. "I'm sorry he played a prank on you, but I'm looking for a woman in her twenties, brown hair, brown eyes, about this tall."

"Serena," the man said. "Harry and Reuben took her to—" Anger returned and he smashed his fist against the door frame, making the whole shed shudder. "I will have him arrested."

Cam did some figuring. The name Harry probably meant Harrison Robeson, and if someone had locked the big man in, it was probably Parsons. "Do you know when they'll be back?"

"No." He seemed too focused on Reuben's trickery to wonder who Cam was.

"Are you Mr. Robeson's friend?"

He dusted off his clothes. "Harry is my boss. Serena and Reuben are planning to take his money. I'm sure of it."

"You got that right."

Finally, the blond frowned at Cam suspiciously. "Who are you, anyway?"

Having exhausted his capacity for subtlety for the present, Cam answered honestly. "I'm a friend of the woman you call Serena, and she's not as bad as you think."

When he'd explained the situation, the blond, whose name was Svein, said, "I knew from the first there was something wrong with this."

"Well, you were right, but I hope you believe me that…Serena was forced to do what she did."

"Do you have a phone?"

When Cam shook his head, Svein began scanning the ground around the shed. "Reuben took mine, and I think he tossed it into the weeds. Help me find it, so I can call the police."

Obligingly, Cam bent to help Svein look. As he did, he tried to construct an argument against calling the authorities. When he found the phone a few feet from the shed door, he handed it over with a plea. "This guy you call Reuben? His name is really Mark Parsons, and he's a real jerk. If there's trouble from the cops, I don't know what he'll do to Serena." After a pause he added, "I know he played a dirty trick on you. He did the same to me, only worse, and I'd like a chance to let him know I'm mad about it."

Svein thought about that. "I suppose we could call the police after we find him."

"We?"

For the first time, Svein smiled. "I too would like the chance to let this man know I'm mad about the way I was treated."

Chapter Forty-Three

An hour after Ned rolled Robin through the doors to surgery, Hua entered the waiting room and introduced himself as Del, the records guy. "I was checking to assure that our information is accurate, and I saw that Ms. Dykstra listed her grandfather as her patient advocate. Which one of you is that?"

"Me," Mark said.

"We need some things from you, sir. Ms. Dykstra signed the forms. Now we need to document your formal acceptance of the role."

"Why?"

"In case something goes wrong." Waving a hand, Hua assured them, "Of course that won't happen. We're incredibly good at our jobs here. Still, hospital policy requires the patient advocate sign his willingness to take on the role and supply two forms of identification."

"Why?" Mark repeated.

Hua's smile hinted he was used to dealing with those who didn't understand the intricacies of medical paperwork. "A driver's license is fine, and then something else: a voter registration card, a passport, something like that. Lily will make copies of the documents for the file and return them to you right away."

Mark took a step backward, betraying reluctance. “You do it, Harry. You’re a blood relative.”

Harry shook his head. “Serena will be more comfortable with someone she’s known all her life making her medical decisions. Besides, I’m so old I don’t even buy green bananas anymore.” He chuckled at his little joke. “She needs an advocate who’ll be around for a decade or so.”

Mark seemed pouty. “I don’t see why I need to prove who I am.”

Hua shrugged lightly. “To be honest, sir, I don’t see the reasons for half the paperwork I’m responsible for every day. It’s much easier if you don’t delay us with minor objections.”

Reluctantly, Mark dug out his wallet, removed his license, and gave it to Luca. Taking a passport from the breast pocket of his jacket, he gave her that as well. Showing no interest in either document, Luca took them to a machine, inserted them, waited until copies emerged onto the tray, and returned to give the originals back.

Once Mark had signed the form Hua handed him, the door behind them opened and a man stepped out. “Ah, here is our resident surgeon,” Hua said. “He will see to Ms. Dykstra’s after-care, since Doctor Alvarro will be leaving directly afterward.” As instructed, Hua introduced only two of the men. “Dr. Allen, this is Serena Dykstra’s great-grandfather Harry Robeson, and his attorney, Anthony Biers.”

Mark’s face had paled at the sight of the new player. While Biers stepped forward to shake hands, he stepped back, his mouth open and his breathing shallow. For a moment, Hua thought he’d turn and run.

Chris Parsons shook Biers' hand, then bent to shake Harry's. "I'm looking forward to helping Ms. Dykstra in any way I can," he said.

"Pleased to meet you, doctor," Harry searched the newcomer's face as if memorizing it.

Stepping so close to Mark that they stood toe-to-toe, Chris said, "And what part do you play in this young woman's life?"

"I—" Mark had to stop and begin again. "I'm her adoptive grandfather."

"I see," Chris said. "Then maybe you can answer a question. Was she from an abusive home? Is that how she came to be adopted?"

"Oh, no." Mark was beginning to recover his poise. "Serena had loving parents. Unfortunately, they died young."

"Hmm," Chris said. "Looking at the X-rays in her records, I thought I saw signs of physical trauma. You're sure no one ever hurt her when she was a child?"

"Of course not. She was very active in sports, so it may have been from that."

Chris took a long time before he spoke again. "It's good to know there wasn't some horrible parent in her past who'd take out his anger on a little girl." Staring into Mark's eyes, he backed away and returned to present business. "I'm told the surgery is progressing well."

"That's good to hear, doctor," Mark had apparently decided his son wasn't there to betray the scheme. "I know you'll watch over my girl."

"She's an amazing woman," Chris said. Meeting his father's gaze again, he added, "We must do everything we can to see that she faces no future problems once this is over."

Mark's face flushed, but he said nothing. Seemingly unaware of the tension between the two men, Harry asked how long Serena would need to remain in the hospital and what type of care she'd require when discharged. Once his questions were answered, the "doctor" said briskly, "We'll let you know when she's in recovery."

As soon as the operating unit doors closed behind Hua and Chris, Hua clapped him on the back. "You did very well, Doctor Allen. He almost fainted when he realized who you were."

"He deserves a shock," Chris muttered. "I'm glad I got here in time to give it to him. When you brought Bennett to our place last night, I realized dog-sitting wasn't enough for me. I needed to be in on this."

"Where is Bennett now?" Hua asked.

"In my car, which is parked in the employee parking lot at the side entrance, right next to your van. He's got food, water, and a blanket. It's warm enough today that he'll be fine until you're ready to head back to Kansas." He smiled. "Not that he was pleased to be left out there."

Hua chuckled. "He is a great vehicle security system, so your car is safe from theft."

Chris scanned the hallway. "Where's Robin? I think it's time we let her know I'm in on this caper."

"Ned says she was exhausted, and since we have a couple of hours with nothing to do, he suggested she take a nap. Around eleven o'clock, he'll wake her so she can put on her patient gown and get her head bandaged."

"Sleeping in the middle of a caper? That doesn't sound like Robin."

Hua realized Chris wasn't aware of Robin's physical reaction to stress, a tendency to feel weak and sometimes actually faint from anxiety. She wouldn't have shared that with her brother, fearing it would make him worry more than he already did.

"Apparently she hasn't slept since all this started, but you can see that she is all right." Leading the way to a door marked Post-op, he opened it to let Chris see his sister, asleep on a gurney. She lay on her side with legs slightly bent and her head resting on one arm.

"If she can do that, more power to her, I guess," Chris said. "What about us—do we try to grab forty winks too?"

"I don't think I can nap," Hua said, "but there's a staff break room down the hall where we can pass the time." He gestured in the correct direction. "Waiting is all we have to do now, but in my opinion, it's the hardest part of any caper."

Chapter Forty-Four

Svein wasted no time getting ready to leave for Indianapolis, though he made a point of checking the doors and windows and setting the alarm before they left Robeson's property. Cam figured that meant the big Swede didn't trust him completely, and that made sense. The story he'd told was strange, and Svein didn't know Cam from Adam's milkman.

"The car I'm driving isn't great," he said as Svein tested the back door a final time. "Any chance we could go in the Ford Serena parked in your garage?"

"Do you have a key for it?"

"I hid a spare key in the wheel well."

It was gone. "Guess Reuben or whatever his name is wanted to make sure Serena didn't drive away and leave him here," Svein said.

Hoping against hope, Cam tried the pickup Parsons had left, but it was locked. "He's nothing if not thorough," Svein commented.

"We'll have to take the junker and hope it doesn't break down."

"Wait." After a brief hesitation Svein went on, "I don't think Harry would mind if we used his second car. This is an emergency, after all."

"If it's better than this hunk of scrap metal, I'd be happy."

"Oh, it is." Svein led the way to the garage, where a car sat covered with a large green tarp. When he pulled it away, Cam's eyes widened.

"It's an MGB III."

"Classic Roadster, 1974." Svein gestured for Cam to get into the passenger seat. That took a little maneuvering, due to Cam's size and the car's compactness. When Svein got in on the driver's side, Cam had to turn his body slightly so their shoulders didn't touch.

He was too impressed to be bothered by that. "Four cylinder?"

"Yes." Svein started the engine. "One-point-eight liters with twin carbs. This was the last model to offer chrome bumpers, which adds to its value as a collector's item. Harry let me add a Retrosound Bluetooth stereo that fits the car's original design but gives excellent performance."

"Interior is in good shape too."

"Yes. Harry discovered it in a barn when he stopped at a farm market to buy sweet corn. It had been stuck in a corner, covered with a tarp, since about 2000, when the owner's kid blew the engine. Harry talked the woman into selling it to him and put a new engine in by himself." Svein chuckled. "Until about five years ago, Harry tells me, he could fix any machine on the planet, and I don't doubt him."

"Whether your boss stretches the truth or not," Cam said, touching the dashboard lightly, "he's got great taste in cars."

"Mr. Robeson does not stretch the truth. He is the most honest man I know." Svein's tone had turned angry.

"I'm not doubting you," Cam said. "Think you should call him?"

"He doesn't carry a cell phone. The lawyer has one, but I don't know if I trust him. He was pretty friendly with the girl, Serena. She might have got him on her side."

Cam longed to say Robin wouldn't do that, but he didn't want Svein to get mad again. He also didn't know enough about the situation to be sure what she'd done. Whatever it was, it was what she had to do.

"But it was Reuben who locked you in that shed."

"Yes." Svein's voice grew angry again. "They mean to trick Mr. Robeson into giving them a lot of money."

"That's what he—the guy's name is really Mark—told me before he left me trapped in this sauna thing."

The mention of a sauna interested Svein, but only for a second. "He will get a surprise, I think."

"What kind of surprise?"

Svein smiled. "Mr. Robeson is not as stupid as that man Mark thinks. He had me…do something last night that will teach him a lesson, even if you and I don't catch up with him."

"That's good," Cam said, "but I'd still like to let the guy know what I think of him."

"*Ja*," Svein agreed. "There's nothing like a personal message to get a man's attention."

Chapter Forty-Five

To pass the time, Chris and Hua played games on Hua's tablet, starting with *Crossy Roads*, trying out *Dots and Boxes*, and finally moving to *Glow Hockey*. Tom stared at the wall, and his anxiety cast a pall over the room. When almost two hours had passed he asked, "Should we wake Robin now?"

"I'll see if she's still asleep." Hua returned a minute later. "She woke up a while ago and went to find the hospital cafeteria."

"What?" Chris and Tom spoke in unison.

Hua raised his hands, palms up. "When she work up, she told Ned she needed something to eat, since she missed breakfast due to the supposed operation."

Tom's gray eyes turned black. "He let her go down there alone?"

"She said there's no reason anyone would notice a woman having lunch by herself. She went out the employee entrance and said she'd knock when she gets back so Ned can let her in."

"I should go down there and make sure she's okay," Chris said.

Tom stood. "We'll both go."

As they left the lounge, Ned exited one of the other rooms. "Your friend is back," he reported. "She's changing into a hospital gown, and when she's ready, I'm going to bandage her head." He held up a roll of gauze. "She said to tell the surgeon here to go out to the waiting room and speak to her fan club. Tell them the operation went well, she's in recovery, and they can see her in about twenty more minutes, when she's fully awake."

Tom had located an operating gown in a laundry hamper, rumpled and stained, and he exchanged it for the clean one he'd worn earlier. He put on a mask, pulling it down around his neck, and flashed his badge at the operating room doors. In the waiting room Harry sat in the same spot as earlier, reading news articles on his tablet. The lawyer dozed in a chair in a corner, his head lolled uncomfortably to one side. Mark stood near the front window, shoulders hunched and head lowered.

"I repaired the aneurism," Tom told Harry. "It was in a tricky spot, as her other doctors predicted, but I don't think we damaged anything important getting to it. She might have some memory loss, but that is a small price to pay, I think, for a lifetime without that particular worry."

"That's true, Doctor, and I thank you." Harry seemed to have been expecting a good result.

"Ms. Dykstra is resting comfortably and should be fully awake soon. We'll let you know when you can come back and see her."

Mark joined them, putting his phone away, and his passing woke Biers, who also came to hear the news. When Harry repeated the message, Mark said a quiet, "Amen," as if his prayers had been answered. Biers pumped a fist.

"Thank you, Doctor Alvarro," Harry said. "We appreciate everything you've done."

Tom took a step back. “Lily over there will admit you to the recovery room when the patient is ready for visitors.”

Chapter Forty-Six

In the time it took for the supposed surgery to be done, Luca had faked busy-ness by playing with the equipment at her disposal. She figured out how each machine in the office area worked, making useless copies that whirred and chugged out of various trays in various sizes. When she discovered a laminating machine, she spent a few minutes learning its capabilities. Mostly for fun, she took a blank badge from a drawer, printed her assumed name and some fake credentials in the correct spaces, affixed a photo of herself taken from her phone, and printed an official looking badge, which she then laminated. She was so pleased with her results that she wished she'd had time to make one for each of them. Not that anyone had questioned their status as hospital employees, but the photo on her "borrowed" badge didn't look like her at all.

Luca maintained a disinterested expression when Tom came out in his Doctor Alvarro role and spoke to the three men in the waiting area. Though she kept her head down, she watched their reactions through lowered lashes, and she imagined her ears extending off her head in an effort to hear everything, like a character in a cartoon. Tom's report of success brought relief to his listeners' faces. When he left the group, Mark Parsons followed him to the doorway of the OR unit and they spoke for a few minutes in private. She couldn't hear any of that.

Harry Robeson had been patient during the two-hour waiting period, showing no overt sign of worry or the discomfort that sitting in the stripped-down travel wheelchair probably caused. Luca had spoken to him briefly once, stepping from behind the counter to offer coffee to serve the guests. Mark had been talking on his cell phone and refused with a shake of his head. The lawyer held up the energy drink he'd brought with him as his way of saying no. Robeson had accepted a cup with thanks.

"Not many customers today," he'd observed when she handed him the cup.

"We don't usually do a lot of surgery on weekends," she told him. "I guess this lady is a special case."

"She is," Robeson observed. Meeting her gaze he said, "I appreciate what you all are doing for her."

Luca couldn't get a sense of the old man. Harry seemed really smart—no, *wise* was a better word. How could he not see Mark Parsons for the crook he was? Why had he accepted the story of "Serena" and her supposed background with so few questions? Robeson seemed to be in full control of his mental faculties, despite his age and the ruin of his physical frame. It was crazy that he was willing to hand over several hundred thousand dollars to someone he'd met only a few days ago.

Family makes us do weird things, Luca concluded. That was certainly true in her case. Her own father had announced when she was fourteen that he'd paid her way long enough, and it was her turn to "support us both on your back." Luca had no one but Daddy in those days, so she'd done as she was told. Harry Robeson had no one at all. The desire for a living relative must have blinded him to everything else.

When Tom disappeared through the double doors, Mark returned to Robeson's side. The lawyer left the window and took the seat nearest the wheelchair. Because Mark faced her, Luca heard his part of the conversation clearly. She also heard most of what the lawyer said, since his voice carried. It was only Robeson's words she had to guess at.

"Alvarro has a private plane standing by to return him to his vacation home," Mark told them. "He'd like us to pay his fee now, so he can leave as soon as Serena is awake and stable."

Harry put a hand to his chin. "Alvarro believes Doctor Allen can handle things after that?"

"He does. He'll perform some simple tests to make sure she's got no lasting damage from the surgery. Once that's established, Allen and the hospital staff will take over." Mark smirked a little. "It's standard procedure, since surgeons don't do much patient care. I've heard it's because they prefer dealing with people who are under sedation."

"I looked Allen up on my phone," Biers put in. "He's got a stellar reputation. Still, it doesn't seem wise to me to—"

"I think…all right," Harry interrupted, but Luca missed some of the words. "I trust…and…trust Reuben."

"Reuben" seemed gratified by the show of confidence. Leaning toward Robeson, he spoke in a low voice. Reading his lips, Luca deciphered "parking lot," "discreet," and something about avoiding notice of the hospital staff. She heard "unaware of" and then a few mumbled words, ending with "arrangement."

"I understand," Harry nodded to Biers, who retrieved a briefcase from under his chair. With obvious reluctance, he handed it to Mark, who accepted it as if the contents were completely unimportant.

"I'll take care of this right away." Looking up, Mark saw Luca watching and gave her a subtle wink. "When I get back, we'll all go in and see Serena."

Chapter Forty-Seven

When Tom returned from reporting to Robeson, Chris and Hua had gone back to playing games on the tablet. "Are we ready for the big finale?" Chris asked.

"Yes. We'll host Robin's post-surgical wake-up, convince Robeson she's going to be fine, and get him to hand over the money."

"It's almost over," Hua said. "Once Mr. Robeson pays, Parsons will tell us where Cam is."

"He'd better," Tom said. "We aren't letting him out of our sight until we know Cam's okay."

Chris followed them out of the lounge. "Once Mark is gone, he'll never find me or Robin again. I'll see to that."

The room where they expected to find Robin was empty. In fact, all the rooms were empty. In the whole OR unit, there was no one but them.

"Where is she?" Chris asked dully. "Where did he put her?"

Hua hurried to the double doors and peered into the waiting room. "I'm afraid the correct question is where did he *take* her. Mark is gone."

Tom looked around wildly, trying to think, wanting to act, telling himself he couldn't afford to lose control. "Maybe he's not gone yet. Harry's car is still out front."

"The employee lot," Chris said, and they hurried down to the smaller entrance at the side of the building. "The van is missing," Hua said, though they could all see that it was true. "Parsons stole our van."

While that sunk in, Tom saw someone moving across the space. Ned, wearing a flannel over his scrubs, approached the driver's door of a small red car. "Wait," Tom called, and the three men rushed outside and hurried toward him. Ned's posture indicated that he considered disobeying, but Tom pushed the car door closed with a slam. Ducking past him, Hua leaned his back against it. Chris arrived last due to his prosthetic legs, but he planted himself at the rear of the car, ready to stop Ned from backing out should he somehow get past the other two.

"Who took the white van?" Tom demanded.

"Reuben and the girl."

"Where did he get the keys?" Hua asked.

Ned pointed to Tom. "I found them in his pants pocket."

"Was taking her part of the plan from the beginning?"

"No." Ned ran a hand over his hair and squeezed the back of his neck. "At first he said we'd be leaving together, and I'd drive him to the airport. About a half hour ago, Mark texted me and said I should find the keys to the van and put the woman in the back."

Chris made an odd sound. "Did she go with him willingly?"

Ned gave him a look that seemed to ask if he was kidding. "She was still out like a light."

"You drugged her?"

Ned leaned back in fear. "Reuben did—I mean, he had me give her some pills when I went out to bring her into the OR."

"She couldn't refuse to take them in front of Robeson," Hua said, "and we didn't see it, so we didn't know what he'd done."

Tom took Ned by his jacket and shook him. "You lied when you said she'd gone to the cafeteria."

"Well, yeah." Ned pleaded his case as a blameless employee. "Mark knocked the girl out because he figured she'd try something, maybe even get us arrested." With a weak grin he added, "He didn't think you all would know what to do if she was out of commission. He said you—"

"Never mind," Tom interrupted. "Where is he taking her?"

Ned shrugged. "I was supposed to call you when I got away from here and say you should go back to the motel. She'll be there later."

"Parsons didn't originally plan to take Robin or the van," Tom mused. "Did something change in the last hour or so?"

"Well, yeah. These two guys were hanging around Brandell, asking about their old fishing buddy Mark, who was somewhere in the area."

"Mark is Reuben," Hua said.

"Oh." Ned's large forehead crunched with the effort of taking that in. So yesterday, those men were filling up at pump 6 when Reuben came in to give me these scrubs. When he left the station, one pointed and said something to his friend. They got real excited. Reuben was already in his car and they were stuck at the pump, so they couldn't follow. It's always crazy busy there on Fridays," he injected irrelevantly. "You work like a damn dog."

At that point Tom wanted to grab the man and shake him, but Hua asked, "These were two large men, dressed oddly?"

"Yeah." Ned snuffled a laugh. "Like they kept putting on more layers, and it ain't even that cold yet. Anyway, by the time they hung up the pump and maneuvered around the car ahead of them, Reuben was gone. The smaller guy came into the store and asked if I knew where he was headed, but I said no. I acted real cool, like Reuben was a complete stranger, but he might have saw the scrubs laying on the counter." Ned seemed to realize there were consequences to what he'd done. "It ain't like Reuben and me are old friends. If this wasn't legal or whatever—"

"The men in the car." Chris spoke through his teeth.

"Yeah, them." Ned shifted his shoulders to get himself back on track. "The guy was irritated, but he didn't give me any grief." Ned had finally reached his point, and he raised a finger to emphasize it. "But when I went outside for a smoke an hour ago, there were those same two guys, sitting out front in that big gray Lincoln."

"They followed you here this morning," Hua said.

"Huh." Ned frowned, realizing for the first time the truth of that. "That must be why Reuben changed things around. I called him and said some guys that asked about him yesterday had showed up here."

"What did he say?"

"He asked what they looked like. Then he hung up. A few minutes later he called and said to get your keys and put the girl in the van."

"And he told you we'd see her later, at the motel."

"Yeah." Ned seemed relieved to be able to report a positive ending to the adventure.

"Okay," Tom said. "Go back to Brandell and forget this ever happened. If you do that, you should be okay. Got it?"

Ned grinned, relieved. "Mister, you don't have to tell me twice."

As he roared away, Tom asked Chris to check the front parking lot. "Those men have seen me and Hua, but they don't know you."

"No Lincoln out there," Chris reported when he came back. "Just Harry's car."

"He thought he could fool them by taking our van," Tom said, "but he had to pass them to get to the street. They must have seen it was Mark driving."

"Why did he take Robin?" Hua asked.

"So we won't chase him," Chris replied

"Right," Tom agreed. "He's got two killers after him. He doesn't want us following too."

"But if those men intend to kill him," Hua said, "Robin could be collateral damage."

Tom stared at the street as if trying to see tire tracks that would tell him which direction they'd gone. "We need to find that van. Hua, can you contact Luca and—"

“Wait.” Hua held up a hand. “She is calling right now.”

“Hello.” He listened, frowned, and listened some more. “Hello, Lily. Are you there?” When he got no response, Hua said, “I’m afraid there’s more trouble inside.”

“What kind of trouble?”

Hua made an impatient gesture. “I don’t know. Luca called, but it appears she wants me to hear what is being said.” Hua listened again. “Someone is requesting entry at the front doors. I think it is the police.”

For a moment no one spoke. Then Chris said, “You two take my car and go after Mark.”

“We can’t leave you and L—” Tom began, but Chris broke in.

“I’m not all that steady on my new legs, so I’ll be no help in a fight. But as Doctor Allen, I might be able to get Luca out of trouble.”

Tom glanced at Hua, who nodded. “Okay. Give us your keys.”

Chris handed them over and they hurried to the car, where Bennett sat in the driver’s seat. That dog seemed convinced he could drive if they’d only let him try.

Chapter Forty-Eight

Luca looked up sharply when someone rapped on the glass entrance doors. Two uniformed police officers stood outside, and one of them gestured for her to come to the door. Quickly, she called Hua's phone and left the line open, so he could hear what was happening out front.

Her legs were stiff as she crossed the waiting area, and she wished she'd taken a sip of water to wet her throat. How should she handle this?

"The door's broken," she said with exaggerated mouth movements. "You need to go to—"

"We got a call there's criminal activity going on here, ma'am," one of the officers interrupted. "You need to let us in."

"It won't—"

The cop pointed to the control module. "Check the settings. I don't see a light, so I'm guessing it got turned off somehow."

Somehow. Right.

She made a show of doing as he said, pressing the wrong switch repeatedly, which got the result she wanted: nothing. The cops seemed puzzled, but the lawyer spoke behind her. "I think it's this one."

He pressed the power switch then the Automatic button, and the traitorous doors slid open. All Luca could do was cover her irritation with fake embarrassment. "Sorry. I don't know how I screwed that up."

The officers entered, glancing around at the quiet lobby. "What's going on here this morning?" the older cop asked.

"The usual," Luca replied. "Surgery." She gestured at the waiting area. "People waiting for it to be over."

"Why does it say there's a biohazard?"

She faked surprise. "It says that? First I heard of it."

The younger officer walked over to the men. "And you folks are?"

"I'm Harrison Robeson. This is my attorney, Anthony Biers."

"And which patient are you waiting for?"

When Robeson answered their questions, the cops turned their attention back to Luca. "We need to see your surgery schedule for today, specifically, Serena Dykstra's medical information."

Though flustered, Luca tried to appear calm. "I've been having trouble accessing our records this morning. I called IT for help, but no one has had time to get here yet."

The older cop gave her a stony look. "Call the hospital manager. He or she needs to confirm that everything here is the way it should be."

"It's Saturday," Luca reminded him. "The manager isn't in."

"Then we'll speak to whoever is next in line. Make the call."

She hesitated, unsure what to do next, but to her great relief, the double doors opened and Chris Parsons came out, looking mildly concerned. “I’m Doctor William Allen, Officer. Is there a problem?”

“We had a report of irregularities here.” Gesturing at Luca, the man said, “This woman can’t show me who’s scheduled for surgery.”

“Our computers are misbehaving, but even if they were working, confidentiality rules apply. We can’t reveal patient names.” Chris appeared to search his mind for a remedy. “When the tech gets here, Lily could print off the times and surgeons’ names. Would that help?”

The cop wasn’t ready to give up. “This call we got said your hospital is being used to perpetrate a scam on an elderly man.”

Biers, who had moved to the desk, gave an audible gasp. Chris seemed stymied by the specifics of the complaint, but surprisingly, Harrison Robeson spoke. “I suppose I’m the elderly man you were told about. I can assure you, there’s no scam being perpetrated on me.”

Leaned toward his client Biers said, “Harry, you need to—”

“It’s all right, Anthony.”

“There might be something to this,” he said urgently. “I mean, where is Reuben? We haven’t seen him since I gave him the—”

“Anthony.” Harry’s voice was thin, but the authority behind it shut Biers up. “As I said, officers, everything here is as it should be. My great granddaughter had surgery. She’s now in the recovery room.”

They eyed the double doors. “In there?”

"Yes." Luca swallowed a squeak of surprise when Harry added, "I've just gone back to see her. She's groggy, but she's doing well."

The younger cop looked to the older one for guidance, and he asked, "Why would someone call and report something like that?"

Chris turned to Luca. "Could it have been your ex, Lily?"

Picking up on his cue Luca said, "It could be him playing his tricks." Faking rising anger she went on, "I thought I saw his car in the parking lot earlier, but I never thought he'd—" She pounded her desk with a fist. "That jerk is always looking for ways to give me trouble." Taking up her phone, she read off the number of Mark Parson's cell. "Is that where this call you got came from?"

The younger cop checked. "It is."

She sighed dramatically. "I don't know what I saw in that—" Pausing as if to force herself to remain professional, she told them, "I'm sorry. His name is J'mal, with an apostrophe. Do you want his address? I'll call his mom, and you can get him for filing a false report." Leaning forward she tapped the cop's shoulder with a finger. "She's the one told me to kick his ass out."

The older cop took a step back, which Luca guessed meant there would be no investigation of the imaginary J'mal. Turning to Chris he said, "Doctor, you're telling me everything is okay here?"

Chris regarded him soberly. "Things are completely normal."

"And Mr. Robeson, you say you haven't been cheated in any way?"

Again Biers seemed about to speak, but Harry beat him to it. "Everything is copacetic, Officer."

The cop turned to Luca. "Let me see your hospital ID."

That made Chris clear his throat nervously. The photo on his own badge showed a much older man. They'd counted on the fact that people seldom look at the ID photos when meeting hospital staff.

Giving him a reassuring glance, Luca handed over the badge she'd made for herself.

The cop looked from the photo to her face, read the job title, and then gave it back. She said a little prayer that they wouldn't ask Chris for his ID. When they didn't, she guessed it was because they thought a doctor was entitled to more respect than a lowly receptionist.

"Okay." The older man took a step back, and his partner followed. "I think we're done here. You folks have a nice day."

When they were gone, Luca came out from behind the counter and approached the man in the wheelchair. "What's going on, Mr. Robeson?"

Chris followed Luca, his expression concerned. The attorney looked lost. Only Robeson seemed to be enjoying himself. "Call me Harry. Your friend Serena told me everything last night." An impish grin appeared as he added, "Not that I didn't already know her story was pure balderdash."

Though surprised by that, Chris kept his focus. "We need to get out of here. Mark took R…Serena prisoner and left with the money. The others have gone after him."

Harry made a quick decision. "Anthony, you drive," he ordered. "We can talk on the way." With Biers still shaking his head, they left the hospital. Biers helped Harry get into his car and stowed the wheelchair. Chris rode up front. Luca came along a few minutes later and climbed into the back seat. Chris texted Hua. "There. They'll know we're out and ok."

"Where are we going?" Harry asked.

"I wish I knew," Chris replied. "Once we're away from the hospital, pull in somewhere and we'll decide what to do."

A few blocks down, Biers pulled into a box store parking lot and put the car into park. "When do I get to know what's going on here?"

"Later," Harry ordered, turning to Chris. "Where is Serena?"

"Reuben took her with him," Chris said. "That's bad, because there are men trying to kill him."

"He could be trying to protect her," Biers said. "They're very close, even if she isn't really a relative."

Chris snorted disdainfully. "You don't know him He only cares about himself."

"Anthony," Harry explained. "The man we know as Reuben is a con artist. He forced this young woman to play the role of Serena in order to get my money." Harry turned to Chris. "How can we help?"

"Our friends went after them, but they don't know where to look."

Harry rubbed at his chin. "I'd suggest that the airport is most likely."

"You're probably right, but he'll have a new identity. In a place that big, he'll be on a plane and gone before we can find him."

Luca took two sheets of paper from her pocket. "Hua tricked him into giving me the driver's license and passport he was carrying. If he meant to leave the country as soon as he got his hands on the money, this is the name he'll be using."

Scanning the copies, Chris took his phone from his pocket. "I can probably hack into the airline's records and find out what flight he's on." As an afterthought he added, "It would be a lot faster if I had a computer."

Anthony pointed at a briefcase on the floor near Chris' feet. "My tablet's in there. Use that."

"Better." He removed the device, handed it to Anthony for unlocking, and began typing. "He's a white-hat hacker," Luca explained as they waited. "He only uses his powers for good."

A few minutes later Chris said, "He's leaving at three o'clock: Indianapolis to Frankfort to Dubai."

"Text the others and tell them to meet us at the airport," Harry ordered. "And let's get there as fast as we can."

As Biers pulled onto the street, Luca asked, "What about the men who want Mark dead?"

"We have to hope he can lose them in traffic," Chris replied.

Luca wasn't optimistic about that. "They're likely to just pull up beside the van at a stoplight and start blasting away. They could kill Clarabelle without even realizing she's in there."

"Maybe Serena will escape somehow," Biers said ingenuously.

Chris gave him a look. "Last we knew, she wasn't even conscious."

"Oh." Biers went silent, apparently done trying to invent false cheer.

Luca added more depressing information. "They want Mark dead. We need him alive. Without him, we've got no way to find the guy he locked up to force her to do this con."

"I'm sorry," Harry said softly.

"The airport," Chris urged. "It's all we've got."

"Yeah." Biers accelerated, causing his passengers to grab onto something for stability. As he drove, he kept shaking his head as if trying to make it work better. "Harry, you knew Serena was a fake?"

"In the first place," Harry replied, "Dolores was a lesbian, which made it unlikely, though not impossible, that she had a child. After she died, I met her friend, possibly her lover, who seemed to be a good person. She'd have told me if there'd been a baby."

"You say Serena confessed about the con?" Luca asked.

"Yesterday afternoon, before Reuben returned to my home. She asked me to go through with the charade so that she could rescue the friend you mentioned. I agreed."

"Why did you let Svein and me think you'd fallen for her story?" Biers asked, sounding hurt to have been left out.

"At first I didn't know who was in on the scheme and who wasn't, so it was best to keep my suspicions to myself." Harry smiled to take the sting out of admitting he suspected everyone. "And besides, it's been years since I did something the least bit daring." He raised his hands. "I could see that neither Serena nor her supposed grandfather meant me any physical harm. She was clearly under duress, and he... Well, he's the type of person who'd rather steal a living than earn it."

“But you gave him three hundred thousand dollars.”

“No. I had you bring me that much, but most of it is in here.” Harry tapped a cooler near his feet. “The valise you gave him has only about three thousand dollars in it.”

After a brief silence, in which only the hum of the heater could be heard, Biers said, “You have got to be kidding.”

“I took the chance that Reuben—Mark, as we now know him—thought he had me well and truly fooled. I withdrew the real amount in case he checked my bank account, but I had Svein make dummy packets for the briefcase.”

Biers ran a hand through his hair. “Where did you get three hundred thousand dollars’ worth of fake money?”

“In exchange for a small donation to her next production, my niece Natalie brought me all the funny money they had in her theater’s prop room.” To Luca and Chris he explained, “Natalie is fond of melodramas, so there are often scenes where large amounts of cash change hands for nefarious purposes.”

“I saw her come and go last evening,” Biers said. “And now that I think of it, she had a purse as big as a suitcase.”

“She was very helpful.” Harry’s tone hinted Natalie had come a long way toward making him appreciate her. “Though he didn’t know my reason for the switch, Svein approved of my caution with the money. He put a real hundred atop each stack of fakes. It looked quite real.”

“You’re pretty clever, Harry,” Luca said approvingly.

“If our con artist had looked below the first layer, he’d have seen the money wasn’t all there.”

"What could he have done about it?" Chris asked, pleased to hear that the conman had been conned. "He couldn't admit he'd sneaked a peek at money meant for the Spanish doctor."

"Speaking of the not-so-Spanish doctor," Harry said, "I got the sense that Serena is fond of him."

"You're good," Luca told him. "She tries to hide it, but we all know."

He turned to Chris. "And judging from the resemblance, you're Serena's brother?"

"Right again." Chris made a throat-clearing noise that hinted at his emotional state. "You might doubt the honesty of our little band, Harry, but never doubt that we love Serena. We'll do whatever it takes to get her back safely."

Biers muttered something at that point, but when Harry asked what he'd said, he insisted it was nothing.

Chapter Forty-Nine

Robin woke to the hum of tires on pavement, becoming aware of stops and starts as the van navigated traffic. At first she assumed Tom was at the wheel, though she wondered why she was lying in the back. Had she fainted during a caper? That usually happened after the excitement, not during. As the ride continued, her fuzzy brain began operating a little better, and she tried to recall the last place she'd been. A hospital. Mark had been there. She recalled taking some pills, and he'd smiled in that way he had when Robin did exactly as he wanted her to.

Drugged. Mark had changed the game, which meant she was in trouble, as were Tom, Hua, Luca, and worst of all, Cam. Mark didn't care that he was locked up somewhere and desperate. She should have expected it, should have done more to keep her friends safe.

During a stop, no doubt for a traffic light, the slider between the cab and the cargo area opened. Robin was not really surprised when her father's face appeared in the gap. "You're awake."

"You drugged me."

"A little dose with your chocolate milk. A bigger dose a while later. I didn't want you to worry about anything, including ways to get out of going through with the con."

"I did everything you wanted—" she began, but he cut her off.

"It's good you're back from La-la Land, because we've run into a snag. I'm going to pull into an alley somewhere along here. Hopefully the men following us will miss it and go on by, but if they don't, you need to be ready to run."

Her brain was still fuddled. "Men following us?"

"I told you about them," he said patiently. "They want me dead, but they won't be shy about killing you too. In fact, they'll probably make me watch and kill me afterward."

The van lurched forward, and his voice faded as he turned back to the street. "They're a few car-lengths back. I'm going to speed up, turn a corner, and go down the first alley I see. Hang on."

A second later the van took a sharp right, then another, hurtling over a curb. It sped up briefly and then came to an abrupt stop. Holding on to prevent being tossed around like a tennis ball, she heard her father swear. His gamble had not paid off.

When the side door rolled open, Robin was already crouched, one hand bracing herself on the roof. Mark stood before her, the case Harry had provided in one hand. With the other he gestured for her to hurry. She exited the van, stumbling a little as she hit the cobblestone paving. An urge to tell Mark something teased at her mind, but she had trouble putting it into words. "Not worth the risk," she mumbled, but he jerked at her arm and she followed, still fuzzy-headed.

"This way." Mark pulled her farther down the alley, but what he'd hoped was an escape route led to a cul-de-sac that was in essence a cage of brick. Around them, a half-dozen delivery doors gave access to the backs of several stores. They stopped, staring in dumb horror. Behind them, a car came as far as the van they'd left behind. After a few seconds the engine quit, and the alley went silent.

The delivery doors were marked with the names of stores that faced the street behind them. One by one Mark tried them, but all were locked. As he made one growl of frustration after another, Robin turned in a slow circle, looking overhead for a fire ladder or a window they might climb to and get away. Nothing. Her gaze stopped at a tiny slit of light, a space perhaps a foot wide between two buildings. “There,” Robin pointed. “Through there.”

Grasping her intention, Mark plunged into the space. It was a tight fit, and his clothes rasped against the rough brick walls, but he kept moving. Robin followed, angry with her father but aware that the most important task at that moment was escaping his pursuers.

Navigating the skinny space was difficult, but it had a big advantage. Neither of the men chasing them could fit into the space and follow them through, “Get around to the front,” she heard one say to the other. Looking back, she saw the first man, whom she dubbed Danger A in her mind, aim a gun in her direction. She gasped out an order to Mark, “Faster!” Muttering something unintelligible, he pushed on.

No shot sounded, and Robin realized they didn’t dare shoot her, even if the gun had a silencer. The tight space would hold her corpse upright, shielding the man’s real target, Mark, from injury. Danger A would wait and hope his partner, Danger B, got around to the other end in time to trap them between alleys.

That brought a thought to mind. “Do you still have that gun you waved at Cam and me?”

“No.” When she made an impatient groan he explained, “It’s under the seat in your friend’s van. I forgot it when we got out.”

“You remembered the money though.”

Mark was chagrined but still offended. “I’m not even sure how to load it.”

Robin gritted her teeth. “Okay. Just keep going.”

They struggled on, their hair and clothes catching with each step, their feet turned oddly sideways as they sidled along. Mark held the case of money awkwardly behind him, and it made a rasping sound as it dragged against the hard surface. Would he drop it if she told him it held only a fraction of the money he was counting on? More likely he’d waste precious time berating her for disloyalty. No sense wasting her breath. Unless they reached the other end before Danger B did, their struggles, with or without the case, would be for nothing.

When they finally pulled free of the walls, Mark groaned aloud. They were in a second cul-de-sac, almost identical to the first. As they paused, sucking in air like marathon runners, Danger B appeared in silhouette at the alley entrance a hundred yards down. He started toward them, his short legs pumping. Mark stood frozen, his cheek and hands scraped from the narrow passage. He seemed unable to think. “Try the doors,” Robin ordered. When he didn’t respond, she gave him a push. “You got us into this, now help get us out.” Mark’s gaze sharpened at her tone, but he swallowed once and turned to obey.

Robin tried Patty’s Pastries—locked. Mark tried The Irish Bridegroom—also locked. They moved apart, trying each door, as their pursuer’s footsteps neared. When Robin heard his heavy breathing as well, she looked at her father. He’d found a door that, though locked, sat loosely in its casing. Rattling the handle, he pushed hard with a shoulder. The door popped open, and he called, “Here, Robbie. In here.”

In seconds they were inside. Closing the door, Robin blocked the base with her foot while Mark leaned his shoulder against the frame and held the knob steady. In seconds someone rattled the handle. Then a body pushed at the door. Next a voice called them names that conveyed the speaker's frustration. Finally they heard the sound of retreating footsteps.

Robin wasn't naïve enough to believe they'd escaped. The problem was merely delayed. Danger B would call Danger A, and they'd find a way to get at them. "Give me your phone, Mark. We need to call my friends."

He pulled the phone from his breast pocket and started to hand it over. When he swore softly, Robin saw that in the trip between buildings, the screen had been smashed to a crazed blur. He pressed the side button hopefully, but nothing lit up.

"Okay," Robin said, trying to sound like it wasn't a catastrophe. "Second best option, we find a place to hide."

Judging from lumber, tile, and other materials piled everywhere, Robin concluded the store was under renovation. She took a short piece of two-by-four from a nearby stack and wedged it under the doorknob as a stopper.

It was dark in the passage they'd entered, but picture windows at the front of the building revealed a large, empty showroom with a stairway ascending the right-hand wall. When a figure appeared at the window, Robin pulled Mark farther into the shadows. Danger A peered in, framing his eyes with both hands to see into the room. At the door she'd blocked, someone, no doubt Danger B, rattled the knob again. How long before her improvised block shook loose?

"Upstairs," she ordered. Mark didn't question her command, but she had no time to reflect on his submissiveness. Right now she had to protect her father's life. Later, when Cam was safe, she might murder him herself.

The staircase was old, with faint depressions on each side from feet going up and down them many times over the years. Mark kept glancing back. "They'll get in," he said.

"Yes," she replied.

"They're going to kill me."

"If they can, yes. We need either a way out or a place to hide where they can't find us."

Mark looked past her, as if trying to guess what they'd find on the second floor. "That's good, Robbie." By the time they reached the top of the stairs, he seemed to have recovered his courage. "I'll go this way and look for an exit. You go the other."

She hesitated. "We shouldn't split up."

"We have to. There's no time." Backing away, Mark said, "I'll get you out of this, Robbie." He gave her his familiar three-finger salute. "Scout's honor."

Robin went to the front of the room, while Mark disappeared into the dark space at the back. Her part of the exploration brought only disappointment. The whole area was empty except for a dozen rolls of insulation awaiting installation. Robin walked all the way around it. Every step she took caused the wood floor to squeak in protest. With no place to hide and a noisy floor to give away their every movement, they needed to get out before their pursuers broke in.

The sound of glass breaking downstairs told her it was too late for that. Hurrying back to the center of the room, Robin peered into the darkness. "Mark?" she whispered. "Mark, where are you?"

There was no reply. Though it was much darker at the back, she sensed he wasn't there. She stepped forward, peering into the dimness. Where had he gone?

Ignoring the sounds of movement on the first floor, she let her gaze sweep the area from right to left. Nothing. Then she looked up, and she knew. There was a metal ladder attached to the back wall, and as she watched, a square of light appeared, changed shape, and disappeared.

A trapdoor onto the roof. Mark had found an escape route and taken it, leaving her behind.

On the ground floor, Robin heard their pursuers speaking in low tones. She had seconds to decide what to do. Her first instinct was to follow Mark up the ladder, but steps on the stairs revealed there was no time for that. Turning, she tiptoes to the rolls of insulation and crawled between them. At the center of the pile she crouched, as still as death, and waited, cursing the day she'd blundered back into her father's crooked orbit.

Chapter Fifty

Svein's phone said they were .6 miles from the hospital when a white van passed them heading west. "Hey, that's ours," Cam said.

"Are you sure?" Svein asked. "Lots of white vans around."

"I bought that one, I modified it, and I do the maintenance. It's ours, but it shouldn't even be in this state."

Braking, Svein pulled to the side of the street. "What do we do?"

"Follow it. Lend me your phone, and I'll ask Bubbles what's going on."

Svein's brows rose at the name, but he dug out his phone and gave it to Cam, at the same time making a neat U-turn. Peering ahead he asked, "Where did it go?"

The van was nowhere in sight, though the light at the next block was red. Ahead of them a gray Lincoln turned down an alley. Svein pointed. "Could it have gone where that car went?"

"Maybe. Turn around again and drive real slow past the entrance." Cam made a call and heard a hesitant, "Yes?"

"Bubbles, it's me."

"Bozo! Are you all right?"

"I'm good. I'm in Indianapolis looking for Clarabelle, and I saw our van go by. Are you guys here?"

"We came to find you, but things have gotten crazy. Where did you see the van?"

"On 10th Street, but it turned off somewhere. We lost it."

"We?"

"A guy's helping me." Svein had done as Cam asked, and they craned their necks to look. "We think it turned into an alley on the 500 block, but now there's this big Lincoln blocking the entrance."

"Give us the street corner nearest your position." Hua's tone was urgent. "Clarabelle is in the van, Bozo. Her father took her to make us back off, but two dangerous men are chasing him."

"Yeah," Cam confirmed. "They're supposed to kill him." Again Svein's brows reacted, but he merely parked the car as near as he could get to the alley entrance. Looking up, Cam told Hua, "The alley is east of 10th and Gardenia." He couldn't avoid a trace of pride as he added, "We're driving a bright blue '74 MGB III. Do you know what they look like?"

"I will find it online," Hua said. "Locate Clarabelle if you can, but be careful. We're on our way."

When he ended the call Cam said, "I'm going down that alley to see what's going on. You can wait here."

Svein's narrow nose got even narrower. "I think Harry is fond of that young woman, Bozo. If you intend to rescue her, I intend to help."

Chapter Fifty-One

As her pursuers climbed the stairs, Robin hardly dared to breathe. They were silent, having apparently worked together long enough to communicate without conversation. They circled the room slowly, and the sound of their steps came close and moved away several times. Once someone kicked the pile of insulation, but she managed to quell any audible reaction. Though the search probably lasted a minute or two, it felt like she hadn't breathed normally for an hour.

As her mind sorted through possible scenarios for the next few minutes, none of them good, memories of the past butted their way into her mind. Robin's father had betrayed her. It wasn't the first time.

"Robbie, we're going to go into this store and look at jewelry."

"For Mom?"

His hesitation should have alerted her, but she'd been young, maybe six. "Yeah, for Mom. When they get out a tray of rings, I want you to say you have to go to the bathroom."

"I don't. I went before we—"

"Say it anyway." His tone was a warning. "Do a little dance, like you can't wait."

The store was small and quiet, and tray after tray of beautiful gems lined the aisle from front to back. When she made her request, the nice woman behind the counter smiled indulgently. Mark acted embarrassed, saying, "I'm sorry. I told her to go before we left home, but sometimes she forgets."

Robin had been upset by that. She hadn't forgotten to go, and it bothered her when her dad made her sound like a baby.

The woman led her to a tiny space at the back of the store with a toilet and a sink. One corner was stacked with supplies, boxes of toilet paper, disposable towels, and soap. "Can you find your way out again?" the woman asked, and Robin nodded.

When she returned, her father was apparently agonizing over his choice. He'd laid several rings on the velvet cloth the woman had spread out on the counter. "I like them all," he said with a disarming smile. "I think we need to take a walk around the block. Once I get away from all this shiny stuff, I'll find it easier to make a decision." Taking Robin's hand he said, "Let's go, Sweetheart."

They hadn't gone a block when a man called out from behind them. "You! Hey, you!"

"Keep walking, Robbie," Mark ordered, but the man caught up. "Sir, I'm the manager at Warton's Diamonds. When you left, we found a ring missing from one of the trays."

Despite her youth, Robin had known what would happen next. Mark turned to her and said, "Sweetie, did you take something from the store? Something really pretty?"

And when her father searched her pockets, the ring was there. The disappointment on his face seemed real, at least it would have if she hadn't known Mark Parsons so well.

Now he'd done it again, left her to deal with the consequences of his crime. What would happen if the men caught her? She'd serve as a delay—and perhaps a sacrifice.

No use dwelling on that. If she remained still and quiet, they might give up. If she didn't sneeze from dust particles or shift the muscles that were screaming at being cramped in an odd position, she might be okay. Since the room was mostly empty, it shouldn't take long. They—

"Come out of there now, or I'll drag you out." The voice was directly above her. When she hesitated, the man kicked a roll, making the whole pile shudder. "Out! Now!"

Pushing her way out, Robin found Danger B, wearing an unfriendly grin and holding a snub-nosed pistol. "Who are you?"

"That man took me hostage." Robin tried to sound outraged. "He stole my van and he—"

"I don't think so." Danger A had joined them, also with a gun. "Mark went into that hospital this morning with you and two men, a young one with a briefcase and an old one in a wheelchair. When you and him tried to sneak past us in that white van, I figured you had some kind of scam going. Where were you headed when he spotted us and ducked into that alley?"

She saw no point in trying to explain that parts of their theory were true but important details were missing. If they'd parked in the visitors' lot at the front of the hospital, they hadn't seen her carried out to the van, unconscious. “You’re wasting your time,” she told them. “Mark doesn’t care about me and he doesn’t confide in me. Never has.”

With a glance to assure that Danger A had his gun trained on Robin, Danger B stowed his in a holster under his arm. That done, he reached out to grab Robin’s hand and took her little finger in his grip. “I wonder if your answer will be the same if I break this and then ask again.”

Though her spine twitched at the suggestion, Robin tried to appear honest. “It won’t change anything. I don’t know what he plans to do.”

He bent the finger far enough away from its mates to make her gasp with pain. “Give us your best guess.”

She could tell them to go to the airport and check flights departing for Dubai. It wasn’t as if she owed Mark Parsons anything. He’d forced her to help with his scam, marooned Cam in some unknown place, and taken her on his escape to keep her friends from pursuing him. Now he’d left her behind with two killers so he had time to escape. Her father always managed to land on his feet—usually by screwing someone else.

And that was the difference between them. Robin could not betray Mark the way he’d betrayed her. She wasn’t like him, and despite her present situation, that made her proud. “I can’t tell you where he is, because I don’t know.”

Danger B rolled his eyes in irritation, and that brought a surprised grunt. “Hey, Gerald, look. There’s a ladder on the wall that goes up to the roof. Do you think he coulda got out that way?”

His partner was skeptical. “And left his little girlfriend behind?”

"I told you," Robin said. "I mean nothing to him."

Gerald frowned at the ladder. "You better climb up and take a look, Ernie."

The guy dropped Robin's hand and rubbed a knuckle across his nose. "What if he's waiting up there with a club or something?"

"Be careful he don't hit you with it."

Reluctantly Ernie went to the ladder, situated his holster more comfortably under his arm, and climbed slowly to the top. With obvious reluctance he turned the latch, pushed the trapdoor open with a sharp movement, and moved to one side, waiting for the blow he expected. When nothing happened, Gerald ordered, "Get out there and look, you chicken."

Ernie's head and shoulders disappeared, stopped for a few seconds, and then the rest of him went. They heard tromping for a while, and then his face appeared in the opening. "Hey, Gerald, I think our job's done."

"What do you mean?"

"I mean our guy is squashed on the cobblestones two stories down."

"Is he dead?"

Ernie made a snorty sound. "I'm supposed to know that from forty feet away? He's layin' real still, all splayed out with blood coming out his mouth. I think dead is pretty likely."

Robin felt an emotion she couldn't define. It wasn't sadness, but she had to accept that there was a sense of loss. It stunned her to think Mark Parsons no longer walked the earth. All her life he'd been there, at first a demanding presence, later an instructive memory. Though he'd shown her how certain goals could be reached, he wasn't the kind of person she'd ever wanted to become. Because of him, her childhood was stained with sorrow, fear, and regret. Rest in peace, Dad, she said in a silent prayer. Now maybe Chris and I can find peace too.

Ernie had started down the ladder, and his question brought her back to the present. "What about the girl?"

Gerald considered. "I think she'd better take a fall down the stairs."

"Right," Ernie agreed without hesitation. "Then let's head back to where it's warm."

Ernie was thirty feet away, his gun holstered. Gerald had lost focus and dropped his gun hand to his side. Seizing the opportunity, Robin braced herself with her back foot and pushed Gerald as hard as she could. His bulk made knocking him down impossible, but he took a step back to regain his balance. Pushing past him, Robin flew down the stairs, expecting a bullet to whiz by her ear—or slam into her back—at any moment.

"You let go of her? What were you thinking?" Ernie demanded.

"Just get her before she gets out onto the street."

"Shoot her!"

"And have everyone on the street come to see what's happening?"

"Well, if it wasn't for your rookie mistake, she wouldn't have—"

"Shut up!" Gerald ordered, and his footsteps began pounding down the stairs behind her. "Take the front door. I'll take the back. Do *not* let her get outside."

Ernie muttered something with the word *dumb* in it, but he joined Gerald on the stairs.

Go ahead, she told them silently. *Waste your breath arguing*. Despite their disagreement, the men clattered along behind her faster than she'd hoped, and Robin tried to think ahead. Should she try to exit the back door, which was closer, or the front, which was an unknown? Since the cul-de-sac at the back limited her options for escape, Robin chose the front door. A public street would make it harder for them to pursue her. She could call for help. She could duck into a store…

The door was locked. Her fingers fumbled as she tried to turn the old-fashioned latch, which stuck a little. She'd just managed it when a hand grabbed her hair. Pulled backwards, she tried to scream, but the other hand covered her mouth. "Nice try," Gerald grunted. "Now let's do the stairs thing again."

Half-dragging, half-carrying her, he moved toward the staircase. Ernie, who was still coming down, tried to grab her feet, but she kicked at him, landing a decent blow to his face and another to his groin.

"Help me!" Gerald said through gritted teeth, but Ernie crouched near the landing, one hand on his crotch and the other on his nose.

One foot found the bannister, and Robin pushed against it with all her might. Gerald toppled backward, taking her with him. They landed heavily, but Gerald hit the floor while Robin had him for padding. His grip on her eased as he lay there, momentarily dazed. Rolling away, Robin got to her feet and ran through the first doorway she came to. It was only a broom closet, but its wooden door was the old-fashioned, solid kind. She'd barely got it closed and propped a broom against it when the handle rattled. Soon she heard Gerald threatening what he would do when he got hold of her again.

Chapter Fifty-Two

When Cam and Svein approached the alley entrance, a burly man had emerged, talking on his phone in an animated manner. They stopped, and Svein pretended to be giving Cam directions. The man spared them only a glance, busy shouting at someone about being slower than a tortoise in the Everglades.

When he was gone, Cam and Svein went cautiously down the alley, each taking a side and watching in case the second man Hua had mentioned was lurking somewhere. They passed the gray Lincoln Town Car they'd seen earlier. Ahead of that was the van, its driver's door and slider wide open. Cam glanced inside, but both the front and the cargo area were empty. "They're probably farther down the alley," Svein said. As they passed, Cam saw the van's keys in the ignition. Pocketing them, he went on.

Before they reached the back of the building, a second large man appeared. When he gave them a hostile look Svein asked brightly, "Is that a short-cut to 9th Street?" He hurried by without answering. Cam considered stopping the guy, but what would he say? *We think you might be a hired killer. Can you tell us where our friend is*? Probably not the best conversation starter.

He and Svein continued down the alley, which turned into a cul-de-sac. An empty one. They stood for a moment, confused, but

Svein pointed to a narrow space between two buildings. "If they went through there, those men could not have followed."

Cam examined the space. "Robin would definitely fit, and her dad is kinda skinny too."

"But we aren't," Svein said.

"So those guys are looking to get at them from another direction." Cam started back the way they'd come, breaking into a trot and then a run. Svein caught up easily and stayed with him until they returned to 10th Street. Stopping, they scanned both directions but saw no sign of Robin, Mark, or either of the big men.

"Let's walk up the block," Cam said. "Keep an eye out for them or for Mark and Serena."

They walked quickly, peering into store windows as they passed. When they reached the end of the block Cam said, "We'll go back down the other side. Different viewpoint." They crossed the street and began walking back toward the car. Halfway down, Svein took Cam's arm. "I saw a woman. There."

Though he followed Svein's pointing finger, Cam saw nothing. "Place looks empty."

"I think it was Serena. It was only a glance, but it looked as if she tried to leave and was pulled back."

Cam crossed the street, dodging cars and ignoring the beeps and swearwords that resulted. He assumed Svein came too, because a second round of insults followed the first. When he tried the door it swung open. Cam felt Svein's presence behind him as he stepped inside. At the back of a large room, the two men they'd seen earlier stood before a closed door. One of them was shouting threats; the other had found a screwdriver and was removing the door's hinges.

Cam glanced at Svein, who read his mind and nodded agreement. Side by side, they moved forward.

Chapter Fifty-Three

Barricaded in the broom closet, Robin awaited disaster. There was no escape, and her pursuers were doing their best to smash in the door. The tiny room shuddered every time one of them rammed it with a shoulder, and Robin's nerves got even more frayed. She had a very short time to live, and she guessed the men's anger would add to the pain she'd experience before she died.

What came next was confusing. There was a *smack!* like a blow, then another and another. After that she heard crashes, grunts, and thuds. It seemed to go on for a long time, but finally the sounds lessened and then stopped altogether. She cowered in her hiding place, unsure what to do, until she heard Cam's voice. "Clarabelle? Are you in there?"

"Bozo!" Removing the broom, she opened the door and was immediately enveloped in a hug that almost left her breathless.

When Cam let her go, Robin looked past his broad shoulder to see Svein grinning up at her. He knelt a few feet away, and he was busy binding the hands of Danger A with duct tape from the renovation supplies. "Your friends are on their way," he told her cheerfully. "Soon you'll be able to go home to wherever you really come from." Robin had to smile; Svein's positivity stemmed partly from victory over her pursuers, but also from the knowledge that she'd soon be out of his life entirely.

"You two make sure these man aren't going anywhere. There's something I need to do."

Leaving behind the *ZZZZRRRRPPPPPP* sound of tape leaving its roll, she went to the back door and looked out into the cul-de-sac. It was empty and still. Though Robin found a stain that might be blood on the cobblestones, there was no sign of her father, dead or alive.

Chapter Fifty-Four

Tom and Hua found the car Cam had described parked in front of a clothing store on 10th. "Now what?" Tom asked.

"He mentioned an alley."

"I see two." Tom leaned forward. "But the Lincoln's in that one."

The car sat empty, and when they got out to look closer, they saw the van, also empty.

"Now what?"

"We need our scent detector," Hua said. Returning to the car, he snapped Bennett's leash onto his collar and led the dog to where Tom waited. "Find Cam, Bennett. Find Robin." The dog went straight to the car, sniffed at it, and then led them down to a cul-de-sac that offered no exit except the way they'd come.

That wasn't completely true. At a narrow opening between two buildings, Bennett whined softly.

"You can't fit down there," Hua said to Tom, "but I can. Shall I see what's at the other end?"

"Yeah. Bennett and I will wait on the street, near the car."

Hua slid into the space and began sidling down, the rivets in his jeans scratching against the surface. Tom started back toward the car, but before they got there, Bennett strained at the leash. He wanted to go up the street, and, trusting the dog's nose, Tom went. Bennett stopped at a door and whined, scratching at it with a paw. As Tom peered inside, Hua came toward them from the opposite direction. "I came out in a second cul-de-sac," he reported. "I had to either return to the first alley or come back out to the street."

"Bennett likes this place," Tom said. "It's dark in there, but—"

At that moment the door flew open and Ernie burst through, his arms fastened behind him with duct tape. Reacting instinctively Tom reached out and caught him. Past coherent thought, Ernie hollered, "Let me go!" over and over until Tom shook him silent.

"Let's see who you're running from," Tom said, shoving him back inside.

At the back of a large room, Cam and another man were trying to tape Gerald's legs together. His hands were bound, but he was giving everything he had to keeping his feet free. The need for both men's efforts to subdue him had given Ernie the chance to run.

"Looks like we came to the party a little late," Tom said, "but we brought you a present."

Robin came in from the back, her face drawn. She brightened when she saw them, and Bennett ran to her. Grabbing him as if he were a life raft, she rubbed his ears and spoke softly in his ear. Once he was satisfied that she still loved him, the dog moved on to Cam, who'd finished making Gerald completely immobile. Patting Bennett's wide head, Cam told him he was a really good dog.

Since he already knew that, Bennett moved on to investigate Svein, who was taping Ernie's legs together while Hua held them still. Finished, Svein let the dog sniff his hand. Having greeted all the important people, Bennett growled at the two men on the floor, letting them know he wouldn't stand for any further attempts at escape.

"Is everybody all right?" Tom asked.

"I could use a shower, but I'm okay," Cam answered.

Robin hesitated before replying, and Tom frowned, unable to read her mood. Finally she said, "Everyone who matters is."

"Hua, you'd better let the others know." With a nod, Hua moved away a few steps, took out his phone, and punched in a number. Before the call connected, he saw something outside and grinned. "Look." Following his gaze, Tom saw a car pulling up at the curb. He recognized the driver as Harrison Robeson's lawyer.

"We'd better go show your fan club you're okay, Clarabelle." They all went out to where Luca, Chris, and Biers exited Robeson's car. The old man peered anxiously out an open window in the back, and his face lit up when he saw Robin. She put on a smile as if donning armor, and Tom wondered which of them would discern that something was bothering her. Chris for sure. The others seemed too relieved to notice.

When Cam and Svein joined them a minute later, they formed a small crowd, which drew notice from passers-by. "Why don't you all head to the first restaurant you find?" Tom suggested. "Text us the address, and we'll come along as soon as we clean up here."

"I will call the hospital and give them the all-clear on their C-diff scare." Taking out his phone, Hua backed away to find a quiet spot.

"I'll move those guys' car out of the way and get our van back," Cam said. "I found the keys in the big guy's pants pocket."

"I'll direct you," Svein offered. "It's difficult to back out of an alley into traffic."

"Thanks. That would be great."

"Wipe away your prints when you're done," Tom cautioned. "At some point we're going to let the police know about Ernie and Gerald. It's hard to say how much they'll share of what happened, but it's best if we erase our presence where possible."

"I did that at the hospital," Luca said. "I figured it was a good idea." Pointing inside she asked, "Should I do the same in there?"

"We didn't touch much," Robin told her. "The door handles, the stairway railing—" she paused. "The ladder to the trapdoor on the roof."

"Use these." Harry held out a pair of cotton gloves. "They're Svein's. He's always prepared for anything."

"I won't be a minute." Luca disappeared inside.

Robin took Tom aside and told him what Ernie had said about Mark. "I need to…walk around the building once," she said. "If he's hurt, I have to—Tom, I can't—" She didn't finish.

"I'll go with you. We'll act like a couple out for a stroll."

She smiled faintly. "Yeah, lots of couples stroll down alleys and explore the trash bins behind stores. It's very romantic."

Tom dropped his voice, though there was no one else near enough to hear. "When you're around, Ms. Clarabelle, any place on earth is romantic."

Chapter Fifty-Five

Robin, Tom, and Hua reached a small restaurant six blocks farther down 10th Street where Luca had texted to say she was waiting with Harry, Chris, and Anthony. Hua had texted Jai to let her know they were all safe and together again, promising a call to explain everything in an hour or so.

As they parked in the lot, Cam pulled the van in next to them. Svein came behind him, but in deference to the vehicle he drove, parked in a remote corner, away from any possible door dings.

Bennett was still excited about the reunion of everyone he loved, and Robin had been dog-kissed repeatedly. He whined at being left yet again in the car, but she promised there'd be a burger at the end of the wait. She could have sworn the dog understood, because he settled down in the driver's seat, curled his tail around himself, and dropped into nap mode.

Luca had answered most of Harry's questions, being mostly honest without giving details like their real names or place of residence. Anthony Biers seemed shocked to learn he was in the company of criminals, but Harry took the news in stride. "It sounds like you all lead a very exciting life," he said once Robin was seated. "I'd love to hear more about it at some time in the future."

"That can be arranged. I'd like to visit you again someday, once I've…processed what's happened."

Harry met her gaze, and Robin realized he understood that she wasn't able to rejoice with the others at the moment. The people who mattered most to her were safe and together again, but she felt a deep sadness at the thought of Mark, alone, without resources, and hurt, perhaps badly. The fact that he didn't deserve her concern wasn't enough to erase or even ease it.

He was her father, and she couldn't forget that. Mark Parsons understood Robin in a way no one else could, and while Chris rejected the idea that he'd ever given them anything worthwhile, Robin knew that she and her father shared traits that had helped her in life. The drive to succeed, though their end goals were completely opposite. The love of planning, of predicting what might go wrong and providing ways to steer around the rough spots. And, though she wished she could deny it, the thrill that came from getting people to do as she wanted. Mark was a con artist, but wasn't she one too? She tricked people, scared them, and nudged them in what she considered the right direction. Suddenly she felt exhausted, tired of being someone else's conscience. Mark's teachings were as good as hers, since his victims learned the same lessons: Don't trust too easily. Don't be greedy. Don't let strangers talk you into being careless with your affections or your possessions.

Tom's hand touched hers under the table, and Robin met his gaze and smiled. He seemed to know what she needed, and while he never pushed, he always made her aware that he was willing to help. She squeezed his hand to let him know she was okay.

Raising her eyes, she saw Anthony Biers watching. His head bobbed minimally, a good-humored salute that hinted at the answer to the question she'd had about him. Biers had no interest in her now that she wasn't Harry's heir. *Not very flattering*, Robin thought, *but at least I won't be leaving any broken hearts behind in Indiana.*

Another question followed. If Biers was a man who'd romance her because she might inherit Harry's money, should she warn Harry to watch him?

No, she decided. Despite her earlier doubts, Harry Robeson was nobody's fool. He'd spent decades in the business world, dealing with ambitious types daily. He'd dedicated a great deal of time to helping people in need of a boost, and had no doubt learned some hard lessons about sincerity. Almost certainly, Harry knew the difference between his lawyer, who was smooth and capable but opportunistic, and Svein, who was suspicious and grumpy but completely dedicated to the welfare of his boss. Though Harry's body was weak, his mind wasn't, and he didn't need advice from a passing grifter. Catching her eye, Harry winked, and Robin wondered if he guessed what she was thinking.

"I want to thank you for this adventure, Miss...Clarabelle," Harry said, raising his coffee cup in a toast. "I haven't had this much fun in a decade."

"It wasn't much fun for her," Cam said in his usual frank way. "Not for me either."

"But you prevailed, young man," Harry replied. "That's the thing." Resting his chin on a fist he went on, "I for one would like to hear how you extricated yourself from wherever you were imprisoned."

"I broke a hole in the roof," Cam said. "I climbed out and—" He stopped, remembering something, and turned to Hua. "We need to go back there before we go home, Bubbles. I can't fix the hole, but I can at least empty my, um, outhouse bucket. Nobody else should have to take care of that."

Chapter Fifty-Six

The final official meeting of the Kidnap Gang happened in the kitchen, where Hua had made French toast with blueberries. Mai ignored the conversation as she worked to keep glasses and cups filled with each diner's preferred drink, but everyone else at the table came to full attention when Robin announced she had something important to say. She'd dreaded suggesting they end their capers, but when she did, resistance came only from Jai, who complained that she hadn't yet had the chance to "stick it to the bad guys."

"You should go to California and live with Em," Robin told her. Indicating Jai's outfit: two pairs of socks, fleece-lined slippers, and a bathrobe over long pants and a sweater, she added, "It's warm there. You'll have friends your age and lots to do."

Jai's expression revealed resistance, and Robin explained the plan she and Tom had made. "We'd like to move to Wisconsin and start a new life together," Robin said. "We'll go back to our real identities and leave kidnapping and all its related crimes behind."

Though they all knew Jai dreamed of someday fighting crime at Tom's side, everyone, even Jai, knew Tom and Robin were in love. "Em's home sounds nice," she said with determined grace. Her voice caught as she added, "But we will miss all of you."

"We'll miss you too," Robin said. "Tom proposes we have an annual reunion of the Kidnap Gang. We can meet at Em's and tell stories of our glorious deeds." Turning serious, she went on. "Tom and I won't leave any of you without a home and a purpose, so the next question for each of you is this: What would you do if there were no Kidnap Gang?"

Glancing at Cam Hua said, "We have talked of becoming full-time gardeners. I would do the business part, Cam would care for the equipment, and we would both do the planting, tending, and harvesting." He paused. "Of course this property belongs to the group. A financial arrangement would be made that is fair to all."

"Count me out on that," Tom said. "You, Robin, Em, and Cam bought it and did the work to make it livable. I make no claim to the house or property, and I doubt Em will either."

"I'll need a share of the cash we have on hand so I can go back to being Robin Parsons," Robin said. "As far as the house goes, I'll gladly sign it over to the two of you."

"What about Luca?" Cam asked. "We can't leave her out just because she wasn't here at the beginning."

All eyes focused on their newest member, and Tom asked, "What about it, Luca? If we give you a share of the cash, you could go back to Tulsa or choose a new place to live."

Luca turned to Cam. "You don't need all of this big old house, right? Could I be your tenant?"

"Why would you need so much space?" Robin asked.

"You been telling the people in town this is an artists' retreat, right? Well, I think that could work for real. I'd need some help from Hua to get the online stuff set up, but we have lots of well-lit rooms, outbuildings for big projects, and sleeping space for quite a few people. I'd like to host retreats for artists, writers, musicians, and whatever."

"I would not mind helping with the meals," Hua said. "I have become quite good at preparing food for large groups."

Cam seemed enthusiastic. "I gotta keep the house in shape anyway, so I'll do the maintenance."

"Could Bennett stay here?" Robin asked. "We aren't sure where we'll be living, and we'd hate for him to be cooped up in an apartment or a tiny back yard."

"It's his home," Cam said. "His job can be keeping the birds out of the strawberries."

With general agreement evident, an optimistic mood settled on the table. For Robin it lasted until Hua asked, "Have you told your brother all this?"

Robin's smile faded. "No, but I'll call him."

Chapter Fifty-Seven

Though she didn't share it with the others, Robin's call to Chris had two purposes. Learning the Kidnap Gang was being disbanded would be both a joy and a sadness for him. Chris believed in the work they'd done and relished his part in it, but he'd worried about his sister's safety. She hoped he'd greet her return to normal life with more relief than regret.

As to the second reason, Robin had deliberated all night about whether to tell her brother what she now knew. In the end she'd decided that she had to. "He's alive," she said when Chris' face appeared on the FaceTime screen. "I got an email."

"What does it say?"

"I knew you'd be ok. I figured I'd lure them away and your friends would be along to help. Good to see you and your brother again."

"Bastard." It was a mutter, but she saw the word his lips formed.

Trying to make Robin feel better, Luca had suggested Mark left her behind to save her life. "He wanted those men to chase him over the rooftops, so you'd be able to get away," she contended.

It was a lovely thought, but Luca didn't know Mark. He could say he'd meant to save her, but he thought of himself first, last, and always.

“How did we survive having a mother with no backbone and a father like Mark?” she asked.

“Like all successful survivors do, I guess. You emphasize the positives you get from your parents and work to minimize their negatives.”

“So you’re saying we’re crooks, like our dad, but we’ve got good intentions, like Mom.”

Chris grinned. “Yeah. I think that’s it.”

“What if we weren’t crooks anymore? What would you do then?”

He looked away for a moment. “I’ve been meaning to talk to you about that.” Surprised, Robin waited for him to go on. “I’ve been offered a job with a watchdog agency, a private group that started up a year ago. They do the kinds of things we do, except without…you know…crime. They use lawsuits, the media, and public opinion to elicit better behavior from people who use their power or position to cheat others.”

“Kidnap.org without duct tape and a white van.”

“Yeah.” He seemed relieved that she took a light tone. “Anyway, they saw my blog posts about corruption in the U.S., and they want me to work for them.” He frowned. “I’ve been struggling with it, because I’m not sure I can do that and help you guys out too.” Clearing his throat he finished. “I decided I’m going to tell them no. I can’t leave you—”

“Chris.” Robin leaned toward the screen. “This morning we disbanded the gang. From now on we’re simply a group of friends with varied interests and shared memories.”

“Really?”

"Yes. Hua, Cam, and Luca are staying here in Kansas. The girls are going to California to join Em. Tom and I are moving to Wisconsin, where we plan to open a detective agency." She blushed. "We figure we can use some of what we've learned the last few years to be successful investigators."

"I'm sure you can. And it's about time you made an honest man of that guy. He's crazy for you."

"I'm crazy for him too. It will be hard saying goodbye to the others," she admitted, "but we're a bunch of amateurs, not cut out to be criminals."

"I think your bunch of amateurs did a whole lot of good," Chris replied. "Now, go pack your bags before Tom decides he can't wait around for you any longer."

Notes

Dear Reader,

If you enjoy my books, please write a review, tell a friend, or pass the book on to someone else who loves to read. It's the nicest thing a fan can do for an author, and we're grateful for the help.

Peg

ABOUT THE AUTHOR

Peg Herring reads, writes, and loves mysteries. As an educator she once set the school stage on fire (just a little one). As a driver she's been so lost that she passed through the same town in Pennsylvania three times in one day. Family and friends have lost count of how many times she's locked herself out of her house. As the award-winning author of several mysteries series and standalone books, it's much safer if she sits in her office and writes, either as herself or as her younger, hipper alter ego, Maggie Pill.

Visit http://pegherring.com for Strong Women, Great Stories

Books by Peg Herring

Books 1 & 2 in the Kidnap Capers (Suspense with cozy tendencies)
KIDNAP.org (Book 1)
Pharma Con (Book 2)
***

The Simon & Elizabeth Mysteries (Tudor Era Historical)

Her Highness' First Murder
Poison, Your Grace
The Lady Flirts with Death
Her Majesty's Mischief
***
The Loser Mysteries (Contemporary Mystery/Suspense)
Killing Silence
Killing Memories
Killing Despair
***Clan Macbeth Historical Romance (medieval Scotland)
Macbeth's Niece
Double Toil & Trouble
***
Mercedes Maxwell Suspense Series with Historical Implications
Shakespeare's Blood
Charlie Dickens' Documents
***
Standalone Mysteries
Somebody Doesn't Like Sarah Leigh (contemporary cozy mystery)
Her Ex-GI P.I. ('60s-era mystery)
Not Dead Yet... ('60s-era paranormal mystery)
***
Standalone Women's Fiction/Suspense
Deceiving Elvera (11/1/2020)
Maggie Pill's Cozy Mysteries
The Sleuth Sisters Mystery Series
Book #1 *The Sleuth Sisters*
Book #2 *3 Sleuths, 2 Dogs, 1 Murder*
Book #3 *Murder in the Boonies*
Book #4 *Sleuthing at Sweet Springs*
Book #5 *Eat, Drink, and Be Wary*
Book #6, *Peril, Plots, and Puppies*
Book #7 *Captured, Escape, Repeat*
***
Trailer Park Tales-Cozy Mysteries
Once Upon a Trailer Park

Twice the Crime This Time (10/1/2020)

www.ingramcontent.com/pod-product-compliance
Ingram Content Group UK Ltd.
Pitfield, Milton Keynes, MK11 3LW, UK
UKHW020131250726
13967UKWH00002B/595